Hidden Intentions

Hidden Intentions

Meisha J. Camm

www.urbanbooks.net

Urban Books
74 Wheatley Heights
Dix Hills, NY 11798

ISBN 1-893196-40-2

First Printing April 2006
Printed in United States of America

10   9   8   7   6   5   4   3

Dedication

To Shakim Robinson, I will always love you and be there for you. We have a bond that is unbreakable. Our daughter, Shamaya a.k.a. Cookie thank you for bringing a priceless joy into my life.

Acknowledgements

I want to thank Jesus Christ for giving me this gift of writing. With the power of prayer and determination, anything is possible.

The easiest part of a book is actually writing it. I have learned struggle, hard work and patience are three vital elements in the process of becoming successful.

Thank you to Carl Weber, Roy Glenn and the Urban Books family for believing in my work.

Thank you to my parents Rodney and Shelly Camm and my sister, Melanie, for watching Shamaya all those hours I spent typing away on the computer. Shakim, if it wasn't for you, I wouldn't be writing. Thank you for always believing in me and showing your support. Shamaya, my baby girl, thank you for showing me unconditional love and always putting a smile on my face whether I needed one or not.

To Jessica Tilles, Carla Dean and Niko Hamm, thank you for pushing and pushing me to write to the best of my ability and critiquing my work.

To my friends and family, Mr. and Mrs. Ballinger, Chunichi, Tiffany Ballinger, Lachele Edmonds, Chrissy Smith, Sara Schiable, Linda Potts, Pat Howell, Calvin Hatcher, Kisha Powell, Valerie Langhorne, the entire Wade family and Renee Bobbs, thank you for your kinds words of encouragement. Rashaad Spencer, I know you'll always be my number one fan.

To the online writing groups RealSistaWriters and writersrx, thank you for always sending me important information pertaining to the book world. A special thanks to Gevell Wagner for taking the time out to read my work.

To Nikki Turner, Tobias Fox, Edwin and Earnest Mcnair, Michael Baisden, Shannon Holmes, Zane, and Mary Monroe thank you for steering me in the right direction.

Chapter 1

Today was a typical day at BankFirst for the first of the month—hectic with lines back to the entrance—until Charles strolled his trifling behind through the revolving door. Feelings of anger and frustration that once consumed me and that I had tucked away into my vault of bad memories resurfaced. I was a volcano ready to erupt, which would allow my lava of feelings to burn his ass up. Fortunately for him, I was at work and had to maintain some type of business decorum.

A year and a half ago, I ate, slept, and breathed Charles. Every ounce of my body constantly craved his touch. He was my world and I was his. Or at least that is what I thought, until I realized I could no longer accept his nasty habit. Charles was a weedhead and probably still is. I gave him an ultimatum—his habit or me. Of course, he chose his bad habit. My heart ached so badly, I refused to look at another man for eighteen months. I clearly was out of my mind and vowed *never* to allow another man to control my feelings again.

"'S up, Nya? Still looking sweet."

"Hello, Charles." I greeted him with a smile, and not because I wanted to. "How are you?"

"I'd be better if—"

I raised my hand and cut off his words before he had a chance to expose my business to the entire bank. "Let's go into my office."

Charles followed on my heels like a puppy dog awaiting a treat. However, he was sadly mistaken. It was my turn to impose a little pain.

"Come in and have a seat," I offered, closing the door behind us. I rested on the edge of the desk and stared down at him. A devilish smile crept across my lips. "Listen, you chose your woman, remember?"

"Aw, Nya, come on. There wasn't another woman and you know it."

"Oh yes, there was. Her name was Philly Blunt."

Charles took a deep sigh. "I've left the stuff alone."

"Don't lie in my face, Charles. I can smell it on you."

Charles held his head down in defeat. "I miss you, Nya."

I stood to my feet, squared my shoulders, and walked around behind my desk. "Charles, I won't dwell on how much you've hurt me because I'm over that now. I am over you. I wish nothing but good things for you. But you and I can never be . . . ever again."

With a broken face, Charles stood to his feet and left my office without an uttered word. However, his body language spoke volumes.

Damn, that felt good.

The gold-faced clock on the wall displayed the time of 1:55 p.m. I grabbed my leather satchel, said my goodbyes, and made a dash to Wal-Mart for the essentials a girl must always have—Summer's Eve, Tampax, and so on.

After driving around Wal-Mart's parking lot trying to find a parking space that was not three miles up the road, I lucked up and caught someone pulling out of a space that was literally at the front door.

"Nya, how is the lovely lady doing today?" a man's voice asked. An eight-man entourage followed closely behind him.

"Hi, Mr. Edmonds. Thank you for the compliment. I am fine, and how 'bout yourself?" I asked, pulling my tired self from my car.

"I'm fine, but I would be elated if you came to my cookout tonight. I'm barbecuing ribs and chicken. The fish will be grilled," he said as a tomato dropped out of his shopping bag and onto the ground.

"I'm sorry, but I already have plans for tonight. Thanks for the invitation though," I said, knowing damn well the only plans I had was for him and his crew to get the hell out of my face.

"Well, you know where I live if you change your mind. And if you do, bring some of your friends."

I threw a forced smile his way. "Have a nice evening," I said, completely ignoring his request and walking into the store.

Mr. Edmonds has a problem with accepting no for an answer. He is handsome, but that's about it. He's been trying to take me out for the longest time, and I've tried to let him down in a nice, easy way. However, I may have to crank up the mean volume a bit.

I love me some Wal-Mart. I call it Wally World, my shopping haven. As I pushed my cart down the juice aisle, a young man, obviously not paying attention to where he was going, slammed his cart into mine.

"Watch where you're going," I snapped, my hands tightly affixed to the cart.

"I see you're a feisty one. Excuse me, Miss, I apologize for *slightly* bumping into you." He had a huge grin on his face and a trace of sarcasm in his voice.

"You should be, and it wasn't *slightly* either." I looked at him out of the corner of my eye as I grabbed a pint of cranberry juice.

"It's a shame such a beautiful woman as you has to look so evil in the face," he said, licking his full, sensuous lips.

Something inside me ignited. It was the middle of July 1998. The weather outside was at sizzling temperatures, but the heat inside of me was at a record-breaking high. He wore a wife-beater tank, jeans, and Timberlands. His outfit was an automatic panty dropper, and mine were just about ready to hit the floor. Besides, the way he licked his lips made me curious to see what else he could lick.

I noticed him when I entered the store, giving me one of those "damn, she's fine" looks. All men do it, especially those trying to run game. His mouth was wide open as his tongue dragged the floor. Still, I paid him no mind and kept walking.

He *is* somewhat cute, even though his tactics worked my last nerve. Nevertheless, I could get lost in those eyes. Of course, he probably hears that all the time from women. Well, he's not going to hear it from me. His body isn't bad either. I like hard muscles, lots of them. I feel safe and secure with a man who is solid from head to toe. My ideal man is one who works out, but who is not a workout fanatic—someone who stays in the gym more than in my bed.

Besides, one fanatic in my life is enough—my sister Leah. She lives on the treadmill and exercises relentlessly. We can't leave the house without her asking me at least four times, "Nya, do I look fat?"

I'll tell her, "No, you look fine," or "Girl, that outfit is too cute." But it must go in one ear and out the other because, no more than five minutes later she'll ask me again. At that point, I will tell her anything she wants to hear just to shut her ass up.

Another thing about living with an exercise fanatic is them thinking they know every damn thing. If I hear "You are not going to have a bomb-ass body by eating French fries and potato bread" one more time, I'm going to scream. Leah is always lecturing me about what I should and should not eat. Hey, I need carbohydrates in my life. I'm not giving up my favorite foods for no-body, including rice. However, once or twice a week, I do try to have a date with the treadmill, when time permits. Hell, I'm a busy woman. Of course, I like to look nice, but being physically fit and beautiful will only get you so far in life. I have my mind on other things.

"If you want a smile from me, you'll have to work for it. I just don't give them out to everyone who looks my way," I said, placing a gallon of apple juice in my cart.

"My name is Tory Sothers." He extended his hand toward me.

I looked at him as if he was crazy. After giving it some thought, I decided not to be rude.

"Hi, I'm Nya Gamden." I smiled, returning the introduction and grasping his hand in a firm, yet feminine shake.

"Allow me to buy your groceries to make up for our bad start."

"No, thank you," I said, knowing damn well I really wanted to say yes.

"Really, I don't mind. It's the least I can do."

"Well, if you insist." *Who in their right mind would turn down a chance at getting free groceries? Hell, since it's free, I think I'll put a few extra items in my cart.*

For the next hour, we talked, walked, and shopped.

During that time, I learned he received his engineering degree from Old Dominion University and currently worked at RADCOM, a major computer engineering company. So far, I liked what I was working with. We were enjoying our conversation so much, we didn't want it to end. So we continued walking up and down the aisles aimlessly. All the while, I tossed items into my cart that he had offered to pay for. Finally, we reached the checkout counter, marking the end of my mini-shopping spree.

"It's been real with you, Nya." He displayed a smile which could melt an iceberg. "I like your name. Does it have a meaning behind it?"

"It means courage and strength." *God I hope he asks me on a date.*

As if reading my mind, he said, "Would you be willing to go out with me? You know, dinner and a movie. I'll pick the movie, and you can pick where we will have dinner."

"I would like that very much," I said with a smile.

"There's my smile," he teased.

"Let's just say you worked hard for it."

He opened the door and placed my groceries on the backseat of my car. His gesture was so sweet, it made me melt inside, but I remained cool, calm, and collected on the outside. If he had a clue as to what I was really feeling and thinking, we'd both be in trouble.

After Tory loaded the last bag, we exchanged phone numbers and set our date for Sunday.

Chapter 2

On first dates, I never let a man pick me up at my house. I have to get to know a person first. You never know, they could be a lunatic waiting to strike. Even though I didn't take Tory to be that type of person, you can never be too careful. By the fourth date, maybe, I will feel more comfortable about letting him pick me up at my house. That's if we make it to a fourth date.

"How do I look?" I asked as I stood before Leah and turned around in a full circle, my arms stretched wide open.

"Beautiful," she responded, her attention focused on "The Real World" instead of me.

Gosh, I hate when she does that. "You know, Leah, it's funny how you only have to tell me once that I look beautiful," I snapped as sarcasm twisted around every word. "If you ask me, I have to say it over and over again." I glanced at my watch. "Dang, I only have a few more minutes. I have to leave here at 7 o'clock in order to get to the restaurant by 7:30."

Wearing a beige linen pant set with brown sandals that accentuated my freshly manicured toes, I was dressed to impress. Leah insisted I wear hoops, but the diamond earrings with the matching pendant made me look more sophisticated. My brown and beige Fendi purse was perfect for the evening. Leah said I needed a change, so she pinned my hair into a cute upsweep. Hair done, clothes tight, eyebrows arched, and feet done, I was ready to shake up Tory's world.

As I sashayed my way to the door, Leah yelled out, "Bye! Tell me every detail when you get back!"

"Maybe I will, maybe I won't."

"Shut up and stop lying to yourself, Nya. You know you're going to tell me everything."

"Bye, girl." I laughed, closing the front door behind me.

I arrived at Aldo's a few minutes early and took a seat on the bench in the foyer to await Tory's arrival. *I hope he isn't late. If you're going to be late, the least you could do is pick up the phone and call. With everyone carrying a cell phone these days, there is no excuse for a breach in communication.*

Aldo's is a nice Italian restaurant with the perfect setting for a first date. The lights are dim, but so dark that you can't read the menu. The décor feels romantic, like in those old movies filmed in Venice. Plastic grapes hang from the terracotta stucco walls, giving the restaurant a special touch. All that's missing is the little man guiding the boat and singing *O Solo Mio.*

At 7:30 sharp, Tory stepped into the foye, carrying a bouquet of pink roses. So far so good. Tory was as smooth as he wanted to be, sporting a black linen suit, a pair of Kenneth Cole shoes, and a gold watch that screamed class. *Plus, there's something sexy about a man who is masculine enough to wear a diamond stud in each earlobe.*

"Hello, gorgeous," he smiled, then softly kissed my hand.

"Thank you." I rose from the bench and reached for the roses. "The roses are beautiful. You look nice yourself. I see we think alike. We both have on linen suits."

"The weather has been so hot that I wanted to make sure I would be comfortable. I like the way linen feels on my skin." Tory licked his lips in a way that sent chills throughout my body and made me wish I were that linen suit.

I gazed at his lips and imagined them caressing my skin. I was getting wet just at the thought.

"I like this spot. It has good food and a cool atmosphere. Shall we be seated?"

"I'm ready," I answered, breaking out of my trance.

As we approached the hostess stand, Tory requested a cozy table for two.

The hostess grabbed two linen-wrapped utensil sets and led us toward the back of the restaurant to a candle-lit booth.

Tory helped me into the booth and then sat across from me.

"Good evening, I'm Gary. I'll be your server this evening. If you don't mind me asking, are you two newlyweds?" he asked, his hands propped on his hips.

I can usually spot them. "No," I responded, wondering if he had some "sugar" in his tank.

"Wrong guess. But I must say the two of you make a great couple." He removed the pen from behind his ear. "Now what can I get the lady to drink?"

Tory and I were smiling, trying to hold back our laughs.

"A glass of water and a ginger ale, please."

Tory ordered a bottle of Moët.

"I don't drink alcohol," I stated, not wanting him to waste his money.

"That's all right. I think it's sexy that you take care of your body."

"I don't smoke either."

"That's even better. Treat your temple right. Me, on the other hand, I do have a drink occasionally. I don't smoke cigarettes, but I do blaze from time to time to relieve stress. Do you blaze?"

"No," I responded sharply.

Just then, the waiter returned with our drinks and a basket of warm bread that I absolutely loved.

"What can I get you?" Gary asked, prepared to take our order.

"I'll have the Grilled Salmon with Angel Hair Linguini," Tory decided.

I ordered my favorite dish. "I'll have the Manicotti."

At first, I was afraid to even eat in front of this tantalizing man. But eventually, I let my guard down and allowed myself to enjoy the good food and good conversation. I felt comfortable around him, but not so comfortable that I forgot my golden rule: do not tell a man everything about myself on the first date.

Shortly after Tory excused himself to the bathroom, my cell phone rang. *Who could this be?* "Hello?"

"Hey, girl. How are things going? Remember you told me to call in case you needed to be rescued from Tory?"

"Thanks, but no thanks." I pulled my mirror from my satchel. "Things are going well. We just finished dinner." I checked to make sure I didn't have any food stuck in between my teeth.

"Since you don't need to be rescued, call me tomorrow with your happy-go-lucky self."

"I will," I promised, laughing into the phone.

Whenever I go on a first date, I always have one of my friends call at a certain time to fake an emergency just in case the evening is not going the way I expected. That way I can make my getaway without looking like the bad guy. I was having such a pleasurable time, though, I had forgotten all about Yvette.

As Tory returned to the table, Gary approached with a variety of desserts displayed on a tray.

"Do you two have enough room for some of our scrumptious desserts?"

"What would you like?" Tory asked, gazing at me from across the table.

"Nothing. Everything was so delicious, and I can't fit another thing in my stomach."

At that moment, I excused myself to the bathroom to freshen up. I make it a point to keep my purse fully stocked with the essentials: Bath & Body Works' Country Apple scented lotion, the Body Shop's mandarin-flavored lip gloss, TUMS, Aleve for headaches, a brush and a comb. In addition, you can always find dental floss, breath mints, chewing gum, but not bubble gum, on the inside compartment of my purse. One of my pet peeves is bad breath. It is such a turnoff to me. I make sure my breath is always so fresh and so clean. It would be the kiss of death if someone ever told me that my breath was funky.

Upon returning to the table, I discovered Tory had ordered a slice of strawberry cheesecake anyway.

"I thought maybe you would change your mind," he said, holding two forks in his hand.

I smiled as I reached for one of the forks so we could share the piece of mouthwatering cheesecake.

After dinner, we decided to go see *Two Can Play That Game*. The soundtrack was hot, so I was hoping the movie would be just as good.

Once we were seated, I leaned over toward Tory. "Thanks for dinner, Tory."

He looked surprised.

"What's wrong with your face?" I asked.

"Nothing, Nya. You just caught me off guard."

"How so?"

"The women I have dealt with don't usually say thanks for anything. My last two girlfriends just expected too much and took me for granted. Don't get me wrong, I don't mind doing nice things for my lady. At the same time, however, a brother wants to feel appreciated. You're welcome, though," he said, displaying a broad smile and standing to his feet. "Do you want some popcorn, candy, or something to drink?"

"No, thank you."

"Okay, I'll be right back."

When Tory returned to his seat after purchasing a soda, he gently placed his arm around my shoulders and the movie began.

Chapter 3

First dates end no later than half past midnight. I wouldn't want my date to make any assumptions. When Leah and I were growing up, Mommy would always say, "There's nothing open after two in the morning, except legs and IHOP." This time, however, I was tempted to break my rule. I was not ready for this evening to end.

"Nya, let me take you to one more place." Tory caressed my hand in his. "Then, I will let you go."

He's such a cutie when he begs.

"Are you game?"

I yanked my hand from his grasp, leaned back, twisted up my lips, and asked, "Game for what?"

"Just follow me," he said, grabbing me by the hand again and leading me to my car. "I will not keep you out long. I promise." His smile looked awfully wicked to me. Tory definitely had something up his sleeve.

After following behind him in my car for a short distance, we ended up at the beach. *How romantic.* It was late, so there were no tourists about, which made for a nice and quiet atmosphere.

Tory stretched out a blanket and turned up the CD player in his four-door, forest-green Lexus GS 300.

"That's my song," Tory said, extending his hand toward me. "Dance with me, Nya."

I took his hand and moved myself into him.

While white waves crashed gently against the shore, Tory embraced me as we slowly swayed under the stars to Jagged Edge's *Gotta Be.*

In my ear, he spoke passionately about his family. It was evident they meant the world to him.

Tory grew up as a military brat with two siblings, a brother and sister, while his mother taught English at Norfolk State University. His dream was to be an entrepreneur and form a computer engineering company, which would serve as a way to ensure job opportunities for minorities.

Tory firmly placed the span of his hand on my lower back and pulled me closer. He inhaled deeply and then slowly blew his warm breath on my earlobe, causing my body to shiver.

"Are you cold?" He pulled me closer.

"No, I'm fine."

"Tell me something about you, Nya. What are the goals and desires of your heart?"

"I want to be a nurse practitioner who specializes in obstetrician/gynecology. I love babies and the whole pregnancy process. Birth is so amazing. I have seen many births and each time was more miraculous than the last. I applied for the nursing program at Old Dominion University and am attending this fall."

He kissed me on the neck. "Congratulations."

My legs felt as if they were getting weak. Tory left me speechless. Somehow, I gathered my composure and mustered a "Thank you" in response. Then, I closed my eyes and rested my head on his shoulder. This felt like a dream come true.

Tory's smile disappeared and seriousness masked his

face. "Tonight was wonderful, Nya. There is something special about you; I just can't put my finger on it."

"I enjoyed myself, too, Tory."

After the song was over, Tory escorted me to the blanket, motioning for me to have a seat. The cool ocean breeze and smell of salt water lent a romantic feeling to the dream-like atmosphere. Obviously, Tory was feeling it, too, because he leaned in and brushed his lips against my neck. The hair on the nape of my neck stood to attention and I let out a slight giggle. The wetness between my thighs expressed interest as well. However, this was neither the time nor the place. I tightened my thighs and suppressed the urge to love this man from head to toe.

Tory released a grunt and reached for his lower back. "My back is killing me. Ever since I pulled a muscle helping my boy move, my back hasn't been the same."

"Take your shirt off and lie on your stomach." I reached inside my purse.

"What for?"

A wicked smile formed across my lips. "Believe me, this won't hurt."

After he turned on his stomach, I straddled his back, poured a dollop of lotion into the palm of my hand, and rubbed my palms together so the lotion would feel warm against his skin. I gently smoothed the lotion in a circular motion on his back, concentrating on his tight shoulders.

"You're quite tense."

"I know. My work stresses me at times."

"Let me see if I can work out the kinks."

With slow, long strokes, I moved my hand from his lower back up to his neck. I separated my hands and then brought them over his shoulder blades to the blanket. I repeated the movement several times.

Tory closed his eyes and basked in the moment, releasing moans and groans at precise moments.

Next, I worked my thumbs from his lower back, up to his neck, and up the sides of his head, stopping at the crown of his head.

"Oh shit, that feels good, Nya."

I smiled at Tory's reaction and continued working him for the next half-hour like a trick working a limp dick.

"Baby girl, where in the hell did you learn how to give a massage?"

"Oh, let's just say I pay close attention."

"You're a damn good student." He sat up. "Thank you so much, baby. You've got me feeling like a brand new man."

"You're welcome."

"May I return the favor?" Tory began to gently rub my arms and shoulders.

Whew! His touch was intoxicating, but I couldn't give in. "No, but I'll take a rain check." I eased away from his grasp.

"Well…," he trailed off in thought, stroking his tongue from one side of his mouth to the other and leaving a glossy sheen.

Damn, him! There he goes licking those luscious lips again. I was getting horny and wetter by the minute. My vagina throbbed and I wanted so desperately to slide down on his python and wrestle with him until the sun came up.

He glanced at his watch. "I don't want to keep you out too late."

When we reached our parked cars, he asked for a hug. As he stood waiting to hold me, I walked into his outstretched arms and exhaled as they enfolded me. After a few moments of relishing in the warmth of his embrace, I decided it was time for our date to come to an end.

After my left leg was inside my silver Toyota Camry, he gently shut the door. Reaching for my hand through the open window, he gently kissed it. The touch of his soft lips against my skin sent chills down my spine.

"Have a nice evening, Ms. Gamden."

"You, too, and thank you for a great evening," I said, trying my best to maintain my composure.

"No, thank *you*."

As I pulled off, I looked at the clock on my dashboard. It was 12:50 a.m., and I had broken my rule by twenty minutes. *Oh well, it was well worth it.* In fact, I looked forward to seeing him again.

During the ride home, I couldn't stop thinking about Tory. As I turned up the volume on Jaheim's CD, my cell phone went off, disrupting my thoughts. I flinched, and then quickly turned down the volume to my stereo system. I reached inside my purse with my right hand to retrieve my phone, smiling the whole time because I knew it could be no one else but Tory.

"Hello," I finally spoke into the receiver.

"Hi, baby girl, this is Tory."

"I know who this is." I was all smiles and I'm sure it was evident on his end.

"I was calling to make sure you got home safe."

I chuckled. "Liar. We just left each other."

"Okay, you got me. Truth is I wanted to hear your voice."

"Tory, you don't need an excuse to call me, baby." *Did I just call him baby? Lord, I must be getting caught up in the moment.*

"When will I see you again?"

"Wednesday night is good for me." I tried not to sound too anxious.

"My schedule is wide open for you, Nya."

"Okay, then, Wednesday it is. There's a play called *Better Days* playing at Willett Hall in Portsmouth. I would love to see it."

"It's been a while since I've gone to a play, but I can tell you have good taste and trust this play will be worth my time." For a brief moment, there was silence. Then he continued. "Well, I won't keep you. It's late. I'll see you on Wednesday. Sweet dreams, Nya."

"I appreciate you calling, Tory. Good night."

I hope I can make it until Wednesday. God give me strength.

Chapter 4

Wednesday slowly but surely arrived. An extra pep was in my step because I was eagerly looking forward to my date with Tory that evening. I even went as far as to schedule a much-needed hair appointment so I would be looking my very best.

When I arrived at work, a bouquet of orange carnations with the most adorable yellow teddy bear was centered in the middle of my desk. The card enclosed read: *Simple pleasures for a beautiful sight to see.*

Hmm, who could have sent these?

Yesterday, flowers were delivered from Tory, so I was sure they couldn't have been from him. *Oh well, I have a stack of work to do and no time to ponder who's the sender.* I placed the yellow teddy bear in the top drawer of my desk and got on with my day.

Two o'clock couldn't get here any faster. I took a tenth glance at the clock. I would be leaving work early in order to allow myself enough time to get my hair done and dress for the evening.

"Thank you, Ms. Jones, for banking at BankFirst. Is there anything else I can assist you with today?"

"No, honey," Ms. Jones replied as she reached for an envelope.

"Have a nice evening," I offered, handing her five twenty-dollar bills.

BankFirst is one of the major banks on the East Coast. I have been here for two years with decent pay. As a rule, my responsibility is to train new tellers; however, my specialty is servicing irate customers. My motto is "kill them with kindness." While they steadily scream at me, I maintain a calm voice and a smile. When the going gets rough, what keeps me sane is the compliance of the bank manager, Ms. Stein, to work around my schedule of classes.

Ms. Stein took me under her wing and taught me everything about banking. To remain on her good side doesn't take much. Just as long as I'm servicing the customers in a timely and correct manner and balancing my cash drawer on a consistent basis. I take much pride in making sure every penny is accounted for. As you can probably tell, I have a very strong working relationship with Ms. Stein.

Now, Ms. Pilom, the teller supervisor, is another story altogether. This woman has struck an everlasting nerve in my body. She's one of those people who always complain about her salary but doesn't want to work for it. She has made a permanent indentation in her seat. Which is what happens when you sit down on your butt all day. Asking her to assist a customer is like speaking a foreign language to her. On many occasions, I have laughed my ass off because Ms. Stein caught her hiding in the back office so she wouldn't have to do her job. She has been employed at BankFirst at least a year prior to my coming onboard and still has no understanding of how to operate the teller system, and Ms. Stein is constantly getting customer complaints about her service.

On this particular day, I was back and forth between working the teller line and being a customer service representative. Ms. Stein and Ms. Pilom were swamped with paperwork for loan documents needing to be completed by five o'clock, and there was a gentleman in the lobby who had been waiting a while for assistance.

With his back turned to me, I asked, "Sir, may I help you?"

"Of course, you can." He turned around to flash an award-winning smile. "I've been waiting to see you and only you for forty-five minutes."

"Mr. Edmonds, so nice to see you again," I greeted, forcing a smile. "What can I help you with *today*?" I asked sarcastically, leading him inside my office.

"I want you to be the love of my life. Let's say we start off simple with a dinner or a nice stroll at Mount Park." He gracefully took a seat in the chair positioned in front of my desk.

I stretched my hand across the desk and inhaled a deep sigh. "Sir—"

He gently covered my hand with his. "Call me Darren, please," he said, cutting me off.

"I can't call you by your first name. My mother would have a fit." I gave a soft chuckle. "Don't take offense. I was just raised not to call an elder by their first name."

"I'm far from an old man. Let me tell you something—and never forget it—the barrel may be old, but the wine is still good."

"Mr. Edmonds, I'm seeing someone…besides, you're a client of mine and I intend to keep it that way. So, what *financial* needs can I help you with today?"

"I need you to transfer two hundred thousand from my first money market account into the new CD advertised at four percent."

"Do you want the interest to come directly to you, or

do you want it to roll over?" I asked while pounding away at the computer's keyboard to bring his account up.

"You can have it."

"Excuse me," I said, halting my keystrokes.

He cleared his throat. "Have the interest deposited into my personal checking account." Next, he looked toward the floral arrangement and said, "Ahh, those are beautiful flowers you have."

"Thank you. I received them today from a secret admirer." I smiled, and then turned my attention back toward my computer to complete his transaction. "Is there anything else you need?"

"What I need is you. It's all right, though. My mother always told me to be persistent and never give up on something I want." Just then, his cell phone started blaring, and without thinking twice, he put it on vibrate.

I figured it was probably some woman calling. *If it were a guy calling, he would have picked up the phone to gloat, like most men do. For the life of me, I can't figure out why he wants me. I'm sure other women wouldn't mind having him. He's just too much of a flirt for my taste.*

I extended my hand. "Enjoy the rest of your afternoon, Mr. Edmonds," I said, smiling.

Before walking out the door, he turned, winked his eye, and said, "You do the same. Enjoy the flowers and teddy bear."

So that would explain who the sender was.

"Nya, could you come to my office, please?" Ms. Stein blared from the intercom, disrupting my thoughts.

"Yes, ma'am, I'll be right there."

While walking slowly to her office, I immediately thought the worst, praying nothing was wrong. I couldn't afford to lose my job. Not that I had given them any reason to give me the ax.

After entering her office, Ms. Stein told me to take a seat.

Oh, boy, here it comes.

"Nya, I think you are an exceptional employee and go beyond your work expectations."

Here comes the ax.

"And I know next month you will be returning to school."

TIMBER!!!

"However, a supervisor position is open.

"I received approval in our budget to have two supervisors. I recommended you as the perfect candidate. Nothing will change except your salary, of course. Currently, you are making $18,500. Your salary will increase to $23,000, effective today, if you accept the promotion."

Cha-Ching!

"I'm still willing to work with your school schedule, and your work expectations will basically stay the same."

I felt so proud she would recommend me. I do work hard for the bank, and I was glad it was finally recognized. *Mommy was right about letting my work speak for me.*

"I will give you all the time you need to think about it, Nya."

"I don't need any time to think about it, Ms. Stein. I will gladly accept the offer."

"Congratulations! Well, since it's already one-thirty, and you were scheduled to get off at two, go ahead and settle your drawer so you can scoot on outta here," she said, shaking my hand.

"Thank you so much for this opportunity, Ms. Stein. I will not let you down."

"You're most certainly welcome. Keep up the good work, Nya."

Chapter 5

Within five minutes, I settled my drawer, grabbed my shit, and was heading out the door for my two-thirty hair appointment with Kendra at Hair Expo in Chesapeake.

Kendra is the owner of Hair Expo and has been doing my hair for years. The salon is small and I like it that way. During the weekdays, it's pretty quiet. I never schedule an appointment on a weekend because I am too impatient and it gets too crowded. Even though Kendra is considering relocating to accommodate her customers and four stylists, I think I will stick with my weekday appointments. Kendra doesn't make me wait a long time either; I have to get in and get out. Also, I despise sitting under the hairdryer. It makes me feel like I'm slowly suffocating. I'm always trying to find a way out of sitting under all that damn heat, but Kendra isn't having it on this visit.

"Nya, since you have a hot date, let me put spiral curls in your hair," Kendra offered.

"Okay, but I don't want to be under the dryer for a long time."

"You won't be, girl. It will only take about an hour for your hair to dry."

I reluctantly gave in as I reached in my purse to respond to my ringing cell phone. From the number displayed on the caller ID, I knew it was Tara, a good friend of mine since we were little women.

"What's up, girl?"

"Hey, Nya, where are you?"

I could tell by the tone of her voice something was not right. "I'm getting my hair done. What's wrong?"

"Raul was supposed to pick me up at 4:30 from my job, but he has to work overtime. You know with my car being in the shop, I hate relying on people to take care of my business. Will you come pick me up?"

"Sure, I just got under the dryer about ten minutes ago. Kendra should be finished with my hair in another hour."

"Thanks, Nya."

"No problem. I'll see you then."

"Bye."

While under the dryer, I dozed off. I had to do something to keep from going crazy under that thing.

"Ms. Sleeping Beauty, wake up." Kendra turned off the dryer and started removing the rods.

I didn't realize how tired I was. That little catnap did me good. I felt refreshed.

"Go get in my chair. Where are you and Tory going this evening?"

"We're going to a play called *Better Days*," I said, lowering myself into the black salon chair.

"My husband and I went to see it on Saturday. You'll definitely enjoy yourself."

"Thanks for the review. How are the kids doing?" I asked as she proceeded to primp my hair.

"They're doing fine and growing like weeds. My kids are a handful, but I love them just the same. There, I'm finished." She turned the chair so I would be facing the mirror. "Your hair is gorgeous."

"Yes, you really outdid yourself this time," I responded, looking in the mirror.

"You always want a relaxer and a doobie wrap. Don't worry, I wouldn't charge you extra if you wanted something else done to your hair."

"Thanks, but no thanks. Every now and then, I don't mind a different hairstyle, but I'm comfortable with the way it is. If I wasn't going out tonight, I probably would've wanted the usual," I said, handing her the money.

"Well, have a good time tonight. Don't do anything I wouldn't do," she teased.

"I will, and you don't have to worry about me doing anything you would do." I chuckled under my breath. "See you in two weeks, Kendra."

Chapter 6

I arrived at Tara's job just in the nick of time.

Tara sold luxury vehicles—Mercedes Benz, BMW, Lexus, and Bentley automobiles—at Steiner's World Class Cars on Virginia Beach Boulevard. She started as a receptionist and, in less than a year, worked her way up to a car service specialist. Tara had always loved cars. Especially fast cars. And a man had to have a nice set of wheels to grace her presence.

For instance, about a week ago, the crew and I went to Applebee's. On the weekends, the place is more like a club than a restaurant. The only difference is you don't have to pay a cover charge. After we were seated, this guy approached our table because Tara had caught his eye.

"May I buy the beautiful lady a drink?" he asked, his eyes affixed to Tara.

Tara folded her arms across her chest. "That depends," she replied flirtatiously.

"Depends on what?"

"The kind of vehicle you drive." She smirked, turning her attention to her manicured nails.

"Well, if you must know, I drive a Tracker."

"No, I do regret that at this time you cannot buy me a drink. Maybe when you get a *real* car, I *might* let you. Bye-bye," she said in the snottiest of tones, waving him off.

We busted into tears of laughter as he walked away looking stupid and embarrassed. It really wasn't funny, though.

Tara can be so blunt at times, especially when it comes to men.

"You didn't have to be so cold," Leah said.

"Please, men come a-dime-a-dozen. My family and friends are all who matter to me. He was cheap anyway. How was he going to ask to buy me a drink and not my girls, too? That was so rude. He would have been smoother if he had gotten the waitress or bartender to come over and ask me instead."

I took a sip of my ginger ale. "You've got a point." I parked my car at the front door and waited for Tara to bring her behind out from her job so I could get home and get ready for my date.

"Hey, girl." Tara jumped in the car and slammed the door. "I appreciate you picking me up."

I cringed. *Damn, could she have slammed it a little harder?* "No problem, girl. How was your day?" I asked as I pulled off into traffic.

"I sold three cars! I'm on a roll. I sold two Mercedes and one Lexus. I think it's time for me to go shopping. I need to reward myself. So how was your day?"

"Wonderful! I got a promotion at the bank. I'm going to be a supervisor with a huge raise to go with it." I smiled proudly.

"Congratulations! This calls for a celebration this weekend." She sighed with joy. "Whew, the do looks good. Nya, you should wear your hair that way often.

It's down to your butt. You just don't know what to do with it. Have no worries, I will help you. I don't mind at all."

Tara is always trying to change somebody, especially me. I like the way I wear my hair. It works for me. "I'll think about it. Anyway, you sounded upset on the phone earlier. What's up?"

"Raul and I had a little spat, but we're okay now. Since I've been working and going to school at nights, he feels I'm neglecting him. Nya, you know the deal— I'm trying to make a future for myself. It requires hard work to get anything out of life. He needs to be more understanding and supportive."

I nodded my head. "I know that's right."

"He has not seen me in three days and already he's tripping. We have not had sex in six days. If Raul goes two days without it, he gets cranky. I will admit the sex is good. He has a big chocolate bar. Girl, I can't mess with a man who has a short stopper." Tara erupted into laughter.

"I thought you liked him for the Mercedes Benz he drives. Are you two getting serious?" I took my eyes off the road for a quick second in order to glance over at her to see her expression.

"We have only been dating for seven months," she answered, rolling her eyes. "At first, it was the car and gift. Especially the diamonds. They're more than best friends to me—those babies are more like cousins." We fell out with laughter. "But now, I'm really feeling him. He can be so needy at times, though." Tara shook her head.

"I think you're the guy in the relationship and he's the woman," I chuckled.

"I give my man space because I need space. Maybe I'm giving him too much. For example, on my lunch break, I went across the street and bought him a rose and the sweetest card." She stopped long enough to sigh, and then continued. "By the way, before dropping me off, can you take me over to his place? I want to leave my boo's goodies on his bed." She rummaged through her purse for the key to Raul's place.

"Sure, I have time to spare."

In all actuality, I didn't. But how could I say no to the best friend I have ever had?

Chapter 7

When we pulled in front of Raul's apartment building, I told Tara I would wait in the car.

'I won't be long," she promised.

"Good, because I've got to tinkle."

"Well, then, come in."

"You sure? I don't want to impose."

"No, I don't mind. Besides, I want to show you his apartment. It's not much, but at least he's not living at home with his momma." She chuckled as she exited the car.

"All right." I laughed, exiting also. "Girl, you are so crazy."

As we strolled up to the building, Tara came to an abrupt halt, causing me to bump into her.

"Hold up, isn't that Raul's car parked down the street? Yeah, it sure is," she said before I could respond.

"Maybe someone else lives out here with the same vehicle," I said, trying to give the man the benefit of the doubt.

"I have lived with two brothers; I know when a man is scheming. I'm not even going to waste my precious energy walking down there to look at the license plate."

"Calm down, Tara. Take some deep breaths."

I could see the fury in her eyes. Tara wouldn't have cared if Raul was seeing someone else, just as long as she was getting hers. All she wanted was honesty from her man.

"Don't black out. Let's go see if he is even in there."

"Let's go," she barked, storming to his front door.

Like a thief in the night, Tara slowly inserted her key into the lock. Once the tumbler turned, we entered Raul's apartment quiet as mice. Standing in the living room, we looked around for anything out of the ordinary. Ginuwine's *Pony* wafted from the bedroom and caught our attention. We glanced at each other, and then Tara nodded toward the bedroom. I followed her lead. As we approached the bedroom, moans and groans of ecstasy sent chills through my bones, so I'm sure Tara was at her freezing point. Tara slowly opened the hall closet and pulled out Raul's baseball bat.

"We're going to need this in case some shit goes down," she whispered. "For him lying to me, I'm going to break this muthafuckin' bat in half. That will make his ass suffer." A satanic grin crept across her face.

Raul was a collector of sports paraphernalia. For his birthday, Tara wanted to give him a special gift. So, she surfed on eBay and purchased an authentically autographed bat. Raul damn near passed out when he saw it was an authentic signature of the great Jackie Robinson.

"I'm about to go psycho on his ass. Talk is cheap. I'd rather show him how I'm really feeling. It's butt whooping-time," she said, getting into position.

On the count of three, I kicked the door open and naked women scattered the room like roaches, searching for clothing sprawled on the floor. My mouth hit the floor. Raul was getting his freak on with two ugly-ass trolls, one riding his dick and the other acting like a damn lollipop getting licked. This was surely a bad scene in a movie I wasn't interested in watching.

"Surprise, surprise, muthafucka!" Tara screamed as she held the bat high above her head, ready to swing down on whatever and whoever stepped in her way.

I took a step back so I wouldn't accidentally get hit in the process of her bashing his skull in. For a split second, she reminded me of the man from the movie *Lean on Me*. I thought she was going to start yelling, "They used to call me crazy; now they call me batgirl!"

"Tara! Baby, I can explain."

Now, didn't he realize a person can't reason with a woman on a mission?

"You lying bastard! You told me you were working overtime!" Tara swung the bat down like an axe, smashing the ceramic lamp that *used* to sit on the nightstand. "Muthafucka, I even went and bought you a peace offering for our argument this morning."

Seeing his lamp shattered to smithereens with his prized baseball bat really pissed him off. "Bitch, are you crazy? Barging in my damn house!"

"Shut the fuck up, Raul! You shouldn't have given me a damn key!" Tara threw the keys toward him, where they hit the wall, barely missing his ear.

"You were neglecting me; I have needs, too."

Tara rolled her eyes at the two ugly-ass women. "I see you were getting your needs met. You can't even keep your fuckin' dick in your pants for one week. All I ever asked from you is to keep it real with me. Don't do sneaky shit behind my back. Worst of all, you're sleeping with other people. Raul, I'm not going to die over some stank pussy you fucked."

"I'm so sorry, baby," Raul begged, slipping into his jeans. "It will not happen again. Let me make it up to you. Please, give me another chance."

"Another chance? When the fuck did you bump your head?"

"We don't want any trouble," one skank replied. "He told us he didn't have a girl." She sounded desperate, scrambling to get on her clothes on strewn about the room. Her drawers looked like a gigantic slingshot.

"Can we go?" skank number two asked as she inched away from the bed.

Tara's head snapped around like something from the *Exorcist*. "You're still here? You bold bitches—get the fuck out!" Tara swung the bat over her head.

The women looked at each other, grabbed their things, and blew past us and out the door. "I hope you beat his ass," they echoed as they jetted from the apartment building.

Tara took about ten swings at Raul while he dodged and cried like a baby. What a pitiful sight to see from a grown-ass man. After she was done with his ass, she took his prized possession to his television, vases, paintings and anything else within swinging distance.

When we left Raul's apartment, it was definitely evident "Tornado Tara" had made her presence known. "He's an official double loser," she said, brushing her hands of him. "This time next week, I'll be getting gifts, cards, and messages saying he loves me with all of his heart and how good my pussy is."

With all the commotion going on, I forgot I had to pee.

We sat at the traffic light in total silence.

"Are you okay?" I asked Tara.

"Yeah, I'll be fine. The best way to get over one man is to be with another. I think I might go out with this guy named Greg. He has been asking me out for months. Stupid ass slowed me down from getting acquainted with new faces." She took a deep sigh and looked out the window. "Girl, you know me—I bounce back quickly. The only thing I feel bad about is not throwing his broken baseball bat in the trashcan. Despite the bat being busted up, I know Raul will still keep it."

When I dropped her off at her place, she said, "Thanks so much for picking me up. Have a good time tonight." She leaned over and gave me a sisterly kiss on the cheek. "Nya, thanks for being my girl and having my back."

Chapter 8

Once I arrived home, I made a mad dash for the bathroom, knowing I couldn't hold it much longer. I had to go ever since we left Raul's place. And after Tara practically tore up Raul's place, I wasn't about to ask to use his bathroom.

After taking a quick shower and exfoliating my skin to make it extra soft, I slipped into my black Donna Karan dress that crisscrossed in the front. The red lace bra and thong ensemble was an added touch. Just in case I got cold, I grabbed a sweater. Besides, there's nothing more class lacking than erect nipples through a Donna Karan dress.

"Hey, Daddy," I greeted as I entered the living room.

"Hi, baby. Where are you going all dressed up?" he asked, turning his attention away from the boxing match he was watching.

"My friend Tory and I are going to see *Better Days* at Willett Hall."

"Your mother and I saw the play on Saturday. It was so funny." Daddy laughed as though he was reminiscing.

"Why didn't you tell me you and Mommy went?"

"You and your sister are never here most of the time. And when you are, you're either studying, on the computer, or on the phone." He chuckled at the truth he spoke.

With no room for argument, I smiled at him and said, "Well, I've got to go. I have a date and I don't want to be late."

"When are we going to meet your new friend?"

"Soon, Daddy. Bye."

"Bye, baby. Have a nice time."

When I arrived at Willet Hall, Tory was waiting for me at the door. I was so excited that I began to feel weak in the knees. Since Sunday, we had talked every night.

"Hey, sweetness," he said, smiling, "you look stunning as ever."

"Thank you," I said, blushing. "You don't look so bad yourself."

Tory donned a casual crème suit and a fresh haircut. He leaned in and sniffed. "You smell good, too. What are you wearing?"

"I never tell anyone what fragrance I wear." Actually, that was a lie, since for a split second I couldn't remember what perfume I had squirted on before leaving home. *God he makes me so nervous.*

"Okay, you like to keep it on the low. I can get with that."

"I'm just kidding. It's Safari—" I responded, as it suddenly came to me.

"By Ralph Lauren, right?" he interrupted.

Impressed, I leaned back on my heels and smiled. "Right, and I definitely know what cologne you have on."

"Tell me. Inquiring minds want to know."

"Calvin Klein's Eternity." I smiled widely because I

was proud of the fact I knew my colognes. *Eternity*, among other colognes, was a serious panty dropper for me. I felt myself becoming aroused, but I was determined to behave.

"Are you ready to go inside?" he asked, taking me by the elbow.

When he slightly moved, I inhaled his scent. *Damn, I have to be good tonight,* I tried convincing myself, knowing damn well it would be mighty hard.

I nodded my head and Tory escorted me to our seats.

Willet Hall is a quaint theater where there are no bad seats and the acoustics are the best I've heard. Once the house lights are dimmed, the only people you see are the actors on stage and your sweetie beside you, giving it the feel of a private performance. Tory draped his arm around my neck, his hand resting lightly on my shoulder. I nestled under his arm and settled in for a wonderful evening.

Better Days is the story of Gena, a woman who had been down on her luck in the romance department, always ending up with low-down men—don't want to work, lazy, cheat, fuck up your credit, cheap, broke, want to be the boss of your house and don't have a pot to piss in them damn selves. Gena found the strength to kick her no-good man to the curb. Afterwards, she met a new man who really nurtured and cared about her mind, body, and soul. He took her out and spent money on her, treated her the way she deserved to be treated. Most importantly, he was a godly man and attended church regularly. At the end, they married and rode off into the sunset.

I learned two things from *Better Days*. First, I will continue to get closer to my Lord and Savior, and secondly, I will not take any mess from a man.

Chapter 9

After the play, I followed Tory to Mr. Wok's, a Chinese restaurant.

"Nya, thanks for showing me how to use chopsticks."

"You're welcome. As a child growing up, I would eat Chinese food at least once a week. My mother taught me how to use them."

Tory dined on shrimp fried rice. It was hilarious watching him try to scoop up the grains of rice with the two wooden sticks.

"How was your day?" I asked, trying my best to hold back my laughter as I watched Tory fight with the chopsticks.

"Fine. Worked hard as usual. I get so wrapped up in my assignments that I forget to take a lunch break at times. Most times, my secretary demands I take at least a fifteen-minute break. How was your day?"

"I received a promotion."

"Congratulations, Nya!" Tory smiled so wide, you would've thought he was the one who got the promotion.

"Thanks! I'm going to be a teller supervisor. The

best part is my manager is still willing to work around my school schedule," I said, grinning from ear to ear.

"I am so proud of you."

"Thank you."

"You seem to really enjoy your job, Nya."

"I love working with the customers. However, at times, I do get tired of counting money that is not mine." We both burst into laughter as we finished enjoying our meal.

After Tory paid the bill, we made a beeline to his home in the River Bay section of Virginia Beach. And, once again, I found myself getting horny.

As I walked inside his home, I asked, "Do I need to take my shoes off?" The wall-to-wall white carpeting was spotless, and the stack of shoes at the door led me to believe he preferred people to walk through his home in their bare feet. *Can't say that I blame him.*

"No, you're fine. But, I have a strange request—may I see your feet?"

"Sure," I answered, a puzzled look on my face. "Do you have a foot fetish or something?"

"No, I just love a woman who takes care of her feet."

I was not intimidated in the least. My dogs are pretty and they don't smell. Confidently, I took off my shoes for him to inspect my feet. By this time, he had led me to the couch. Instantly, he started rubbing my feet. It felt so damn good. Still, I tried to keep my cool.

"You have nice feet. They are so soft."

"Thank you. I like how you're working my feet."

"I can make you feel even better if you allow my hands to caress your delicate skin," he said in a seductive voice.

"Is that so?"

"I know so. But first, I want to give you the grand tour of my home."

"Okay."

His house was laid out. He had four bedrooms, three-and-a-half bathrooms, spacious closets, pool table, bar, Jacuzzi and a swimming pool. I fell in love with the bathroom because the tub and the shower were separated. His home definitely had a woman's touch.

"Your home is gorgeous."

"Thank you, baby girl. My mother helped me decorate."

See, just as I thought.

Tory pulled out a white T-shirt and a pair of boxers from his dresser drawer and handed them to me.

"Put on something more comfortable. I know you don't want a rub down in that sexy dress you have on."

"Thank you. I'll go change in the bathroom," I said, dying to get one more peek of my favorite section of the house.

"Take your time."

I took my bra off, but kept my thong on. When I emerged from the bathroom, candles were lit. Massage oil and lotion was on the dresser. The radio was tuned into Hot 96's *Quiet Storm,* and Joe's *I Wanna Know* wafted throughout the house. Tory was trying to set the mood. He was working it, too. Still clothed, Tory was lying on the bed. I was relieved. If I would've come out and seen him in nothing but his drawers, I would've known what time it was. And I didn't feel I was quite ready for that . . . at least not yet.

"Come lie down. I wasn't finished with your feet."

As he poured lotion on them and continued his rub down, I found myself floating on cloud nine. If Tory kept this up, I would soon be in heaven. He moved to my neck, and slowly, the kinks diminished. I didn't want him to stop. The massage oil, which smelled like sweet mangoes, was arousing to my senses. Next, he conquered my hands and arms.

"Did you go to school for massage therapy?" I asked, taking pleasure in every stroke.

"No, my mother gets migraine headaches and back-aches due to a car accident she was in five years ago. Since the painkillers were not helping, she tried massage therapy. It reduces her pain and helps her cope with the migraines. She taught my father, sister, brother, and me how to give rub downs."

"You must have gotten an A+ in her class."

"I aim to please, Nya. Now, relax, close your eyes, and enjoy the music."

It was already midnight, but I didn't care. I wanted him to finish what he had started.

Tory massaged my back and worked his way down to my legs. His fingers then traveled their way to my hair, massaging my scalp and sending me to la-la land.

"I love your hair. Plus, it's real. You're a true natural beauty." He paused. "Hey, if you're sleepy, you're more than welcome to stay here for the night."

"No, thank you. I appreciate your hospitality, though."

"Well, at least let me drive you home."

"No, that won't be necessary. I'm going to get to stepping," I said while rising from the bed.

After I finished dressing, Tory escorted me to the front door.

"Keep coming back for more, Nya. The ride is only going to get better. I am a smooth operator," he said, smiling.

He gave me a hug, but it wasn't an ordinary hug. As he wrapped his arms around me, I could feel the sexual tension between us. I didn't want to let him go. I wanted to stay in his arms for the rest of the night.

On my way home, I thought, *how long should I make Tory wait before I let him sniff the punani?*

Chapter 10

After two days, my body still felt rejuvenated, thanks to Tory. I rose out of bed floating on air. My evening with him was unbelievable.

I showered, threw on a sweat suit, and glided downstairs toward the smell of turkey bacon and pancakes. I was starving and thankful that my mother had cooked.

Yvette and I planned on taking a little detour from our Saturday routine. She begged me to go with her to see a psychic. I wouldn't dare tell my mother. She would rebuke the devil out of me. My mother thinks everything is evil and the works of Satan. When Leah and I were little, we were not even allowed to watch cartoons such as the Smurfs because the shows had magic in them. Sometimes, we would sneak and watch them anyway. If she caught us, though, she would say, "You girls cannot watch the works of the Devil. I will not have it in my home. This is the Lord's house. Turn it off. Now!" I can still hear her preaching.

"Hi, girl," I said, pulling up in Yvette's driveway.

"Hello yourself. I appreciate you going with me to see this psychic."

"You're welcome. But, whatever you do, please don't slip up and mention this to my mother. If she finds out about this, she'll go crazy on me."

"My lips are sealed."

"Are you nervous about seeing this woman?"

"No, I'm not. Her name is Safar. What I *am* nervous about is my future. I want to know if Jarvis and I are going to last, my career, a family, and pure happiness."

"You already are happy, Yvette."

"Girl, I know, but I want to stay that way," she said, admiring a picture of Jarvis in her hand.

"Well, I will be waiting outside while Safar and you get the session on."

"No, Nya, you have to come in with me."

"I would rather not," I said, shaking my head.

"Please."

"Don't whine. You better be glad I'm in a good mood to even be taking you."

"Okay, I will admit I am kinda scared."

"You think I'm not. All right, I'll come in with you . . . but just for a minute. I don't believe in this mess anyway."

Once we arrived and stepped inside, we were greeted by the receptionist.

"Good morning, ladies. Welcome to Safar's Psychic Crossroads. May I help you?"

"I have an appointment with Safar."

"Your name please, ma'am."

"Um, Yvette Carson."

"Here you are," she said while looking down at the sheet. "Please have a seat. Ms. Safar will see you shortly."

"Thank you."

This so-called place of business was dark inside and had a strong smell of incense burning. After a few minutes, the receptionist announced, "Safar will see you now." Pointing down the hall, she said, "Walk down the corridor and enter the first door on your right hand side."

"Thank you," Yvette replied.

Upon entering the room, Yvette made an attempt to introduce herself. "Safar, my name is—"

"I know who you are, my child. You and your friend have a seat," she answered, cutting her off. "So, how did you come to hear about me?"

"Mandy, a girl in my yoga class, recommended you to me."

"What are you looking to find out?"

"Basically, the general questions regarding love, career, family. My future as a whole."

"I could tell when I first gazed at you, Yvette, that you are full of laughter and joy. Your smile and attitude are two of your biggest assets."

"Thank you," Yvette replied, displaying a big grin.

"Your friend over there is quite skeptical of me." Safar, looked right into my eyes.

"Me? I'm just here for emotional support, ma'am. Isn't that right, Yvette?" I asked, nodding my head up and down.

"Yes. I don't mean any disrespect, but can we begin?" Yvette asked, eager to find out what her future held.

"All right, then. Hold out your hands for me. The eyes are the windows of your soul; however, the hands tell me a lot about an individual's life. I see lots of people around you all the time. You enjoy helping people, but a special kind of people. You like extending a helping hand with people who are less fortunate. It is your calling and your passion. You will make a lot of difference in many people's lives. You have surrounded yourself with people who truly love you. The day will come in which they will prove their love for you."

"What about my boyfriend, Jarvis and I? Will he and I jump the broom?"

"I see a tall, chiseled, black man who will be your mate. There will be some bumps in the road, but you will make the marriage work. As a matter of fact, both of you beautiful ladies will go through trials and tribulations, but it is nothing each of you cannot handle."

"When will we do it?"

"You are already doing it now, young lady," Safar said in a joking manner. "I am just kidding with you. Loosen up. I won't bite you. I can't tell you everything, my dear. You have to look forward to something. Do not worry, Jarvis and your little ones will keep you busy."

"Thank you so much, Safar," she said, giving the woman a hug.

Me, I didn't want to go near her. She looked evil and scary. I knew she could feel my apprehension.

"Now, it's time for your friend to have a turn."

"Thank you, but no thank you. I appreciate it, though."

I refuse to pay for someone to make up shit about my future. Besides, this woman charges one hundred dollars for the first session. It was a waste of money, if you ask me. Shoot, Yvette could've given me the money and I would've told her whatever she wanted to hear. No different than what Ms. Safar did. *Humph, I could do a whole lot with one hundred dollars. People should stop playing around with other people's emotions. There is only one who knows my future, and that's God.*

As if reading my mind, Safar said, "Young lady, I will not charge you."

"Let her see into your future. Please, just for a few minutes," Yvette pleaded, attempting to negotiate a deal.

"Since you will not come to me, I will come to you." Approaching me, she looked me dead in my eyes. "You are very special and different from other people. Child, you have the heart of a young, bold warrior. You will have to fight a few battles in your life. However, you will be well prepared. Listen to me carefully. Listen to me good. In the near future, someone will put your promising future and freedom into jeopardy. Do not let him take it from you," she proclaimed with a stern look in her eyes.

Who could it be? I know it's not Tory.

"Open your eyes. Always keep them open. I will see you one more time." Safar tried to touch my hands but backed away quickly because my hands were trembling so. "Your strength is too powerful for me. Do not be frightened by it. You are a Scorpio. When is your birthday?"

"It's November 13th," I replied, trying not to appear amused.

"I would hate to be on your bad side."

"Well, I think we should be on our way. Thank you for your time," Yvette said, quickly heading toward the door.

I stood there in front of that woman and put up the biggest front, as if I didn't believe anything she said. Deep down, I was petrified. She had given me a mouthful to think about.

Chapter 11

"Nya, I'm truly sorry I dragged you into this," Yvette said as we walked toward my car, on our way to the local gym for our weekly workout. "She was probably just talking to you like that because you were acting like you didn't believe her. It is strange, though."

"What's so strange?" I asked as we entered the car.

"Whenever I introduce you to someone, they always tell me there is something special about you. Maybe we just can't see it."

"I'm not going to worry about it. No apology needed. I'm not upset. Let's go get our workout on."

I was dying to burn off some of the anxiety I had built up inside of me. Yvette and I ran around the track at least eight times, and then rested for twenty minutes. Next, we worked our arms, butts, and abs. Afterwards, I was tired, sweaty, and wanted a cold can of Sprite. I knew it would quench my thirst. I also knew Yvette would have a fit about it, so I just settled for a cup of water.

By the time we finished our workout, it was almost 2:30. By now, I was starving. An order of Buffalo wings with blue cheese dressing and a salad would definitely hit the spot. Leah and Tara planned to meet us at Applebee's for a late lunch.

"What can I get you ladies to drink?" the waitress at Applebee's asked.

"I'll have a glass of Sprite and some water," I replied, sitting down in the booth.

Yvette requested a glass of ice-cold water.

Tara and Leah both ordered amaretto sours.

"Ladies, I do need to see your IDs, please."

"No problem," Tara said, opening up her purse, while Leah kindly handed over her driver's license.

The fact that they had just produced fake IDs didn't matter; the waitress could not tell the difference.

"Thank you. I'll be right back with your drinks," she said while picking up the menus.

"So what have you two been up to on this beautiful day?" I asked.

"I woke up around noon and cleaned my junkie room," Leah said.

"I slept in late myself. I had a bumpy night with my new friend, Eric. I gave him a ride he'll never forget. I didn't get home till five o'clock this morning," Tara said.

"Your father doesn't get upset that you don't walk in his house till the next morning? My mother would have a pure fit," Yvette said.

"He doesn't like it, but I'm an adult. He always tells me I'm a woman. He even pays for my boxes of condoms and my birth control pills in hopes I will not get pregnant. Besides, not since my little rebellious stage back in high school have I given my dad any more trouble. I know he's proud of me. If I go to school, work, or just be a productive person, he's happy. I want him to be proud of me instead of looking down on me. Plus, I want to do right by my mother. We miss her so much. This is the time when I need her the most."

"I know," I empathized, patting Tara's back.

"We're here for you," Leah consoled.

"On a lighter note, has Raul been trying to win you over?" Yvette asked.

"You know it, girl! I keep receiving flowers, candy, and card deliveries at the house. I called and threatened him, saying if he didn't cool it with the bullshit I was going to sic my big brother Larry on his ass. Let's just say the nagging has ceased," Tara said. We busted out laughing.

"So, how was the visit with the psychic extraordinaire?" Tara asked, diverting the conversation away from her.

"It was a lot to swallow," Yvette said.

"What did she say?" Leah asked.

"Basically, she told me Jarvis and I are going to tie the knot and my career will have to do with me helping people."

"Both are two definite possibilities," Leah responded.

"I know. I'm so excited. She did a reading for Nya, too," Yvette added, smiling.

"What did she say?" Tara and Leah asked in unison.

"Just a bunch of crazy nonsense," I said, rolling my eyes and trying to blow the question off. "She tried her best to work me up, since I don't believe in psychics."

"Safar said Nya has the heart of a warrior and will have a few battles in her life. Oh, one more thing, she said she would hate to get on Nya's bad side," Yvette added.

"Again, she was just talking out the side of her mouth."

"Did she say anything about your family, particularly me?" Leah asked.

"No. She made it seem as if I'm pure evil when I get angry. That's so crazy," I said, shaking my head.

Everyone else around the table gave me a strange look.

"What? Why are y'all looking at me like that?" I glanced into the eyes of each of them.

"Well, Nya, when you get mad, you *can* go too far," Yvette said, crossing her arms.

"Revenge is your middle name," Tara added, rubbing her knife against her fork.

"I second that notion. When someone rubs you the wrong way, you can be ruthless," Leah said.

"Back it up with an example," I demanded. I sat back in my chair and displayed a look that said, "*I'm waiting to hear this.*"

"How about the time we went to Subway and there was a strand of hair in your food. You threw the food at the manager and demanded your money back," Leah said.

"He didn't believe me when I told him it wasn't my hair, accusing me of trying to get free food. Last time I checked my hair was brown, not blonde."

"You called the health department, the local TV station, and the local newspaper about your poor treatment. After the TV segment aired, the manager and the district manager were fired. I'm not agreeing with how the manager treated you, but, damn, you didn't have to get the man fired, Nya. He could have had a family to support," Leah argued.

"I would've been happy with an apology," Tara said, leaning back into her seat.

"Some people have to be taught lessons of respect. I bet the next time the former manager is faced with a similar situation he won't treat the customer like that."

"My turn," Tara said, holding up her hand. "How

about last summer when the police officer pulled us over because he thought we were the missing models for the Covergirl photo shoot. After the mix up, he wanted to check out the car to make sure it was running properly. We all wanted to get on our way, but no, Nya went crazy on his ass."

"He was trying to flirt with us while on the job. No, I don't think so. I told him I would have his badge. He was inconveniencing us. His dick got hard, and he wanted to make up an excuse to see if one of us would bite. That prick should've been chasing the bad guys, not tits and ass."

"You ended up calling his supervisor and the governor, accusing him of sexual harassment," Tara continued. "That four-page complaint letter got faxed to every police station in the Tidewater area."

"The verbal and written apology plus his badge made me feel much better. He should've been grateful I didn't sue his ass."

"I have one," Yvette said, chiming in. "Your junior year of high school . . . you were in Mrs. Watson's honors English class and your paper was due. She took ten points off everyone's paper because it was not double-spaced. Mrs. Watson didn't tell you and the other students it had to be double-spaced. Of course, everyone was pissed. Nya, your eyes turned red with anger. The next day, you took pictures of Mrs. Watson kissing a man in the classroom who was not her husband and mailed them to her house and her husband's job. Then, you sent them to the principal. Two weeks later, Mrs. Watson resigned."

"Wait a minute, how did you even know where her husband worked?" Tara asked, puzzled.

"It was a piece of cake. I use to dread the first day of school every year because it really should be called 'tell-me-about-yourself' day. Well, Mrs. Watson decided she wanted to show us a picture of her beautiful family and tell the class all about herself. How she had been teaching for twelve years, married for ten years, and how her husband worked for Verizon as a computer analyst at the Virginia Beach location. She even told us that she had three children, a boy and two girls, and about how the family absolutely adored Muffy, their cocker spaniel dog. I have a good memory," I said, smirking.

"You're a mess," Yvette said, laughing so hard she almost choked on her water.

"I worked really hard on that paper and deserved an A. Besides, you know I was trying to get into the National Honor Society. Hey, she shouldn't have shared her personal business with the school. I was on the yearbook committee assigned to take pictures randomly with my Polaroid camera. The pictures were to be placed in the yearbook. I was unclear about the homework and decided to drop by. After school, I showed up to the classroom to get my questions answered about the homework assignment and discovered her tongue-tied with a man."

"You're one of the sweetest people I know. However, if someone crosses you, hell has no fury like a woman scorned," Yvette said.

"Ruthless, ruthless, ruthless," they all said in a laughing chant.

"Great, the food is here. Let's eat," I said as the waitress approached the table, taking the focus off me.

The salad and wings were delicious. Now, I definitely needed a nap. Once I work out and then eat a decent meal, what else is there to do but sleep if I have the opportunity to do so? A girl has to get her beauty rest, ya' know. Funny, when I was little, I dreaded naps. I would've rather been playing with my dolls or playing dress up with Leah. Now, I try to get catnaps in, whenever time permits.

As we sat around waiting for our food to digest a bit so we could walk without tumbling over, we engaged in some girl talk.

"What's on for tonight?" Leah asked.

"One of my customers is hosting a party at The System. You know that means we get in for free and will be in VIP. Everyone and their siblings are going to be trying to be up in the club tonight," Tara said.

"Ladies, please make sure you have your 'shut-it-down' outfits in order. Dress to impress," Yvette instructed.

"I already got mine picked out," Leah replied.

"How are you and Tory doing, Nya?" Tara asked.

"So far, things couldn't be better. Right now, he's away on business in California. A day doesn't go by that I don't speak to him. He's the one who's been doing most of the calling, though—I'm not trying to run up my phone bill—but I do miss him a lot."

"When is he coming back?"

"My baby will be back this Thursday. I have to pick him up at the airport that afternoon. Luckily, I am off that day. I have plans to fix him a home-cooked meal."

"Hmm, what did you have in mind, big sis?" Leah asked, licking her lips.

"I think my specialty, roast beef with gravy and all the trimmings, will hit his spot."

"You should be letting him hit *your* spot," Tara said, laughing.

"You're so crazy!" I said, shaking my head.

"You're doing it right. A way to a good man's heart is through his stomach. I don't know what is up with my luck in the romance department. I keep ending up with savages. I haven't given up hope, though. My African prince is somewhere out there," Tara proclaimed, holding her hands together in a praying manner. "But getting back to the subject at hand, have you two done the 'do' yet?"

"No," I answered curtly.

"I told her she should've been broke him off some of that tasty stuff a long time ago. But, no, she wants to be stingy. If you had, maybe you would be in California kicking it with him, instead of here missing him," Leah said.

"At times, I wonder where your head is at."

"You need to stop hesitating and please yourself. You know you want to have sex with him just as much as he wants to with you," Leah added.

"I have something called self-control. Do you and Tara know what that is? If you don't, look it up in the dictionary."

"What are you waiting for, Nya?" Leah pressed.

"First of all, I have to make him wait at least three weeks so I would be considered wifey material. I always want the men I date to think of me as a long-term relationship, not a fuck buddy or a booty call. No man wants a woman who will give it up too fast. They like a challenge. It's so confusing to me. A man doesn't want a woman who is willing to have sex with him on the first date, yet, he will fuck her. After the 'do' is done, he looks at the woman as if she is a whore. If the woman is a whore, so is the man. As far as Tory and I—yes, I want to rip his clothes off, have him spank my ass, pull my hair, and make me come at least six times before sunrise, but it's not the right time. Believe me, the time will come. And when it does, y'all will be the first ones to know."

"Do you think you'll give him some on Thursday?" Tara asked, being nosy as usual.

"I don't know," I replied, growing irritated with all the questions. "Yvette, you're kinda quiet over there. Are you all right? What's on your mind?"

"I'm not worried about the matters at hand, because I already found my man," she said.

"You've been with Jarvis since you were fourteen years old, and you mean to tell me that you haven't once thought about dating or screwing someone else?" Leah asked.

"Of course, I have thought about putting the moves on someone else, but I'm not going to act on those thoughts. I know Jarvis is the only one for me."

"Good for you. Most high-school sweetheart relationships don't usually last. However, Jarvis and you may be the exception to the rule," I said.

"We *are* the exception to the rule," Yvette said.

"Okay, okay, don't go getting all defensive," Tara barked.

"Sorry, I'm not trying to sound all snappy, but I'm just thinking about what Safar said. What if her predictions don't come true? What if one day I stop loving Jarvis or vice versa? I will be crushed if Jarvis and I don't get married."

"Do you love him now?" Leah asked.

"Yes, with all my heart and soul."

"Then go on what you have now. Have faith. Everything will work out. We'll always be here for you. Besides, you know it's a sin to worry," I said.

Chapter 12

Lunch with the girls was quite tiring. When I arrived home, I headed for my bed and napped for a couple of hours. Afterwards, I felt refreshed and ready to take on the world. It was 6:45, and we weren't leaving out till 11:00, which left me plenty of time to dress. I'm one of those people who don't like to be the first one at the club.

Once again, I was faced with the task of deciding what to wear, so Leah came to the rescue. "Help me get dressed, please!" I said, juggling three different outfits in my hand.

"Okay, give me five minutes so I can put on my makeup," Leah said.

I don't wear makeup. I believe in something called natural beauty. All I need is a dime-size portion of Johnson & Johnson lotion on my face and I am good to go. Of course, my friends have tried to give me a makeover, and I ended up looking like a clown.

Dissatisfied with my selections I had lain out on my bed, Leah looked in my closet and picked out a denim top with matching pants.

"You got to rock this outfit with gold. Wear your gold

hoops and gold chain with the cross. A ring is optional.
Put on those Kenneth Cole sandals that I just bought.
I'm going to put your hair in soft spiral curls," she ordered, as if she were a costume director for some major
production on Broadway. "Since I am hooking you up,
you're driving, right?"

"All right," I said with a touch of attitude. I had already figured that much. Since I don't drink, I was always chosen as the designated driver.

When we arrived at Yvette's, Tara was already there. I
was glad because that saved me the trip of having to go
get her. Before going out, Leah and Tara had a few
drinks. No, let me back up . . . a lot of drinks. Yvette will
drink occasionally, but I am a sipper. You know, a sip of
Alizé or a sip of rum and coke. I have seen those two
chicks drunk enough for me not to do the same. I can't
stand the nausea and throwing up all over the place.
Most of the time when they go out, I guarantee you a
date will be made where their face meets the toilet
bowl.

At 11:20, we arrived at The System, the place to be
seen. I could always tell who the movers and shakers
were in this area. My theory is quite simple—the men
who are really bringing in the dough are behind the
scenes. If you're lucky, you may spot them at the bar or
the pool table.

"We'll be out here waiting forever and a damn day,"
Yvette said, looking at her watch.

The line to get in was wrapped around the building.
I was ready to assume the position at the back of the
line when Tara eased my mind.

"No need to fret, girls. We're VIP, remember?" Tara
bragged.

As we walked to the front of the building, Tara
flashed the pass to the men. She even knew Butch, the

security guard. He gave her a hug as if they were family, and we glided past the guards and right through the doors.

"I can get used to this," Yvette said.

"How do you know him?" Leah asked.

"His boss, Mr. Govers, purchased a car from me. He's the owner of this club. Govers told him about me. A few weeks later, Butch bought a vehicle from the lot. Let's just say I gave him an offer he couldn't refuse. You know how it goes . . . I rub your palm and you rub mine. I saved him a lot of money for the vehicle he's cruising up and down the streets in," Tara said, boasting.

Once inside, Tara and Leah headed straight for the bar. I followed closely behind since I could use a drink myself, non-alcoholic of course.

"What can I get the beautiful ladies?" the bartender asked while wiping down the counter in front of us.

"I'll have a virgin strawberry daiquiri with whipped cream and two cherries."

"Live a little, Nya. Have a drink. It'll make you feel nice. You can be such a square, you know that?" Leah said in disgust.

"That's quite all right. I'll be a sober square," I said, laughing.

Tara ordered a sour apple martini, and Yvette had a thirst for a Sex on the Beach. Leah wanted her favorite, Hpnotiq.

"I just need to see some IDs, please," the bartender said.

"Sure, no problem," Yvette said.

Again, they flashed their fake IDs, and it was on. For twenty dollars, this guy named Sonny can name you the president, if you want. They look identical to the real thing. The money spent for the IDs is well worth it since we don't like to party with people our own age. There's always too many fights and drama that come along with the territory. Older people, on the other hand, like to party and have a good time, always dressed in their finest clothing. In the summertime, before we got our fake IDs, we would cruise the Virginia Beach strip. But the disrespect we had to endure from the men became tiring and old. Just because you see a beautiful girl in a bathing suit doesn't mean you can touch it, smack it, lick it, or suck it.

With drink in hand, Leah grooved her way to the dance floor. The DJ was playing her song. DJ Rock was in the house, so I knew we would get served up right with all the hit bangers.

Tara, Yvette, and I decided to find a table. You had to stake your claim up in here. It was 12:15, and in another forty-five minutes, it would be crazy. On many occasions, I've been there when you can hardly move because there were so many people. When it gets like that, I leave early. If I wanted to be in a sauna, I would go to a spa.

I love going out and hanging with my girls. More importantly, I love feeling sexy. I got to work what my momma gave me. Speaking of working it, the DJ was now playing my song, The Ruff Ryders' Anthem. Instantly, everyone stopped what they were doing and proceeded to the floor to shake their booty. Afterwards, he played some reggae, and proud of my moves, I had to break my wind down. It took me forever to learn how to wind. Leah was the one to teach me. But not liking to bring a lot of attention to myself, I refrained from doing it often.

After six songs and finding myself breaking into a sweat, I decided it was time for me to exit the dance floor and get another drink. Leah, of course, remained on the dance floor. I don't know how that girl does it.

When I got back to our table, I motioned for the waitress to come over. Yvette and Tara had a thirst for another round of drinks, too.

"Ladies, I'll be right back with your drinks," the waitress said.

"Thank you. Don't rush. Take your time. There are so many people in here," I said.

"You got that right. We haven't been this busy in a while," the waitress said while picking up our empty glasses.

"Is there a celebrity in the house?" Yvette asked.

"No, but Darren Edmonds is up in the place. He's been here for about an hour. That gentleman is definitely a ladies' man. Women go crazy over him for his good looks and all that money he has."

Darren Edmonds owned a lot of real estate properties, ran a multitude of convenient stores, and a major vending-machine business. He had accounts with many of the corporations in the Hampton Roads area.

"Those quarters, dimes, and nickels add up to the money that folds. Dollar-dollar-bill, y'all," Tara said, laughing.

I always kept this to myself, but I admired him from afar. I was so attracted to him, not because of his looks or his money—which didn't hurt—but for his ambition. He made something out of nothing. Mr. Edmonds even visited my university this past February for Black History Month to encourage other minorities to reach for the stars and consider being an entrepreneur. Beneath that suit, I knew he was a thug at heart.

"Whatever Edmonds wants, he gets at the car lot. Mr. Stein, my boss, and he are very tight. I love to see black men large and in charge," Tara continued.

"Yeah, he *is* fine, but he's not better than my Jarvis," Yvette said.

"No one said he was," Tara said.

The waitress returned with our drinks, and I couldn't have been more grateful. It was getting hotter by the minute in there.

"How much do we owe you?" I asked, pulling a twenty-dollar bill out of my pocket.

"Ma'am, your drinks have already been paid for, compliments of Mr. Edmonds," she said, pointing at me. "He also said he wanted me to give you a little message."

"Well, what did he say?" Tara asked.

Hell, Tara wanted to know what he said more than I did.

"He wanted me to tell you that you're stunning and that he's going to make you his lady," she said in an unenthusiastic tone, as if she could take him up on the offer instead.

"Well, you tell Mr. Edmonds, 'Not in this century,' " I responded in a snooty manner. I could tell men of his stature liked a challenge.

"Aren't you going to give him your number?" Tara asked in disbelief.

"No. Remember, I'm with Tory."

"It's not official, yet. Besides, his ass won't be back until Thursday. What he doesn't know won't hurt him," Tara responded.

"I agree with you, Nya. Don't give him your number; you're a one-man woman," Yvette said, giving me a high-five.

"Shiiit, I would be talking to him now, having dinner tomorrow, and fucking him on Monday," Tara said, laughing.

"I like to take things slow," I said, sipping on my cold bottle of water.

"Y'all, I think I danced a hole in the ground. Let me

have some of that water," Leah said, returning to the table out of breath.

Glancing around at my surroundings, I noticed Edmonds staring and smiling at me from across the room. His smile gave him an air of mystery. I didn't reciprocate. Instead, I acted as if I didn't even see him. He had plans for me, but I was not co-signing. In the meantime, Leah and Tara kept ordering more drinks. By the time I looked at my watch again, it was 2:15 a.m. and time to go.

After dropping Yvette and Tara off at their houses, Tara called her latest beau, Kenny, so he could come pick her up from her house. "Alcohol makes me so horny. I'm going to fuck Kenny's brains out," Tara stated on the way.

Me, I had a date with my bed.

Chapter 13

It was Tuesday and another day at work. When I arrived at the bank, white roses were sitting on my desk. I wondered who they could be from. I searched for a card throughout the vase. The card read: *I just wanted to brighten your day.* I was grateful and wished I could tell the person, Thank you, but I already have a special someone. Yes, I was claiming Tory as my man. He just didn't know it yet. I figured the roses was probably the work of Mr. Edmonds, even though he'd seen me with my baby on several occasions.

I had just two more days before my baby would return from California, and I couldn't wait. I was so excited.

Today, I had on my power suit, a.k.a. grown-up clothes. I didn't particularly like wearing business attire. However, my manager preferred that I did, especially with me being part of management now. I would be setting an example for the teller line. I have to admit when I have on my suits, I feel like I can take on the world. Our bank was business casual. However, effective in two weeks, the dress code would be business professional. When I made the announcement, my tellers wanted an explanation for the change. The reason was simple—no one wanted someone dressed in street clothes handling their money. It's very bias, but that's the way it is.

I was a cool manager, just as long as you worked when we were busy. Otherwise, I didn't care what they did. If the line would get too long for my girls to handle, I had no problem lending a hand and getting my behind on the teller line. The girls respected me for that.

"Good morning, Ms. Pilom, what is on the agenda for today?" I asked with a pen in my hand.

"Child, we have got lots of work to do," she said.

She really means that she is going to shove all the work on my shoulders.

"Here are ten pages of customers that bounced checks. We need to decide whether or not we will pay them by eleven o'clock today. Twelve customers have already left messages begging for us to pay their checks. Let's divide this up."

"Okay."

"After this fiasco, we need to audit all the girls on the teller line. Do not give them heads up. This will be a surprise, Nya."

"I have confidence that all their drawers will balance."

"I really hope so, 'cause I do not need any drama today," she said, laughing.

"Excuse me, there is a call for you on line 3," Ms. Doris said.

"Who is it?" I asked.

"It's a Mr. Hodges."

"Thank you. Please tell him that I'll be right with him."

I hurried to my desk, anxious to get this day over with.

"Good morning, Mr. Hodges. What can I assist you with?"

"Well, I bounced about five checks, but if you can have some mercy and pay them, I'll bring in a deposit by two o'clock this afternoon."

"I'm looking at your account now. I'll pay on your checks, but you will be charged twenty-five dollars for each check. Unfortunately, I'm unable to refund the check fees like I have done before in the past."

"I understand, and I appreciate you working with me."

"You're welcome. Just make sure to bring in that deposit."

"I will."

"You have a good day, Mr. Hodges."

"Thank you."

"Goodbye." *One down and twenty-nine more to go.*

I looked down at my watch and discovered it was lunchtime already.

"Ms. Pilom, I'm going to audit Ms. Deborah first before heading off to lunch."

"That's fine, baby. After lunch, we just have one more teller to audit," she said while adding up several figures on the calculator. "Did your tellers balance?"

"Pretty much . . . a few cents short here and there. It was nothing major."

"I'm going to Wendy's. Do you want anything?"

"No, thank you."

I was in the mood for toquitos, a side order of Mexican rice, with a tall glass of Sprite and a sip of water. As soon as I did a Speedy Gonzales through the next audit, I was going to fill my tummy with some of that spicy food from the Mexican restaurant next door to us. The paperwork was in my hand, and I was ready to count some money.

Ms. Deborah is the assistant head teller, which means her cash drawer limit is fifty thousand. It may sound like a lot, but really, it's not. Besides, our money counters come in handy at times like these.

"Surprise, surprise, Ms. Deborah, the audit patrol is on the prowl," I said jokingly.

Her mouth dropped and I could see fear and apprehension in her eyes. I hoped she had her drawer together.

"Well, I'm going to lunch," she said quickly, while grabbing for her car keys.

"No, you're not. It's my turn to go. I came in before you," Heather stated, rolling her eyes.

"Oh, yeah, that's right," she said, laughing.

I'm glad she found some humor in the situation 'cause I sure the hell didn't.

"All right, let's get to it. The sooner I start, the sooner I'll be finished. Then we both can go to lunch."

"My drawer is a mess," she said, making excuses.

"That's okay."

"May I use the ladies' room, first?" she asked, swinging from side to side.

"Yes," I answered with an attitude. I was trying so hard not to cop one. I needed something to eat and here she was stalling. Ms. Deborah better be glad I hadn't called in my order already. She wouldn't have liked it if I wrote her up as a result of my ass having to eat cold food.

After twenty minutes, she finally returned.

"Are you all right?" I asked with concern.

"No, my stomach is feeling queasy. I think I have a

temperature. It's getting cold in here," she said, tightly hugging herself.

"I hope you're not coming down with anything." I already knew the deal and was ready to play along. "After this audit, I'll let you go home."

"No, I don't think I can make it. If you don't let me leave now, I'm calling Human Resources," she said, slamming her fist against the counter.

This woman was trying to get bold with me. Ms. Stein overheard us talking, and before I could get a word out, Ms. Stein said, "Deborah, please let Nya audit you. It has to be done before three o'clock this afternoon. If you can work with a broken arm, then you can certainly work with an upset stomach for another ten minutes. Afterwards, go home. I want to see you in my office first thing tomorrow morning. Are we clear?"

"Yes, Ms. Stein," Ms. Deborah replied timidly.

Immediately, I knew something was not right.

Ms. Deborah's drawer better add up to the correct amount, or I will fry her behind. "Can we begin now?" I asked while looking dead in her eyes.

Her melodrama was starting to irritate me. She unlocked her drawers. She was right; they were messy. I quickly began counting her money, determined to get this over with. It took another fifteen minutes to count and add up my figures. Sure enough, Ms. Deborah was short five hundred and twenty-five dollars. I reviewed all of her transactions from that morning and recounted her money twice. She had only done straight deposits and handled no cash.

"Ms. Deborah, you are short in a major way."

"What are you talking about? My drawer settled fine yesterday," she said in shock, her hand over her mouth.

"Well, today, you are short over five hundred dollars."

I called Ms. Stein over to recount the money.

"Maybe you miscounted."

"Believe me, I can count. Besides, I can't count something that is not here to begin with."

"What are you trying to say?"

"You tell me."

By this time, Ms. Deborah looked white as a ghost. I wanted to burst into tears of laughter, but I kept my composure. Ms. Stein came up with the same total as me. Now, I was pissed because I knew I would not be going to lunch any time soon. When situations like these arose, we had to call security. Ms. Deborah was not able to go back into her money. Instead, Ms. Stein told her to go sit in the lunchroom and try to recall any transactions that involved amounts of $500.00 or more to give an explanation as to why her drawer was short. By the time security arrived, it was 2:45. Two representatives from security came and did the same things we did. At this point, it was not looking good for Ms. Deborah. When I went into the lunchroom, she was sweating profusely. She had been short before, but never by this large of an amount, which led Ms. Pilom and me not to think anything of it other than honest mistakes.

The representatives decided to talk to her, and after forty minutes, Ms. Deborah confessed to stealing the money. She was one dumb lady. I would've never admitted to taking the money. She was in tears, not because she felt remorse for stealing, but from fear because her behind had just bought herself a first class ticket to the Norfolk City Jail.

As the police escorted her out to the paddy wagon, Ms. Deborah said, "I am so sorry, Nya."

I'm sure the only thing she was sorry about was getting caught. I knew she was having trouble making ends meet, but I didn't think it would come to this. You never know what a person might do once their back is up against a wall. It was now six o'clock, and I was relieved this day was finally over.

"What's going to happen to Ms. Deborah?" I asked Ms. Pilom.

"Nothing really, honey. As long as she pays the money back, the bank will not press charges against her. You have to look at the bigger picture. BankFirst will just want her out. It would probably be more costly to hire an attorney and prosecute her. Now, go home, get yourself some rest, and take tomorrow off."

"But I'm off on Thursday, as well. I don't want the rest of the employees to think that I'm getting special treatment."

"The other employees will mind their business," Ms. Pilom said in a cocky tone.

"She's right. As a new manager, today was traumatic for you. As a matter of fact, I have made the decision to close the branch tomorrow. I think we all need a rest from the events of today," Ms. Stein said.

"Relax, get your mind right, girl. We'll see you back on Friday, baby," Ms. Pilom said.

"Well, if you insist."

Once I left the bank, all I wanted to do was go home and crawl into my bed.

"Hi, baby. How was your day?" Mommy asked while sitting down on the couch.

"Hey, my day was crazy."

"What happened?" Daddy asked, taking a bite out of his chocolate éclair.

"Sit down and have some dinner. There is spaghetti on the stove," Mommy said while patting my back.

"To make a long story short, I had to audit the tellers today. Everyone's drawers balanced except Ms. Deborah's."

"How much was she short?" Mommy inquired.

"A little over five hundred dollars. You should've been there when I told her I had to count her junky drawer. She turned even whiter than she already was. When the big bosses came, she confessed to the crime. Ms. Deborah was arrested and hauled off to jail. One good thing came out of the fiasco today, though."

"What's that, baby?" Daddy asked.

"Both of my managers gave everyone the day off tomorrow. Mmm, Mommy, you put a hurting on this spaghetti. It's so good," I said while eating the spaghetti wrapped around my fork. She always seasoned the meatballs just right.

"Thank you."

"Where is Leah?" I asked.

"She is just now getting off work. That girl should be walking in the door any minute now."

One of Leah's best qualities is talking on the phone. That's why she works for STARVISA, a credit card collection agency. My sister brings in the dough, but has a hard time keeping it.

"Night-night, Mommy and Daddy."

"Goodnight," they said in chorus.

In the next half an hour, I had taken my shower and was ready to go to sleep. Just as I laid my head down on my pillow, the phone rang.

"Hello?"

"Hey, sweetness, how was your day?" Tory asked.

"Hi, I'm glad you called," I said with a big grin plastered on my face. "My day was insane. I will tell you all about it when you get home on Thursday. How was yours?"

"You know I had to check in to get my daily dose of your beautiful voice. I have been in meetings and seminars all day . . . matter of fact, all week. I seriously think RADCOM wants to expand its horizons out here on the West Coast. I've been working out here non-stop. When I get back, I'll have the same workload. I finally had the chance to hire an assistant by the name of Tracy, though. Well, you sound tired, and so am I. So, go get your beauty rest and I'll talk to you tomorrow."

After we said our goodnights to each other and hung up, I laid back down thinking about Tory. We had only known each other for a short period of time. But already, I felt as though I was being quickly swept off my feet. I tried to convince myself that it was too soon to be feeling this way. We hadn't even been dating for three months yet. I had to keep my cool, see how he was feeling first before putting my feelings out on the line. The last thing I wanted was for my feelings to get trampled on.

Chapter 14

Tory's flight was due in at six o'clock and it was now two o'clock. Therefore, I had a couple of hours to prepare a wonderful meal. Tory would be so surprised and thankful. I'm sure he hadn't had a home-cooked meal since he'd been gone. So, I planned for us to have dinner at his place after I picked him up from the airport.

While preparing Tory's meal, Leah entered the kitchen.

"Something smells good," she said.

"Thanks. You know what they say, one way to a man's heart is through his stomach," I chuckled.

"Well, that's what they tell me. What's cooking?"

"Tender roast beef with baby carrots and diced potatoes simmered in homemade gravy, fresh string beans, and rice."

"Dang, Nya, you are throwing down!" Leah removed the top from the casserole pan. "May I?" she asked as she reached for the fork.

"Just a taste, Leah. Don't even think about making a plate!"

"I won't, geesh. We can't have Tory starving," she

teased. She stuck the fork in the roast beef and pulled off a small piece, tasting it. "Damn, girl, I didn't know you could cook like this."

I wanted tonight to be perfect for my new boyfriend, or my man as my friends called him. I've yet to bring him home. My friends can hardly wait to meet Tory in person due to the fact that I can't keep my mouth shut about him. He is everything I've been dreaming about. I couldn't be more blessed. His hazel eyes mesmerize me, his rock hard body is to die for, and I just know when the time comes, he is going to be a wonderful lover as well. He is slightly rough around the edges, but nothing I can't smooth out. Besides, I like a little "bad boy" in my men. Aside from being intelligent, he's also kind and easy-going. Tory stimulates me mentally and brings balance to my life. He wants to be somebody and has goals. He is simply a dream come true.

Tonight is our third date, which brings me one step closer to getting my freak on. And yes, I'm strictly under-cover about that.

Chapter 15

I met Tory at the gate with yellow and white carnations. His flight was delayed fifteen minutes and butterflies had taken up residence in my stomach. For a moment, I thought I was going to hyperventilate.

After pacing the floor and spending a majority of the fifteen-minute delay in the ladies' room, the arrival of his flight was announced. I took a deep breath and positioned myself so that I could spot him quickly.

Damn, he looks good enough to eat, I mumbled under my breath.

When he spotted me, he added pep to his step and made his way toward me.

"Hey, baby," he greeted as he dropped his bags to the floor and embraced me. His hug was intoxicating.

"Hey, you," I whispered in his ear. "You are a sight for sore eyes."

He broke our embrace. "And so are you, girl."

"These are for you," I said, extending the flowers.

"Baby, they are beautiful. I've never been given flowers before. Thank you so much."

"You're welcome," I said, smiling a wide-ass grin.

After arriving at the car, we tossed his bags in the

trunk and headed for his house. "Something smells good. What is that?" he asked, looking into the back seat.

"Dinner. Are you hungry?"

"Starving! I've been eating crackers all day."

"Good, because we are going to throw down." I released a soft chuckle.

"What's for dinner?"

"It's a surprise."

He leaned over and kissed me on the cheek. "I like surprises, Nya." A mischievous grin crept across his lips.

"Great, because tonight I want you to obey my commands," I said with a hint of seduction in my voice.

Chapter 16

"Dinner was scrumptious, Nya," Tory said, patting his stomach with satisfaction as he stretched his long legs out before him. "The roast was so tender. I needed a home-cooked meal. You even washed the dishes. I have to admit you really did your thing tonight."

"Thank you," I said bashfully. "It's not over yet. Dessert is in the oven right now."

"I was hoping dessert would be you with whipped cream on top. I would definitely do the honors of licking it off of you."

I felt a tingle travel down my spine. "You get the bowls and I'll get the spoons," I responded, giggling.

Tory held up his index finger. "You mean one spoon."

I smiled and winked at him.

"Let's get it on, baby girl," he said, heading toward the kitchen.

Since it was a cool summer night, we decided to take a stroll around the neighborhood. I didn't want to be out too long, though, because the mosquitoes might start looking for a free meal ticket.

"I certainly enjoyed myself this evening, Nya."

"The pleasure was all mine," I said while taking his hand.

"Growing up, I was so fascinated with the stars. Some nights, I would go out on the balcony and watch the sky."

I looked up at the stars and Tory leaned over and kissed me, catching me off guard. His lips were soft and full. I closed my eyes as our tongues danced together. It felt so good.

He led me back to the house with a trail of kisses behind us. Upon entering, we made a beeline to the bedroom. "You won't need this," I said as I slowly removed his wife beater.

He started kissing me, working his way down to my neck. *Oh my God, he's at one of my spots, my ear. It's driving me so crazy. I'm getting wetter and wetter. I can't give him any tonight. It's too soon.*

I glided my hands across his shoulders. "Ooh, baby, you're feeling tense."

"I guess I am feeling a little jet-lagged."

"Why don't you let me take care of that for you? Lay down on the bed, and I'll be right back," I said, running down to the living room to get my purse, where I pulled out the strawberry-flavored massage oil.

As I stood in the doorway of the bedroom, I asked, "Are you comfortable?" while staring at his bulging muscles.

"Not yet."

"Well, let's take care of that." I smiled wickedly. "Turn over on your stomach, baby."

"Is this dessert *after* the dessert?" he asked.

I wished I could've said yes, but I was sticking to my "no sex" rule. I had to maintain my focus and not allow his cobra to sidetrack me.

Tory's bed looked like it stood damn near six feet off the floor. A three-step wooden ladder sat at the side. I kicked off my shoes, climbed the steps, and straddled his back. Rubbing my toes against the cream silk duvet, I sprinkled massage oil on his back and rubbed my hands together. Then, I let my fingers take over.

"Your hands feel nice," he moaned.

Dismounting him, my fingers traveled down toward his waist. I was tempted to suggest he take off his pants, but I was not even going to go there.

After thirty minutes, the Sandman had come and gone. Tory was fast asleep. I took that as my cue to exit.

I kissed him on the lips and then whispered goodnight in his ear.

Before I could make my escape, he opened his eyes, grabbing me and gently motioning my body to lie on the bed. He started kissing my ears again as I tried slowly to ease away.

"Your skin is so soft. Don't go. Stay a little longer. I'll drive you home or to work tomorrow. Whatever you want, Nya. Please, baby, don't leave me. You're so special to me. I don't know what it is. All I know is that I feel so good when I'm around you. I can be myself. You make me feel so comfortable," he said, bringing my body even closer to his.

I don't know who was hotter, him or me. He was beginning to touch a tiny place in my heart.

"You are so sweet to me," I said, forcing a smile, uncomfortable that this may go where I was not ready for it to go. Well, mentally, I was not ready, but my body was craving this man.

"I bet you taste even sweeter," he said, unzipping my sweat jacket.

"Tory . . ."

"Shhh," he whispered, completely undressing me.

Next thing I knew, I was standing before him naked as a jaybird. Funny, I didn't feel awkward like I thought I would.

"Damn, your body is driving me wild," he said while looking at me up and down.

I was caught up in the rapture of his seduction as he cupped my perky breasts in the palm of his strong hands.

I moaned deeply, lying back on the bed and closing my eyes. I exhaled deeply.

"Your breasts are so soft."

I was too much in awe to reply. Tory played and teased my breasts with his tongue. Afterwards, he took my erect nipple in the warmth of his mouth. My swollen bud summoned his finger.

"Do you want me to stop? I will if you want me to," he panted.

The heave of my body answered for me.

He stopped, hopped off the bed, and jetted down the stairs. Before I knew it, he was back and the coolness of whipped cream on my neck, ears, breasts, and clit was driving me crazy. He licked and sucked places, finding erogenous zones I never knew existed.

"Oh, Tory, don't stop," I said as he frantically flicked his tongue across my clit in an unexplainable manner. "Oh, shit, don't stop! Don't . . . don't . . ." I trailed off, exploding inside his mouth as my body shook uncontrollably.

"Nya, baby, I know you're not ready to make love tonight. Still, I wanted to give you a taste of ecstasy. You know that I had to show you what you're dealing with. One of these days, I will take you all the way . . . whenever you are ready."

If you only knew. You've just taken me there, back, and there again.

"I like to please you, even if I don't get anything in return. You already have done too much. My baby picked me up from the airport, cooked me a nice meal, and gave me the best rub down. I'm peeping you out—I like your style, Ms. Gamden. I want to make you mine. That is if you'll have me. Are we official yet?" He kissed me on my hand ever so gently.

I managed to nod my head, still laying there trying to recover from the major orgasm I had just experienced.

Tory went to the bathroom and returned with a hot cloth to wipe me down. "I don't want you to go home all sticky. Would you like to take a shower?"

"No, I'm fine. I'll take a quick shower when I get home. If I don't leave now, I won't leave at all. Tory, I want to thank you for respecting my decision to wait."

"When can I see you again?"

"How does Saturday work for you? There is a new art gallery opening up in downtown Norfolk. Plus, I want to catch that movie, *Barbershop*."

"Sounds like a plan. May I pick you up at your house?"

"Sure."

"Let me walk your fine ass out."

"Okay," I said, grinning from ear to ear.

Chapter 17

"Mommy, we have already discussed this. Don't ask Tory to give you a life story on himself. Daddy, I don't want you to scare him away."

"Does he go to church?" Mommy asked while looking in the Bible.

"Yes, his family attends Mount Grove Baptist Church."

"That church sounds familiar," Daddy said, turning the channels on television.

"William, you know Mr. Rose's oldest son is the pastor of that church."

"Okay, now I remember."

"Praise the Lord! Another soul is saved from the clutches of the devil." Mommy lifted her hands in the air.

"He should be here any minute," I said, looking at the clock on the wall. And that minute couldn't come fast enough.

"While we're gone, remember to lock up this house and set the alarm," Mommy showed me a list of other things to remember.

"Don't worry. I've got everything under control. You

two just don't forget to bring us something back from your Bahamas trip."

My mom and dad would be gone for two weeks. That meant I was going to have to take care of the house. Leah was no help in this department. She had a hard enough time taking care of herself. Mommy and Daddy traveled a lot. If they got fed up with the daily stress of life, Daddy would take Mommy and get away.

He always told me, "Baby, enjoy your life to the fullest, because you only get one chance."

My daddy is my hero. I love the way he treats my mother. They never argue in front of us, he never laid a hand on her, and there's nothing he wouldn't do for her.

At 7:30 on the dot, the doorbell rang.

"Great, he's here," my daddy announced.

"Good evening, Mr. Gamden. I'm Tory Sothers. It's an honor to meet you, sir," he said, shaking his hand.

"Willie, don't let the boy just stand in the doorway. Come on in."

"You must be Mrs. Gamden. It's a pleasure to meet you. Now I see where Nya gets her radiant beauty from."

"Thank you." My mother blushed at his compliment

Daddy snapped his fingers. "You look so familiar."

"That's probably because my father played football with you in high school, sir."

"That's right, we called him 'sock-it-to-'em' Sothers," Daddy said laughing.

"Pop said your nickname was 'go-for-the-gusto' Gamden."

"How's your father doing?"

"Fine. Working hard and growing old gracefully."

"He's a good man."

"I'll be sure to tell him that, sir."

"You are a fine young man, Tory. Nya tells us that you work for a major engineering company and have aspirations for your own business."

"That's right, sir."

"I know your parents are proud of you."

"Thank you, sir."

"Now, don't take this to heart, but I tell all men that come through my castle door not to hurt my baby, or I will hurt you."

"Daddy!"

"Well, it was nice meeting you, Tory. We've got to get going now. Your aunt and uncle are waiting for us," Mommy said, turning towards me.

Mommy and Daddy usually traveled by themselves, but I guess this trip was going to be a family affair.

"Have a nice evening," Daddy said with an apologetic look on his face.

When Leah got off the phone for two seconds to say bye, we exchanged hugs with our parents and then I proceeded to introduce her to Tory.

"Well, well, you must be Tory. I've heard a lot of things about you. Good things, of course," Leah said with a smirk on her face.

"It's a pleasure meeting you, as well," Tory said, shaking her hand.

"I won't keep you two. Besides, my call is waiting. See you later," Leah said, running up the stairs.

Little did Tory know she meant that literally. The whole gang was making an appearance at the art gallery just to get a sneak peek at him.

"Daddy was just playing. I hope he didn't scare you," I said.

"No, not at all. Leah and you are his babies, his pride

and joy. Your father was not playing, either. When I have my daughter, I know I'll be the same way. Your sister and you deserve nothing but the best. I was surprised not to see a shotgun or an AK-47 greet me at the door," he said, laughing. "Besides, my father had already prepared me. He told me that your pops doesn't play around."

"Are you ready?"

"I'm ready when you are, baby."

"Then let's go."

"I am so excited about tonight," I said, fastening my seat belt.

"What is supposed to be jumping off at this gallery?" he asked while pulling out of the driveway.

"Well, Visions Art Gallery is showcasing a lot of local minority artists. I love black art. Tonight, the theme is family. I enjoy looking, but I certainly cannot afford to take home every piece that I want. These wonderful paintings will range from a thousand dollars on up. The painting in your living room of the young mother rocking her precious child in the chair caught my eye. It's a gorgeous piece."

"Thank you. My mother gave it to me for a housewarming gift. See, that is what I mean, Nya—most of the women I meet are not interested in art; you, on the other hand, are unpredictable. What I am really trying to say is you are one of a kind."

"Thank you. You're not too bad yourself, Tory."

"It's Mr. Sothers, if you're nasty."

We both busted out laughing.

Outside, there were paintings showcased with a crowd of people hovered around them. A brochure of the artists and their pieces were given to us as we entered the building. Inside, the lights were dim with lines of people waiting to see the featured painting of the evening. There stood a fine piece of art. A black man was embracing his woman. While he held her tight, she was resting her head on his chest and wiping away her tears. It stirred something inside of me that I just couldn't shake.

"I see your eyes gazing and the expression on your face. It seems that you definitely like this painting. What's on your mind, Nya?"

"It represents love, pain, and struggle. This man and this woman represent a union. By the looks of it, she seems to be relieved. He is there for her now to take care of her, physically and emotionally. I want the same union. When two people are in a relationship, there has to be a team effort. If I fall, you pick me up; if you fall, I pick you up."

"Interesting observation," he said, giving me a soft peck on my lips.

The painting was twelve hundred dollars, which amounted to almost one of my paychecks. When it comes to art, I like to splurge. Already, I have five pieces hanging around in my parents' home. They sure were not that expensive, though.

"How did you come to love art so much?"

"It's funny you ask . . . because I cannot draw a lick. On Saturdays, my mother would take Leah and me to different art galleries, plays, and musicals. She always wanted to expose us to many things. I appreciate her for that."

"Nya," I heard a voice calling me from the crowd.

It was Yvette, and she was amongst the whole gang. A woman who looked very familiar was following closely behind on their heels, but I couldn't recall where I knew her from.

"Hey, girl," I said.

"These paintings are off the hook."

"Not to mention the free food and drinks," Tara said, laughing.

"How long have you two been here?" Leah asked with a glass of champagne in her hand.

"Um, we've been here for a little while."

"Tara and Yvette, this is Tory Sothers. Tory, these are my best friends. We all go way back," I said, pointing my thumb behind me.

"This is Michelle, my cousin." Tara pointed to the girl who had finally caught up with the rest of the group.

"No wonder you look so familiar. I remember when you would come down here for summer vacations. We would all play together. How have you been?" I asked, giving her a hug.

"Fine, I'm currently working in Richmond for the state tax department. I'm looking for an accounting job in this area. I love to visit Virginia Beach."

"I see you have a bun in the oven." I pointed toward her protruding stomach. "Congratulations! How many months are you?"

At this point, Tory cleared his throat, and his palms were starting to get sweaty inside of mine. I found this to be strange but dismissed it as him just being caught off guard about meeting my friends.

"Six months," she said, rubbing her stomach.

"It was nice meeting you ladies," Tory said, excusing himself to get a glass of champagne.

"Where are the guys?" I asked after Tory had walked off.

"They went to find us more drinks." Noticing the expression on my face, she said, "Don't worry, I'm not going to get too tipsy up in here," and sipped her glass of wine.

"These paintings with all these sexual innuendoes are making me hot under the collar," Leah said while fanning her face.

"Tory and I are going to walk around a little bit more, and then go catch that movie."

"I already saw it. I give it three stars," Yvette said.

"My baby's daddy, Ice Cube, is in the movie with his sexy ass," Leah giggled.

"Girl, you need some help," I responded, laughing. "Bye, y'all. Tell the guys I said hello," I said as I walked off in search of Tory.

"I can tell you got lots of love for your crew. I can also tell that Tara and Leah are the wild ones out of the bunch," he said as I approached him. He was standing near the entrance with drinks and appetizers in hand.

"You've got that right," I said while smiling and taking a glass from his hand.

Tory and I looked at ten more paintings, with each of them moving me, not only emotionally but also financially. I wanted to pull out my wallet to buy one of those babies. Oh, who the hell am I kidding? I wanted all of them. But I had to maintain my self-control. With each painting we looked at, it was getting more and more difficult to resist the stroking of my bank card. I finally decided it was time for us to go.

"You ready, baby?"

"Yeah, do you want to grab a bite to eat before the movie?" he asked.

"No, I'm fine. The drinks and appetizers filled me up."

"I'm stuffed, too. I couldn't stop eating those Swedish meatballs and fruit sticks. I had to ask if you were straight, though. I have to take care of my baby in all areas," he said, kissing my hand while gazing into my eyes.

I want him to kiss something else. And maybe tonight might just be the night.

Chapter 18

Barbershop was off the hook.

"What a night!" Tory proclaimed, looking down at his watch. "Are you hungry?" he asked.

"A little."

"What are you in the mood for?"

"I have a taste for a sandwich."

We made our way to Sourdough's, a trendy coffee, tea, sandwich, and salad restaurant that is open late on the weekends.

"I'll have the smoked turkey sandwich with lettuce, tomato, black olives, sweet pickles, hot peppers, and a smidgen of Italian dressing with bottled water," I ordered.

"Let me get the roast beef sandwich with a Sprite."

"Is this for here or to go?" the cashier asked.

"To go," Tory said, looking at me with a devilish smirk.

"Penny for your thoughts?"

"These thoughts in my head will turn into reality. Babygirl, I have a surprise for you. Don't ask any questions. All I want you to do is ride in the car."

"Okay," I said, eagerly waiting for what was coming to me.

* * *

After we left the restaurant, Tory took me to the exclusive Odyssey Hotel. Even though I was excited, I kept my composure.

"We're almost there," Tory said as we stepped onto the elevator.

The room was spacious and immaculate, with candles lit all in the bedroom and white roses everywhere.

I took a seat on the bed. "How did you know that I like white roses?"

"Last week, when I called you, Leah picked up and told me."

"That doesn't surprise me."

Chocolate-covered strawberries were sitting on the table. The room included a mini-bar, refrigerator, microwave oven, and a cozy Jacuzzi laced with rose petals.

"When did you have time to do all this?"

"Babygirl, I didn't have time. That is what friends are for."

"It *is* the thought that counts," I said, smiling.

"I have one more thing for you. This is from the heart," he said, kissing me on the cheek. "Read this while I go turn on the music."

Luther Vandross' *Because It's Really Love* started to play. It's my all-time favorite song. Someday, I will play it at my wedding.

I sat back to read the poem, which read:

I hope you do not feel I come on too strong
Baby girl, what I feel cannot be wrong
You make me smile and brighten my day
I am so grateful and blessed that you swung my way
I want to hold you in my arms and squeeze you tight
I pray that tonight is the night
Love, Tory

* * *

As I read the poem over and over, several Stevie Wonder, Pebbles, and Babyface sultry songs played in the background.

"The radio is on point tonight," I said, smiling.

"It's not the radio. I made this CD last night for you."

"How did you know——?"

"Let's just say that a little birdie told me. Sit tight. I'll be right back."

While he was gone, I replayed the words of the poem in my mind.

He had touched the depths of my soul. I wasn't going to let him know that, though.

"Did you like it?" he asked, coming back into the room.

"I love the poem, this room, the roses, everything," I replied as I stood and took a slow spin around the room.

I knew he had spent at least a thousand dollars on the room alone. This hotel was not one of those cheap, rent-by-the-hour joints.

"Thank you so much," I said, hugging him.

"You're welcome. Believe me, it was all my pleasure."

As we stood there in a tight embrace, I rested my head on his chest just like in the painting. We both knew what time it was—I wanted it; he wanted it—and we were about to do something about it. Our lips embraced and our tongues began to play tug-of-war.

"Nya, baby, you do not have to do this if you don't want to. I can wait until you are ready. I don't want you to feel as though I'm rushing you."

"The time *is* right," I said, clawing off his shirt, pants, and boxers.

Tory did the same to my clothes, pausing only for a moment to admire my lingerie. The pink bra and boy-short set I wore especially for tonight reeled him in.

"You look gorgeous. Turn around for me one time."

Boy shorts had a way of enhancing my booty.

"Hmm, come here," he said, licking his lips.

As I moved in closer to him, a wild animal instinct came over me, causing my dripping wet pussy to want his python pulsating between my thighs. I placed his two fingers in my vagina so he could feel the wetness, while my right hand stroked his penis. When reaching the tip, I twisted it as if I were opening a jar of chocolate sauce. My left hand gently caressed his balls.

Tory undid the front clip of my bra. My nipples were hard as rocks. He did not seem to care. I wanted them to be teased and played with, again and again. He poured tiny drops of MOET on my breasts and devoured every drop. The sounds of his licking and slurping caused my pulse to quicken. Suddenly, he started massaging them until he worked his tongue down to my vagina. It felt so good. My knees began to weaken, and I could hardly stand up any longer.

"Nya, I'm going to make you so happy."

And I'm going to fuck the shit out of you.

With each lick, he brought me closer to climaxing.

"Oh yes," I moaned, closing my eyes.

I had resisted for longer than I could stand. I came so hard that I shivered profusely. I didn't even try to tone it down. At that point, I didn't care. I fell back on the bed, and Tory climbed right on top of me. He was kissing my neck while quickly putting on the condom. Finally, his python was where it belonged.

"I won't hurt you. I'll go slowly."

Our tongues were intertwined. Each stroke got better and harder. Our pelvises had developed their own sexual rhythm.

"Nya, yes," he moaned.

"Keep it coming," I said out of breath, grabbing his hand.

We rolled over. I barely managed to get on top of him. Tory was against the headboard of the bed while I rode him like a true urban cowgirl. I was giving him the hardest blows as he continued to suck my nipples.

"Give it to me. Don't stop," Tory chanted.

"Yes," I gasped while rolling over so he could be on top.

"Damn, girl, your pussy is so tight."

"Harder," I demanded while giving him a smack on his ass.

He called my name again erotically. It was music to my ears.

"Oh ooh," we both said in chorus.

We couldn't hold it back anymore. Tory and I came at the same time. Once again, I shivered.

"Thank you for the ride," he said, rolling from on top of me and wiping the sweat from his forehead.

"Anytime," I replied, damn near out of breath.

I couldn't stop smiling at Tory.

"What is that face for?" he asked while gently stroking my cheek.

"I am so happy right now. I needed to be reached out and touched."

"That's my job."

"I forgot all about our sandwiches."

"Don't sweat it. We can always order room service or go get something else. Whatever you want."

"No, that's all right."

"I'll heat the sandwiches up, but first, would the beautiful lady like to join me in the shower?"

"Yes," I said as I took his hand.

The bathroom was enormous. The shower and the tub were separate. At least four people could fit comfortably in the tub. Sweet vanilla filled the room. It even came with His and Her bathrobes. Which came in handy since I didn't have an overnight bag with me.

"Which would you prefer, a shower or bath?" he asked while pointing to both.

"A shower."

Oil of Olay soap, Johnson and Johnson baby lotion, Bath and Body Works White Gardenia lotion, Dove deodorant, a toothbrush and toothpaste were all sitting on the countertop. These are all products that I use. Instantly, my eyes looked toward Tory.

"By the way, I picked you up a few items," he said, as if reading my mind.

"Thank you."

The little birdie had told him quite a bit about me, hadn't she?

"This water feels soothing against my back," I said after hopping in the shower.

As Tory began washing himself, I took the washcloth and soap out of his hands.

"Let me, Mr. Sothers." Gently, I caressed his skin, including the almighty python. He returned the favor and lathered me up, then started playing in between my thighs. "Hmm," I moaned. I hungered for my love to come back down. "I want you," I said, whispering in his ear.

He grabbed the condom that was on the bathroom counter next to my hygienic items and lifted me up, wrapping my legs behind his back. I slid down on his python and held on tight as he rode me to ecstasy.

"I get high off of you," Tory said.

I bit into my sandwich. "Like a weed high?"

"No, it's even better; it's difficult to put into words."

"Come on, try me."

* * *

"I love being around you. Time quickly passes by when I'm enjoying our moments together. Nya, you stimulate my mind, body, and soul. Baby, you don't even realize how sexy you are. I have never felt this way before," he said, kissing my cheek.

"Promise me something."

"What's that?"

"I like that you feel comfortable enough to share your feelings with me. I want us to always keep the lines of communication open, no matter what."

"I feel as though I can talk to you about anything, Nya."

"I feel the same way, Tory."

"How did you like the bra and panty sets that I picked out for you?" he asked, pointing to the gift box. "I saw you peeking at them."

"You didn't do too badly. My favorite is the red set with lace."

"There is more where that came from. Now that I have kidnapped you for a couple of days, it's my duty to provide you with shelter, food, and clothing," he said, smiling.

"Thank you for the bare necessities."

"I have some outfits in the closet for you. If you don't like them, we can go pick up something else."

While looking in the closet, my eyes lit up with glee. This man was going all out for me. Tory had purchased six outfits. Three were casual, and the others were sexy. He even got me a Chanel dress that I had been dying to have, but which my small pockets were deterring me from buying. He definitely knew my style.

"These next few days, I just want to relax and savor my time with you. We're going to live it up."

"I have no problem with that," I said, giving him a hug.

"Right now, all I want is to be next to you," Tory said while caressing my face.

Soon, we were fast asleep in each other's arms.

Chapter 19

"Hurry up, Nya!" Leah yelled up the stairs.

"Yeah, I'll be right down," I yelled back.

"Now, you know I raised you young ladies better than to yell in my house," Mommy said from the other end of the phone. Even though she was thousands of miles away, she called home often to check on us.

"Yes, ma'am," I said in a low-toned voice.

"Drive carefully. And before you even ask, I don't have any money to send you. Don't even toot up those lips you were born with to ask me for some. Things are tight since your father and I are footing the bill for both of you to get an education."

"Yes, Mommy," I said.

"I love you. Y'all are my babies, the only babies I have."

"We love you, too, Mommy," I responded before ending the phone call.

I had already made up in my mind I was not driving. I always drive everyone everywhere. I desperately needed a break from driving. It would be nice for a change to cruise down the road sitting in the passenger seat with the wind blowing through my hair.

"I'm not driving," I mentioned, letting it be known ahead of time.

"I don't want to drive either," Leah said while putting on her jacket.

"Well—"

Before I could finish, she said, "I'll drive 'cause I don't have time to argue with you. I've got to get to the mall. But, you're paying for the parking."

"Deal!"

My mother's not fooling me. My parents are loaded. She just tells us not to ask for money so Leah and I can work and buy the things we want ourselves. I must admit, though, if I buy something myself, I appreciate it much more. Besides, I'm not the one who asks my parents for money. It's Leah. Her butt is always broke. Well, I may ask my parents for money sometimes. You know, twenty dollars here or a hundred dollars there. My sister and I used to be spoiled. Today, we are reformed spoiled young women. When we were younger, our parents gave us everything—toys, books, and clothes galore. Leah and I always kept up with the latest trends. We didn't want for anything. The reason why I say we are reformed is because we had to learn to pay for things ourselves. It taught me to be independent. Leah, however, is still learning.

We are like night and day. Her ass is buck wild and I am always in a book. She loves to party, and I love to read and relax. Don't get me wrong. I like to party sometimes, just not as much as she does.

"Are you going to the Lauryn Hill concert and after-party tonight?" Leah asked, jamming in the driver's seat.

"Yes, we are going to the concert."

"Who are *we?*"

"Tory and I are going. He asked me about a week ago to accompany him to the concert. Don't worry. I got my "shut-it-down" outfit together. I just have to find a pair of banging shoes to go with it. Help me, please."

"All right, don't beg. I hate it when you do that."

"If anybody asks you for your help with something, they have to beg you. You know you like it."

"Shut up," Leah said, laughing.

"See you're laughing because you know it's the truth."

"Enough of that, and back to the matter at hand. I'm elated that you have your "shut-it-down" outfit. You know you have to represent me. When you look bad, I look bad, and vice versa. I always look good, because you never know who you will run into. You, on the other hand, have to realize that sweats and velour suits are not the only clothing on the face of this earth."

"I'm comfortable in sweat suits. I know how to make a sweat suit look sexy. I like to get dressed up every now and then, but not all the time."

"I will say this—those bras and panty sets are off the hook. Too bad no one ever gets to see them or take them off of you. Oh, let me correct myself. *Tory* gets to take them off of you when he gets the chance to see you."

"Now, you shut up," I said, laughing. "I'm twenty years old, and the three fingers I'm holding up represent the number of people I've slept with. You know my rules and standards. I have to be in a committed relationship. No one-night stands, casual sex, or just kicking it with someone. My twat-twat is priceless and someone special has to be penetrating it."

We both busted out laughing.

"I understand what you're saying, Nya, but I'm young, a little wild, and just want to have some fun."

"You are *very* wild."

"I see nothing wrong with giving a man a little some of my twat as long as I use protection. Your problem is you allow your emotions to get involved, Nya, and I make sure mine do not."

"I can't help it if after engaging in sex with someone my feelings become stronger for that person."

"Another matter at hand is being able to dress a little sexier for you. You have a nice body. Show it off a little. Skirts down to your ankles in the summertime are pushing it. You know you got it, so flaunt it."

"I will not let all my precious goods hang out or pop out because my clothes are too tight or too loose. I want to keep him in suspense. Tory had to put in work to get in between these legs. And I must say he is doing a good job. Just thinking about him and that body, I have to restrain my legs from springing wide open," I giggled.

Chapter 20

We pulled into the Dillard's parking lot of Lynn-haven Mall. As we exited the car, I heard someone honking at us. It was Tara and Yvette.

"Hey, y'all," Yvette shouted.

My sister and I have been friends with Yvette ever since the 5th grade. Well, she was Leah's friend first, and then mine. We met in the spring of 1990 during school recess for the fifth and sixth graders. Yvette was the new girl and she looked out of place and nervous. She was in Leah's class with Mrs. Smith. Leah introduced us. Yvette was the fashion stylist of the group, and the reason why Leah, Tara, and I kept up to date with the fashions.

I didn't meet Tara until I started the 7th grade. It was my first year of junior high school. Tara was in my science class, and we hit it off instantly. Aside from my sister, she's one of the closest people to me. During tenth grade, Tara's mother died of bone marrow cancer. Ever since her mother passed away, Tara's never been the same. Afterwards, Tara became very rebellious against her father. Through the never-ending drama, she managed to graduate from high school on time. Even though Tara is hot in the ass, and has been with so many guys that she and I have stopped counting, she will always be my girl.

"What store are you headed to?" Yvette asked.

"Now, you know the answer to that, girl," Leah said.

I was known for frequenting the exclusive clothing store, Vickie's. That store had the best looks. I liked Vickie's a lot because of the versatility of her clothing. She had conservative, to casual, to club, to downright raunchy clothing. Each of us had different clothing styles. However, all of us could go in there and find something hot. In Virginia, it was about what you wore, and more importantly, how you wore it.

"I guess we're going to the same spot then," Tara said.

"I just need shoes," I informed them.

Getting ready for a night out can be so stressful. You got to have a banging outfit, shoes, purse, hair tight, nails manicured, and toes pedicured. I never liked getting acrylic nails. The one time I got my nails done, I hated it. Because my nails were so long, it hindered me from working on my computer. Now, getting my toes done is a different story. It's so relaxing to get my toes pampered, with all the clipping and trimming. I get a soothing massage on them, as well. I treat myself to a pedicure at least twice a month. I would rather have a pedicure than a manicure. A manicure I get once a month. A sistah's gotta budget those pennies, ya' know.

After leaving Vickie's, the girls and I walked down to the food court.

"So how was your little rendezvous with Tory?" Tara asked.

"Very nice."

"I was beginning to get worried since we hadn't heard from you in a few days."

"I definitely had a good time," I said, grinning from ear to ear.

"I will cut the crap. Did you get some?" Tara asked eagerly. "I don't mean a good meal, either," she said, laughing.

Yvette and Leah had the same inquisitive looks on their faces.

"Yes, we rocked the boat all night long," I answered, blushing.

"Well, it's about time. I was going to strongly suggest you get acquainted with Pete to eliminate some of those cobwebs in your kitty kat," Tara said.

"I don't need a vibrator."

"I must have Pete and I must have the deep long stroke. Y'all know I have needs," Tara added.

"Did you dress sexy for him, showing what our momma gave us, or did he have to rip the sweatpants that you practically live in off of you?" Leah asked.

"I looked more than presentable to him," I barked, rolling my eyes. "I was sexy for the occasion, believe me," I said with pure confidence. "Plus, I showed all of my assets. Are you satisfied?" I asked with an attitude.

Leah prodded. "The question is did he satisfy you?"

"Yes, he did over and over and over again."

"What else did you two do?" Yvette asked.

"We took walks in the park, ate the finest cuisine, and went shopping."

"Since you gave him all of that good loving, he *should* have taken you shopping. I know you were sore down there after that night. I bet you're still recovering," Tara joked.

"Girl, you are so crazy!" I said, cracking up.

"You're laughing because you know it's the truth," Tara added.

"Other than sex, what's been going on with you guys?" I asked.

"I got a huge raise for my outstanding evaluation. I just have a knack for getting people to pay their credit bill," Leah said.

"The crisis center just got approved for federal funding. With all the extra money coming in, we will be able to help more families," Yvette said.

All four of us clapped for joy.

"That's wonderful," I replied.

"I'm the top car salesperson for this quarter. If I play my cards right, I will be getting a two-thousand-dollar bonus at the end of this month. I plan to be a sales manager in six months," Tara said.

"How are you and Rico doing?" Leah asked.

"We were fine until last night," Tara said, shaking her head.

"What happened?" Yvette asked.

"I've been with him every night this week. You know we went to dinner and the movies, the usual typical dates. Both of us were in the mood for seafood and decided to go to Fisherman's Wharf. I only brought enough cash with me to pay the bill. I figured a hundred dollars would be enough, but Rico ended up ordering at least six drinks. Coming up a little short on cash, I asked him to leave the tip for our waitress. With a wad full of money in his hand, he told me he couldn't leave the tip because he didn't want to break a five-dollar bill."

"You're kidding, right?" I asked in disbelief.

"No, and that's not even the icing on the cake. On Tuesday night, he had a craving for a Wendy's frosty. He had the nerve to ask me for a dollar and twelve cents because he didn't want to break a twenty-dollar bill."

"Did you give it to him?" Leah asked.

"Hell no!"

"Maybe he's trying to save money," I said, laughing.

"If that's the case, the money he is desperately trying to hold on to should be stashed somewhere, or in a bank account. Needless to say, he was a great screw with a huge python. Still, I had to dismiss his cheap ass."

"I don't know what is worse, a cheap man or a man with a pencil-sized python," Leah said.

"Both," I said, holding up two fingers.

"Rico and any other man should know there is no romance without finance," Tara said, rubbing her two fingers together.

"I know that's right," I said, giving her a high-five. "I had a strange dream last night," I said, changing the subject.

"What was it about?" Leah asked.

"I dreamt that our two goldfish died. Did you feed them over the weekend while I was gone?" I asked Leah.

"When I ate, those fish were fed as well. Wait a minute . . . three nights ago I was at Nelson's place all night and did forget to feed them the next morning."

"You *have* had them for a while. Maybe they are about to die," Tara said.

"It's no big deal. We'll just buy two more fish if they do," Leah said.

"All this talk about fish is making me hungry. I'm going to the Cajun Grill. Would anyone else like anything from there?" Tara asked.

"I want the bourbon chicken with vegetables and rice. Here, let me give you some money," I replied while reaching into my wallet. The Cajun Grill food is so delicious. I eat there so much that the cook always gives me extras.

"I want the blackened fish with potatoes and vegetables," Tara said.

"I'm going to get two slices of cheese pizza," Leah said with her eyes fixated on the sign.

"I'll just grab a cup of soup. Lately, I feel like my stomach has been turned upside down. Yesterday, I couldn't get my head from out the toilet," Yvette said.

"If you are vomiting that much, please go to the doctor. You could be at risk for dehydration," I said, worry filling my voice.

"It's probably just a forty-eight-hour bug," she responded with a slight shrug of her shoulders.

Chapter 21

As I was getting ready for the concert, I listened to Lauryn Hill's CD, *The Miseducation of Lauryn Hill*. I have played it so much that I had to buy another one. There's not a day that goes by I don't listen to Lauryn Hill, Faith Evans, or Kelly Price. When I get down and out, I let the music lift my spirits up to a higher, positive place.

Tonight I wanted to keep it simple with boot cut jeans, a wifebeater, and crème sandals that matched perfect with my ensemble. Now, underneath my clothes was a different story. I had a yellow and orange bra and a G-string set that Tory gave me. Looking at myself in the mirror, I felt sexy.

"Are you finished in there?" I asked Leah while impatiently waiting at the locked bathroom door.

"Hold on. Give me two more minutes."

"Hurry up. I need to finish getting ready."

Some finishing touches on my hair, brushing of my teeth, and I would be ready to roll out.

"I know you're not getting an attitude 'cause you need me to do your hair. Relax. Don't you know it takes time to get beautiful," Leah said, posing in front of the mirror.

"I will not be needing your lovely assistance tonight. I already did my hair."

"It's probably in that tired ponytail that's older than the Jheri-curl," she said, opening the bathroom door. Leah was shocked. "Whoa, this day will go down in my history book. My sister Nya did her own hair."

"I do my hair everyday," I said, running my fingers through it.

"Ponytails don't count. It looks decent for a change, though," she said, trying hard not to laugh.

"Whatever."

"I'm just playing. It looks great in those curls. What brought on the sudden change of hair appearance? I thought you were ponytail for life."

"Don't get it twisted. I will always be ponytail for life. I just wanted to give myself a different look now that I have a man."

"So, you *have* had men before," she remarked with her arms crossed.

"I need to switch up my hairstyles once in a while." I let her sarcastic remark slide. "Tory would never admit it, but he likes to see me in different styles. He can't seem to stop complimenting me when I do switch up. Besides, he is being a good boy, so I will do my best to look nice for him."

"For his sake, I hope he never messes up," Leah said, shaking her head.

"Me, too, because you know I would look a straight mess with my hair not combed." If my man messes up, I don't waste my valuable time looking nice for him.

The phone rang.

"It's Mommy," Leah announced.

"Let me talk to her."

"No, I want to talk first."

"You talked first the last time Daddy called." I yanked the phone out of her hand.

"Hey, Mommy."

"Hey, baby, what's all the commotion about?"

"Nothing, Mommy."

"Stop that petty fighting. I told you time and time again you two are sisters. Sisters are blood. Family is supposed to stick together and not fight."

"Yes, Mommy."

"Now, let me speak to Leah."

After she gave Leah an earful, she wanted to talk to me again.

"Your father and I have decided to stay another week here. We are having the time of our lives," she said, giggling. They don't want to come back, and I don't blame them. Fun in the sun will do that to you.

"There is a check for a hundred dollars on my dresser payable to you. Cash it, please, and buy groceries. Leah can eat us out of house and home. Are you getting enough to eat?"

"Yes."

"Take care of the house. Try hard not to kill each other. Have fun at the concert. Leah told me that you fixed your hair up real nice. I am so proud of you."

"It's not a big deal," I said, rolling my eyes at Leah.

"Next Saturday, pick us up at the airport at 9:00 in the morning. The flight number is 18264 on American Airlines. If anything changes, I'll call you."

"Okay."

"I love you. See you soon."

"We love you, too."

Chapter 22

Lauryn Hill's concert was remarkable, well worth the thirty dollars spent. And I felt Mr. Sothers was definitely a trooper for sticking it out with four women. Leah and Tara tried to be on their best behavior, but after 10:45, there was no holding back the freak within them. Despite their current men trying to keep them occupied, they managed to find new beaus at the concert.

"Nya, Tory, and Yvette, this is Quincy and Davon," Tara informed.

"We found these two cuties by the Heineken stand," Leah giggled.

"We are headed to the beach, and then they are taking us home. Don't wait up," Tara said, waving good-bye with her left hand, her right hand wrapped around Davon's.

"Bye. Be careful," I said, pulling Leah in for a hug before they drifted off.

"I'm going to make my exit as well," Yvette said, giving me a hug. "Jarvis will be home soon, and I want to be there to greet him with a big kiss. He's been working a lot of overtime at his job."

"Well, it's just the two of us," I said, grinning.

"Hey, I don't have any qualms. Spending quality time with you is a priority for me," Tory said, gazing into my eyes and caressing my right cheek.

"Before going home, let's stop at Tony's for a slice of pizza. By the way, your hair looks gorgeous."

"Thank you. Sounds good to me."

"How do you like yours?" he asked. "I like cheese pizza; pepperoni and sausage is way too greasy for me."

"I feel you on that one."

"I prefer their broccoli pizza."

When we got there, luckily, it was not packed. We were seated at a cozy booth overlooking the Chesapeake Bay. A slice was not going to fill up either of us, so we ended up ordering a large half-cheese and half-broccoli pizza.

"I have some questions for you."

"Okay," I said in puzzlement.

"How do you feel about marriage and children?"

"I would like to be married, of course. You know, a man to call my own. My wedding will be small and simple, inviting only family and close friends. The colors will be white and lavender. Four bridesmaids and grooms-men accompanied by the ever-so-cute flower girl and ring bearer."

"How about your reception?" he asked eagerly.

"I would love to have two ice-carved swans. An open bar, tea, soft drinks, and coffee will be offered as beverages. The main course will be chicken, steak, or maybe a buffet. I hate vanilla cake. Therefore, five layers of chocolate cake would be served. At the top of the sweet delight will be my new husband and me embraced in a kissing pose.

"I saved the best part for last, my dear. What about your honeymoon?"

"The Bahamas, Jamaica, or Barbados all are good choices to me. This is the only decision that I will leave up to my husband," I said, laughing. "As far as my child-bearing years, I want at least two children, a girl and a boy. They will have my good looks and their daddy's good sense of humor and charm. Now, it's your turn, sweetie."

"Well, I really won't worry about the wedding arrangements. I will leave that up to my wife-to-be. I have to admit that we are on the same path, 'cause I would prefer a small wedding as well. Short, simple, and sweet. As long as I have the woman I want to spend a lifetime with in my arms, I will be fine. Besides, I know the fun part of the wedding will not begin until the honeymoon." He grinned and rubbed his hands together.

Under the booth, Tory kept rubbing my inner thighs and it was driving me crazy. "Would you two like dessert?" the waiter asked.

"Nothing for me," I said while shaking my head. "Could you put the rest of the pizza in a to-go box?"

"Sure, no problem."

"Yes, I'll have one of your fruit bowls to go." Tory gave me a seductive look.

While he waited for the dessert and paid the bill, I excused myself to the restroom. I feared that my period was coming down, and Lord knows, the last thing I wanted to see was my period, especially on the night I was planning to get my groove on. And to make matters worse, I wasn't prepared. I didn't have any pads or regular panties on. I locked the bathroom door and quickly unzipped my jeans to investigate. To my relief, my wetness was from Tory making me so damn hot.

* * *

While walking from the ladies' room, I decided to call Leah's cell phone to make sure she and Tara were all right.

"Hello."

"Hey, it's me. Is everything okay?"

"Hi, we're fine, Mother Goose. Hold on, I'll give the phone to Leah," Tara said, sounding drunk.

"Things couldn't be better. We just left the beach. Now, we're headed to their place," Leah said.

"Leah, you don't even know them."

"Don't hate, because I know you're about to get some python. Shit, I want some too."

"Me too," Tara shouted in the background.

"Just be careful, please."

"I think I heard you the first time at the concert. By the way, I'm not coming home," Leah stated.

"I wasn't planning on, either. Have a good night. I'll see you later."

"Bye, you too."

"Baby, are you ready?" he asked with the pizza box and fruit bowl in hand as I arrived back at the table.

"Yeah, let's go."

"I look at you and think I'm so lucky to have you," Tory said, giving me pecks on the lips as we strolled from the entrance.

He stopped to put the key in the ignition of the car. Little did he know he had already started mine. I pulled him closer to me, my tongue meeting his. Then I kissed on his neck while he reached for my butt and squeezed. The windows of the car were beginning to fog up.

"I love your ass."

In one fluid motion, he pulled my shirt up and managed to pop one of my breasts out of my bra. I was so damn turned on that I didn't even care we were still in the restaurant parking lot.

"Give me ten minutes, and I can get us home," he said in a heavy breath.

"All right," I said, massaging his erected python through the fabric of his pants.

Tory got us to his place in eight minutes flat. After I grabbed the bag of food and my overnight bag from the backseat, and after Tory slammed the front door behind us, I started kissing him and tugging at his belt while we stood in the foyer of the house. Once I unfastened the belt, I unzipped his pants. This time, we were not going to make it to the bedroom. We landed on the carpet in the middle of the living room. The dessert came in handy as I poured it all over his muscular chest. Each piece of fruit I ate off of his lean, muscular body led me closer to his python. Once face to face, I took hold of it, making a tight ring with my finger to stroke up and down his shaft. Tory was becoming harder as he waited for me to lick his dick up and down, and I couldn't wait for him to be inside of me.

"Mmm," he moaned.

With tender care, I massaged his testicles while gliding the python in my mouth to sensual pleasure. Round two, three, and four followed one behind the other with no breaks in between. Last week, I loved him giving it to me doggy-style. This week, I loved giving it to him in a chair. The orgasms were more intense. We didn't stop till four in the morning. Thank God I didn't have to go to work the next day.

I slept like a baby. Good loving will do that to you. I looked at the clock; it was eleven. I gave Tory a kiss on the cheek, and then grabbed my overnight bag to pull out my thin navy-blue jogging suit. I wanted to be comfortable. When I looked into the bathroom mirror, I discovered that my hair didn't look too bad since I had wrapped overnight. However, it was going to be in a bun today. I took my time in the shower. There was no rush. Tory and I had the whole day to spend together.

Feeling refreshed, I decided to make breakfast for my baby. It didn't take much time to prepare pancakes, eggs, and turkey bacon. Any leftover fruit that hadn't ended up on Tory's body I placed on the side of the plate.

"Something sure smells good up in here," Tory said, hugging me from behind and kissing my neck. His Eternity cologne filled the air. "The aroma of the coffee woke me up. You sure know your way around the kitchen."

"Have a seat," I said while fixing his plate. "Would you like coffee, orange juice, or apple juice?"

"I'll take a tall glass of orange juice. What time did you rise and shine?" he asked, passing me the blueberry syrup.

"I woke up about an hour and a half ago. You were still in la-la land, so I let you get some more rest. After last night, both of us were worn out," I said, grinning.

"Thank you for making me breakfast," he said, caressing my face.

"No problem. You were incredible in bed and on the floor."

"You're my innocent angel; however, in the bedroom, you're my little devil," he said, taking a bite of bacon.

"I aim to please," I said, kissing him on the lips.

"Keep it up and you'll soon find yourself in rounds five, six, and seven."

"Why don't we just round it off to ten?" I said jokingly.

"What's on the agenda for today?"

"Well, I would like to jog a few laps around the lake. What would you like to do?"

"Besides being with you, I didn't have anything else planned. A jog sounds great. I am in the mood to watch a couple of movies, though. Later this afternoon we could go to Blockbuster—"

"Or watch the Lifetime channel," I said, interrupting him.

"Isn't that the channel for women?"

"Yep," I replied.

"I catch interesting movies on there from time to time. Okay, I don't have a problem with watching Lifetime with my woman," he said, embracing me.

God, I'm in heaven and I don't want to come down.

Chapter 23

It was seven a.m. on my first day of nursing school, and I was a nervous wreck. My parents arrived back home from the Bahamas the night before, and even though my mom was tired from the trip, she sat with me and tried to calm my nerves before going to bed.

"Take a deep breath," I said to myself in the mirror.

There was a knock at the door.

"Yes?"

"It's me. May I come in?" Mommy asked.

"Sure."

As soon as she entered, she strolled over and gave me a kiss and hug. "I know you have butterflies in your stomach, but you'll be fine, baby. You know I am here to help in any kind of way."

"Thanks, Mommy. I needed to hear that."

"Go on downstairs and get you some breakfast. I made your favorite—heart-shaped pancakes with scrambled eggs."

"I can't eat at a time like this."

"Nya, you heard me."

"Yes, ma'am."

"You need something on your stomach. Your orientation is quite long. You will not get a break till noon."

"How did you know?"

"I looked at your curriculum. I have to make sure ODU is treating and teaching my baby right." Mommy always believed that a good education would give Leah and me the key to better opportunities. She would scrub toilets, if need be, just to put us through school.

"I need to head to work now," Mommy said, strolling toward the door.

"Bye, have a nice day."

"By the way, you look nice in your uniform, Nurse Gamden," she said, smiling and walking out of my bedroom.

I was the first person in Room 343. That was okay, 'cause I would rather be early than late, especially on the first day. As I was waiting for class to start, I decided to read a book to calm the butterflies in my stomach.

One by one, students filed in to take their seat. Some faces looked familiar from previous courses that I had taken.

"Hello, Miss lady." Someone tapped me lightly on the shoulder.

"Hi, Carla. Long time, no see," I said, giving her a hug. She and I were once in the same anatomy class together. "How was your summer vacation?"

"If you want to call it that, my summer was too short. Besides working the majority of the time, I managed to scrape up enough money for the kids and me to go with my sister and her family to Disney World. We had a good time. They nearly drove me crazy, though," she said, laughing. "Autumn is starting kindergarten this year; Byron is starting to walk. They grow so fast."

"How's your family doing?"

"Everyone is just fine. But, hey, before the teachers come in, I'm gonna sit my butt down. Look, we're study partners till the end, so call me if you need me."

"Ditto, kiddo," I said with a smile.

Promptly at nine o'clock, ten women dressed in nursing uniforms came in. All eyes were on them.

"Good morning, class. My name is Mrs. Wellington. I am the head director of the nursing department. First and foremost, I would like to congratulate all of you for making it to this point. It takes hard work and dedication to tackle those prerequisites. Give yourselves a round of applause."

I have to admit, I felt good reflecting on what I had accomplished.

"Rest assured we will do everything in our power to make sure every person in this room becomes a registered nurse. Now, we have a ton to go over with you, so let's get started."

I had been ready to start since the day I found out I was accepted into the nursing program.

Each teacher stated their name, gave us a short personal and educational background of themselves, and the specific nursing courses they would be teaching. Every student had to do the same thing. I hated standing up, especially in front of people I didn't know. Next, Mrs. Wellington went over the curriculum for the entire semester, informing us of what she and the other instructors expected from us, and what we as the students should expect from the nursing staff.

Mrs. Wellington wrapped things up early and let us out at 1:30 p.m. As I was climbing into my car and fastening the seatbelt, my cell phone rang. I quickly fumbled through my purse, not even getting a chance to see who it was first.

"Hello?"

"Hi, baby," Mommy said.

"Before you even ask, school was wonderful. The instructors are very nice and more than willing to lend a hand for extra tutoring, studying, and counseling."

"I'm glad to hear that. You know I had to check on my oldest baby. Are you headed to work now?"

"No. Since this is the first day of school, Ms. Pilom was kind enough to give me the day off."

"It must be nice. Well, let me get back to my patients. Mr. Jamison, bless his heart, is having troubles with his bowels. He refuses to use a bedpan, so he just does his business on the bed. He did it again. I can smell him from all the way out here in front of the nurses' station. This will be my fourth time cleaning up his nasty pile of feces. None of the other nurses will go near him."

"Maybe you're his favorite," I said, laughing.

"Very funny, Nya. Have a good day."

"You, too. Bye, Mommy. I love you."

I headed straight home. Hell, it had been a while since I had the pleasure of taking an afternoon nap, and it wasn't sounding like such a bad idea.

Chapter 24

"Lord, we give thanks to you on this day of Thanksgiving. Please reach out your blessing to everyone around the world. We thank the hands that prepared this feast, in Jesus name, Amen," Daddy prayed. Afterwards, everyone around the table stated one thing they were thankful for. I had a lot to be thankful for. Most importantly, my classes were going well. My lowest test score was an eighty-six.

My parents had decided to have the whole family over at our house for the holiday. The holiday spirit was definitely in full force. My little cousins were running rampant, tearing up everything in their path. My daddy, uncles, and mostly every other man in the house were tuned into the football game and patiently waiting to be served.

"Is it time to eat yet? I'm starving," Leah said, walking into the kitchen.

"Did you help?" I asked.

"No."

"Well, you just got your answer," I snapped, pulling the homemade rolls out of the oven.

"Nya is just teasing you," Mommy said.

"No, I wasn't. Her butt shouldn't have missed the blessing."

"The food is on the table," Mommy said, ignoring my remark.

"Happy Thanksgiving, Grandma Cora," I said as she entered the kitchen.

"Same to you, sugar." She smiled and picked up a plate.

When it comes to Thanksgiving, it's no holds barred. This is the day, the only day, I go back for three and four helpings of food.

Daddy did the honors of cutting the turkey. All day, he had been trying to nibble on it. Each time, Mommy would smack his hand away. There was so much to choose from. The spread was fit for a king: smoked turkey, baked turkey, duck, country ham baked with sweet honey and brown sugar, and fried fish; string beans, collard greens, macaroni and cheese, corn on the cob, corn pudding, asparagus casserole, broccoli casserole, tossed salad, mashed potatoes, sweet potatoes, and carrot soufflé. I made the rice pudding. Two dishes were baked with raisins and one without. Oh, I almost forgot about the chicken and dumplings right beside me. Aunt Alberta brought over the melt-in-your-mouth Golden Corral rolls. Also, we had bread pudding and cornbread. If I manage to have room for dessert, spiced peaches, cherry Jell-O with nuts and fruit cup, blackberry cobbler, peach cobbler, key lime pie, apple pie, sweet potato pie, chocolate éclairs, red velvet cake, carrot cake, chocolate chip cookies, and sugar cookies were there for me to choose from.

After everyone had finished eating, I asked, "Mommy, do you need me to help clean this pile of dishes?"

"No, baby, your aunts will help me. Besides, before I

put any food away, I want people to make their take-home plates first. Go ahead, have you some fun; this is the first real break you've had since school started."

"Thanks, I only have two hours to get ready before Tory picks me up. I am stuffed," I said, patting my stomach. "I will make room for some more dessert, though."

"Where are you going tonight?"

"All four of our beaus and us are going to Expressions. It's a new jazz club in downtown Norfolk. Tonight, they are having open mike for poetry."

"How romantic."

"Things between Tory and I are going great. I think I could love him." I smiled bashfully, wondering if Tory felt the same about me.

"I know."

"How do you know, Mommy?"

"I see the look in your eyes when you talk about him or when he comes to pick you up. He looks at you the same way."

"You really think so?"

"Yes, I know these things. My gut tells me Tory is the one for you."

"What do you mean?"

"I mean, you are going to marry him."

"It's a little too soon for that," I said, standing up against the kitchen counter with my arms folded.

"I'm not saying to rush it. Take it slow," she said. "Mark my words, though—your daddy is going to give you away to him."

"Whatever you say," I said, brushing off her comments. "Where's Leah? She can lend her hands to wash these dishes."

"She is probably upstairs 'sleep. Let her be. You can be so hard on her."

"You have a point there, but she doesn't do anything

around this house. You and I have been up since four o'clock this morning cooking. Leah did not help lift a finger," I heatedly stated.

"You know she's the baby of the family," Mommy said, taking a bite out of her chocolate éclair.

"Last time I checked, my six-month-old cousin Camille was the baby of the family. Leah is not a baby anymore. She is spoiled, and you let her get away with everything."

"Give her some time. She'll come around and take some responsibility."

"Yeah, right," I mumbled under my breath.

"What did you say?"

"I said this peach cobbler sure hit the spot. It is so delicious," I gasped, taking a bite.

"Mmm hmm."

I gave her a kiss and ran upstairs to dodge possibly getting hit upside my head.

I had not spent any quality time with Tory in a week. He had been away again on business in California. These days, I could not spare a whole lot of time either. My nose had been stuck in the books. Before Thanksgiving break, I took three exams. We've talked on the phone every night, though. The times when we did talk I could sense something was bothering him. I asked him once, but he said nothing was the matter, so I left it alone. Mommy always told me, "Give a man his space and he'd come back."

The temperature outside was freezing, damn near twenty degrees. Good thing I had watched the weather on the news last night and already picked out my clothes the night before. I didn't want the hassle of having to decide what to wear after having helped cook all that food. I chose to wear my red Fendi sweater and a pair of Baby Phat jeans with my brown boots. My beige cashmere coat would be fine to wear over top.

"You look presentable," Leah said, barging into my room.

"Thank you," I said.

The doorbell rang, and seconds later, I could hear Tara and Yvette speaking to the family. We'd all been friends for so long that they were practically part of my family and vice versa.

"Yvette and Tara are here," my mother called from the bottom of the stairs.

"Hey, Happy Thanksgiving," I greeted as Leah and I descended the staircase and gave each of them a hug.

"Did you eat till you were stuffed?" Tara asked.

"I sure did, eating at least three plates of food and dessert," Leah said.

"Would you two like a plate to take home?" Mommy asked.

"No, thank you," they both said.

"We've got enough food to last us at least two weeks," Yvette said.

"Okay, then, I'm going to get back to washing those dishes. After my family leaves, I'm heading straight to bed. I need to get my rest for tomorrow. There will be some major sales going on, and I need to save my energy for the battle," she stated.

"What battle?" I asked.

"The battle between the other Wal-Mart shoppers and me for the DVD player on sale for $39.99," she said. We all started laughing.

"The guys are at the club keeping our seats warm," Yvette said.

"It's going to be packed," Tara stated.

"How do I look?" I asked.

"Cute," Yvette said.

"I see you have on those show-stopping boots," Tara commented.

As we sat in the living room waiting for Tory to arrive, Aunt Marie asked Tara and Yvette for the fifth time if they wanted something to eat. And for the fifth time, they declined.

"He's here," I announced as my baby pulled into the driveway. With Mommy hot on my trail, I got up and opened the door.

"Happy Thanksgiving, Mrs. Gamden. I brought over a bottle of Merlot and a box of Cuban cigars. I noticed Mr. Gamden was enjoying one the last time I was over," Tory said.

Great, all my hard work down the drain. I had been trying to get Daddy to stop smoking those things. I wanted to do everything in my power to help prolong his life.

"Thank you. That was kind of you," Mommy said, giving him a hug. "Would you like something to eat or a take-home plate?"

"No, thank you. I am good to go," he said, patting his stomach.

Before being whisked away by Mommy, Tory turned and handed me a card. I immediately opened it. On the front of the card was a picture of a black woman caring for her patient. Inside the card, it read:

A stunning, intellectual and independent woman as you needs a little help at times.

Baby, I know you have been working hard at school and working less at the bank. So, here's some change to help you pay a bill or buy something nice.

Love,
Tory

My eyes were wide, and my mouth even wider, as I gasped for air. This was a complete surprise. The "change" he mentioned turned out to be two hundred dollars. Shit, with that amount of money, I could pay a bill or two, and may even have a little left over "change" to buy a shirt or some new lingerie.

"Let me introduce you to the family," Daddy said, ever so delighted Tory brought him those death tickets. "This fine young man is my future son-in-law," Daddy said, telling anyone who would listen.

"Okay, we've got to go," I said, pulling Tory by the arm to rescue him.

"It was nice meeting everyone," he said.

"Thank you for the card and the money," I said, smiling as we walked out the door with the girls following closely behind.

"You are certainly welcome," he replied, gently squeezing my hand.

I had already had the pleasure of meeting Tory's parents about two months ago. We had dinner at their house. I didn't realize his parents banked with Bank-First. Prior to meeting Tory, I had assisted Mrs. Sothers with rolling over her 401k and setting up an annuity for Mr. Sothers.

"I want to ride up front," Leah said.

"Is this your man?"

"No."

"Do I ever ride in the front of your man's car?"

"No."

"Okay, then," I said, closing the front passenger door.

"This is a nice Lexus you have. I know Nya would look good cruising down the boulevard in this ride," Tara said, checking out all the details inside the car and throwing hints.

"Thank you," Tory said.

"Do you mind if we drink in the car?" Leah asked.

"Nah, you're good," he said.

"What are you two drinking?" Yvette asked.

"It's just a little Bacardi," Leah said.

"Would you like some?" Tara offered.

"No, thank you," Yvette replied.

"Hey, you guys, my new man's name is Rob. We've been seeing each other for a week now. I can't wait for you all to meet him," Tara said.

"You change men like the shoes on your feet," Yvette said.

"If the shoes don't fit me, they go right back into the pile with the other ones," she giggled.

"I know that's right," Leah said as we all erupted in laughter.

I began to get a funny feeling in my stomach. It was probably from me eating too much.

"Nya, there is something I need to talk to you about," Tory said as we walked into the club.

"Is everything all right?"

"Yes, I'll tell you later on tonight."

"Okay," I said, not really meaning it. The truth is I hated to be left in suspense.

"Good evening, brothers and sisters. Happy Turkey Day! I am sure you all got plenty of delicious food courtesy of your mama or grandma's cooking today. I am your host for the evening, Emmanuel. Sit back, relax, get a drink at the bar, enjoy the band and tonight's festivities, open mike."

Everyone clapped. Nelson, Jarvis, and Rob were happy to see Leah, Yvette, and Tara. Rob was a physical therapist and owned his own practice. He seemed to like Tara. She usually preferred the wild ones; however, Rob was more on the subtle and calm side. Nelson owned the Caribbean restaurant, Sass. At times, he and Leah were inseparable.

After four poets had spoken on pain, struggle, healing, and giving thanks, the host stepped back up to the mic. "Now, we are going to take a quick intermission. I hope you enjoy this next song by the band that was written by me."

"Those were some deep poets," I commented.

"I'm so glad we came," Yvette expressed.

"I'm going to get another drink," Leah said.

"I could use another one, too. I'll go with you. We'll give the guys a break since they got three drinks for us already. But it still doesn't mean I don't need any money," Tara said with an outstretched hand.

Obediently, Rob handed her a fifty-dollar bill.

"Now, that's what I'm talking about," she said, walking to the bar. Leah and Tara knew how to hold their liquor. Me, I was still working on my glass of ginger ale.

As Leah and Tara returned, Tara's cousin Michelle was following closely behind.

"Hey, long time no see. Happy Thanksgiving," I said.

"Likewise to you all."

"How's the baby doing?" Yvette asked her.

"Getting big."

"He is so cute," Tara chanted.

"Thanks," she said. Michelle had her eyes fixated on Tory, who was trying his best to avoid eye contact with her.

What the fuck is going on here?

"Tory, did you tell her?" she finally asked after a moment of uncomfortable silence.

"Tell me what? You two know each other?" I asked while standing up.

"Michelle, this ain't the time or the place," he replied.

"Oh, yes, it is," she yelled while placing her hands on her hips. "Tory may be the father of my son," she blurted out.

So she was one of the fish in my dreams. But who did the other fish represent? "Is this true?" I looked Tory dead in the eyes.

"Baby, I was trying to tell you."

"You certainly didn't try hard enough!"

"I know that you were studying hard for your exams; I didn't want to break your concentration with some bullshit." He looked at Michelle.

"No man's drama will break me down—I would have passed my exams anyway.

"As for you, Michelle, you are straight playing yourself. You don't even know who the father of your baby is, yet you want to come over here and try to interfere in Tory's life. It's obvious that he doesn't want you." My eyes were getting red. *Who does this girl think she is?* "First and foremost, I am a lady, and I'm not even going to stoop down to your level."

"You just want to cause a scene. No one is even paying you any attention," Leah gawked, shaking her head at Michelle.

"I told you before, Michelle, if the baby is mine, we can work out custody arrangements and child support with my lawyer. I will step up to the plate and be a father," Tory stated.

"Speaking of child support—I want five thousand dollars a month." Michelle crossed her arms.

"I didn't know your baby was for sale," Tara remarked. "Damn, girl, you should have gotten pregnant by one of those NBA players. At the baby shower, you told me Bryan was David's father. Oh, wait a minute, I bumped into him last week at the gym. He told me that he had just gotten laid off from his job. I guess he can't afford you anymore, so now you are trying to pin the baby on Tory. My Aunt Barbara couldn't have raised a gold digger like you. It would break her heart to see how you have been acting lately. David is not a rag doll. Your son needs stability and a good home. Since the age of fifteen, it's only been about the money with you, Michelle. Damn, make your *own* money and stop trying to bank on everyone else's."

"Whatever."

"I see right through your innocent role," Tara added.

"You're just mad because I screwed your boyfriend Tommy in your car five years ago. You actually fell for all that bull he was talking about getting married and having a family. I didn't mean to put an everlasting dent in your plans," Michelle said with a smirk on her face.

Tara balled up her fist and started to swing, but Yvette held her back. "She's not worth it."

"I can forgive, but I don't forget. Aunt Barbara always wanted us to be close like my mother and she were. And you wonder why I keep my distance from you. Your mother had to beg me to invite you to the art gallery. Now I see why she said you were having trouble making friends. You probably fucked your friends' men too."

"I still don't understand how I could've gotten you pregnant. I used a condom," Tory interrupted.

"Any fool knows they aren't a hundred percent effective," Michelle said, directing her attention back to Tory.

"They were effective before."

"You just fell for the oldest trick in the book. You didn't want me anymore, so I purposely got pregnant. I got you drunk one night and the rest is history. The one we used—well, let's just say it turned out to be defective."

"Breaking the relationship off with you was one of the best decisions I've made in my life. You play too many games. You are too conniving for me."

"I'm not finished with you yet, Tory."

"Yes, you are. Keep walking. This table is not reserved for gold diggers." I stood up.

"We'll know the results of the blood test tomorrow. Then we'll see who's not finished with who," she said, rolling her eyes at Tory.

As Michelle walked off, a waiter accidentally bumped into her, causing her to fall right on her ass. The drinks he was carrying fell all over her white dress. After the waiter helped her up, everyone busted out laughing at the sight of her dress covered in brown, green, and red tints.

"What are you doing?" Leah asked as Nelson got on his knees in a praying position.

"I am praying I will never have a baby mamma like her."

"Get up, Nelson. You're so crazy," Leah said, laughing.

"I need a drink. Does anyone else want one?" Tory asked, looking around with an uncomfortable expression still plastered on his face.

"Yes, I will have one," Nelson said with Rob and Jarvis following behind them both.

I was fuming that Tory hadn't told me sooner. I thought we were close enough where we could talk about anything.

"Nya, I know you are pissed, but at least hear him out," Tara said.

"I guess this is what he was going to tell me later on tonight. I don't understand why neither came clean about knowing each other when we saw her at the art gallery."

"You have a point," Leah said.

"Maybe Tory didn't know at the time," Yvette said.

"Yeah, but he *did* know he had fucked her."

"He's a good man. Please let him explain first," Leah said.

"All right, I will, but he's still not getting any tonight."

"Yeah, right," Tara said.

"Shut up," I said, laughing.

"I want to apologize for the ordeal back at Expressions," Tory said while letting the car warm up. He retrieved a blanket from the car trunk and put it over me.

"Thank you."

"I'm not one for bringing bullshit to the table. When we saw Michelle at the art gallery, I was surprised to see her pregnant. Prior to bumping into you at Wal-Mart, Michelle and I broke up two months before. I knew she was out to get me. I broke up with her because of her foul ways and because she tried to have sex with one of my good friends. The girl took me through so much that I'm sorry I even know her. Please don't let her nonsense ruin our night," he said, gently kissing me on the lips.

"Is that what's been bothering you this past week?"

"Yes. Michelle didn't even tell me until two weeks ago. A lot has been going through my mind. First of all, I know that I used a condom with her. Secondly, I began thinking about being a father. No matter how much I don't like Michelle my potential son deserves to have a good father. I'm scared and nervous. I feel as though I have no control over the situation because this was not planned. I haven't even told my parents about it. A child is a big responsibility. I want my kids to be made out of love, not spite."

"I'm angry that you didn't tell me the deal when you first found out. However, I understand why you didn't. To be honest, I would be stressed out too."

"Believe me, I wanted to pick up the phone and tell

you, but you don't need any unnecessary ruckus in your life. I don't need it, either."

"My main concern here is communication. I want us to be able to talk about anything. Don't hold back from me."

"From now on, I will talk to you about everything, no matter good or bad."

"Always remember, we are a team."

"I didn't want to hurt you."

"You hurt my feelings more by not telling me."

"Fair enough. What can I do to make it up to you?"

"I don't know, but I'm sure you will think of something. Still, I want you to know that if David is yours, I will be right by your side." Lord knows I didn't want to deal with Michelle's ass, but I wasn't about to give up Tory.

"Thank you. That means a lot to me." He reached over and kissed me.

We returned to his house and snuggled up by the fireplace until we decided to go to bed, the perfect end to a not-so-perfect evening.

Even though Tory asked me to go to the hospital with him the next morning, I decided not to. This was between Michelle and him, so I patiently waited at his house.

"Hello," I said, answering my cell phone on the first ring.

"Nya."

"Yes."

"I'm not the father of David; Bryan's the father." Tory sighed with relief.

In the background, I could hear Michelle screaming and demanding another DNA test. Inside, I could not stop laughing.

"I'll see you when I get home."

"Okay, I'll be here, baby," I said in a tone that expressed my relief, also.

"Hello, Mr. Sothers. Do you feel as if a ton of bricks have been lifted off your shoulders?"

"You got that right. I want to thank you," he declared, coming in the door and giving me a hug.

"For what?"

"You have been there for me through this whole ordeal. Most importantly, you had my back the whole time when Michelle was spitting her venom at me."

"That's what I'm here for."

"Get dressed. I just thought of a way I can make it up to you."

"Give me twenty minutes," I said and ran upstairs.

Tory took me to Gigi's, my favorite spa, and treated me to a full body massage, bikini wax, manicure, and pedicure. Afterwards, we ended up at the mall to do some major shopping. Hell, if this is the type of treatment I'll receive whenever he messes up, he should mess up more often. Nah, I'm just kidding.

Chapter 25

"Yvette, you have taken this test three times," I said, shaking my head.

"Let's go get another one."

"We have tried EPT, FACT PLUS, and CLEARBLUE EASY. Face it, girl, you're pregnant."

That answered my question as to who the other fish in my dream represented.

"Thank God that it's not me," Leah said.

"Hey, guys, I got here as soon as I could. Now, there better be a very good reason why I was whisked away from shopping at Nordstrom's with Rob's American Express card," Tara said. She lay her purse down on the bed.

"I'm pregnant," Yvette mumbled with tears in her eyes.

"I can see that from the double lines in the tests. So, little mama, what are you going to do?" Tara patted Yvette's back.

"I don't know."

"You have options," Leah said.

"I know one thing for sure—I'm not having an abortion; my heart couldn't take it. A lot of things are going through my mind, like my parents, college, the future, and Jarvis," she said, wiping her eyes.

"Do you think he would want the baby?"

"Yeah, he will want this baby. He loves me and I absolutely adore him. You know we want to get married sometime in the near future. I'm just so scared right now." Her hands shook as she spoke.

Just then, the phone rang.

"Hello," Yvette spoke into the receiver, and then she turned to us and whispered, "It's Jarvis."

"Hey, how's my favorite Care Bear doing?"

"Baby, I need to talk to you. Can you come over?" she said in a shaky voice.

"I can get away for a little while. Let me just tell Jerry the deal. Is everything okay?"

"Yes, everything is fine. I just need a hug right about now," she said, crying.

"Give me fifteen minutes. I'm on my way. You know I can't stand it when you cry. Hold tight, baby."

After hanging up, Yvette ran to the bathroom.

"Are you all right in there?" I asked.

"This afternoon sickness is killing my stomach. Can you get me a glass of ice cold water?"

"Sure." When I returned, I had brought her some saltine crackers, as well. "Eat these. They will help calm your stomach."

"I guess I'm gonna have to get accustomed to this for nine months," Yvette said, slowly sipping her water.

"Feeling bloated, acne, mood swings, weight gain, and belly swelling all come with the territory. Yvette junior is going to be so beautiful," Leah said.

"The baby will have good hair, too," Tara said.

"I don't have a clue as to how we will raise this baby."

"Have no fear. You've got three babysitters and helpers at your service," I said, trying to calm her nerves.

"You mean two. What? Don't give me that look, Nya." Tara touched up her hair in the mirror. "You know I don't do babies."

"You know that we are *all* here for you," I said, comforting Yvette.

"Rest assured, though, the little crumb-snatcher will have my keen sense of style if a girl or a boy." Yvette shook her hips, adding some humor to the situation.

Jarvis barged in the door out of breath to find Yvette with dried-up tears still lingering on her face.

He hugged her. "Baby, what's wrong?"

"I missed my period; I'm pregnant."

Jarvis' eyes got wide and his mouth dropped.

"Are you sure?"

"Yes, she took the test several times," Leah said.

"Whoa. Yvette, I'm happy but in a state of shock. What matters most, though, is that I love you and I want us to have this baby," he said, kissing her on the lips.

"I want the baby too."

"We can do this."

"I think that it's time for us to go. Yuck, don't kiss again until I leave. My eyes and tummy can't take it," Tara said.

"Shut up," Yvette said, laughing.

"I knew I could get a smile on your face."

"Call us if you need anything," Leah said.

"Thanks, I will."

I couldn't believe Yvette was going to have a baby. It seemed like only yesterday we were all in my backyard playing jump rope and eating Fun dip. Now, we're all grown up. It was kinda scary. Sort of like a reality check. I didn't consider myself a grownup just yet. But having a baby is definitely a grownup thing.

Chapter 26

"Yes, sir, Mr. Johnson, I will be right back with a blanket for you," I said.

Mr. and Mrs. Johnson were the proud parents of a healthy 7 pound, 11 ounce baby boy. After I finished with them, my workday would be over. I had been at work since 5:30 in the morning and been going nonstop. Mrs. Johnson pushed for at least two hours. Her husband held one hand while I held the other. I didn't realize how blue a hand could get from someone squeezing it relentlessly. She apologized over and over again. I was fine after the ice pack cooled the swelling down. Witnessing the birth of a child for the first time put life into perspective for me. It made me realize what's truly important. *Birth is a priceless gift in itself.*

"I am quite impressed by the way you handled yourself in there," Ms. Tatem, my instructor said, patting me on the back.

"Thank you."

"What is the baby's name?"

"Scott Abraham Johnson."

"And how is our new mommy doing?"

"As well as to be expected. I assessed her vaginal area. Mrs. Johnson does have swelling and bleeding."

"It's normal."

"Also, she was having difficulty with the baby latching on to her breast, so I consulted with the head nurse to request a lactation consultant."

"Good job. I love it when the students use critical thinking to make decisions; it's what nursing care is all about." Ms. Tatem smiled.

"I'm on my way to say good-bye to the Johnsons. Here are my medication worksheets," I said, handing them to her.

"Great. I'll see you next week. Have a great weekend. You certainly deserve it."

"Thanks, again." I headed down the hall to my patient's room. It made me feel good to know Ms. Tatem felt comfortable in allowing me to make some medical decisions on my own.

My second semester of nursing was going to be over in less than a month. My grades were all right: three A's, two B's and a strong C in pharmacology. *Tomorrow, I have one more test in drug dose calculations. There is a chance I can pull that C up to a solid B.*

What a nice afternoon, I thought, cruising down the road in my car. Last night, Tory informed me that he received a promotion and would be the new project manager. Today, I sent him yellow roses with a card congratulating him. The phone rang, and as I answered, he didn't even give me a chance to say hello.

"I must say that you are full of surprises today. I'm sitting here staring at my flowers now. You started an uproar at my office, ya' know. The ladies are wondering what I am doing to be getting flowers from a woman."

"Maybe the ladies are full of envy because they haven't

received flowers in a while. I feel sorry for their husbands tonight."

We both started laughing.

"The celebration is not over yet. Tonight, I'm taking you to dinner at P.F. Changs, one of your favorites."

"Thank you."

"Just my way of showing my man I'm proud of his climb up the corporate ladder. So be ready at eight o'clock."

"Will do."

"Bye."

Before I could hang up, Tory called out my name.

"Yes?"

"I love you."

"Baby, I love you, too."

I almost hit the curb when he said those three little words that had such a mighty impact. That was the first time Tory had told me he loved me. Two months ago is when I had confessed my love to him. I take those words very seriously. I just don't just tell anyone that I love them. Deep down, I knew he did and would tell me when he was ready.

My phone rang again as I was entering the house.

"Hello?"

"Hey, girl," Yvette said.

"Hi, how are you feeling today?"

"You are the eighth person that has me asked that. I am fine, but my bladder is not. Natalie has been dancing on it all morning. I gave a seminar at the women's shelter and I had to stop three times to go pee. The women were quite understanding. Jarvis is another issue, though. I swear he will not let me do a thing. 'Rest, rest, rest. I want our baby to be healthy. Leave the work to me,' he says. The man will not even let me wipe my behind without wanting to help."

I couldn't help laughing. "Girl, you are too much for me."

"Well, it's the truth."

"What are you sipping on?"

"You mean *gulping*. I cannot seem to stop drinking apple juice. Natalie loves it. After I go to the bathroom, which seems like the sixth time within the last hour, I'm going to try to take a nap. I'll study for my exams later. I have one more month before I drop this load. I hope I can make it."

"Don't worry. You will."

"Momma is so excited about Natalie. She comes home with a new toy or blanket everyday. At the rate she's going, I won't need a baby shower."

"You can never have enough stuff. Especially diapers, wipes and onesies. Speaking of studying, I need to crack open the books myself because I have a test at eleven o'clock tomorrow morning. I want to get my studying out of the way because Tory and I are going to dinner tonight to celebrate his promotion at RADCOM."

"That's wonderful. Tell him I said congratulations."

"I will."

"Chick, I will call you later."

"Bye."

After an hour of studying, I became hungry. A turkey sandwich with a glass of iced tea sounded good. While in the kitchen preparing my snack, I heard singing coming from the back porch. It was Mommy. I didn't even hear her come in.

"Hey, Mommy," I said, kissing her on the cheek. "When did you get home?"

"Hi, baby. I walked in the door about forty-five minutes ago."

I loved the month of May with its spring glow.

Everything seemed so new. The birds were chirping and the flowers blooming. Oftentimes, I would come out to sit and enjoy my surroundings, needing that time to relax and keep sane from the daily pressures of life.

"I brought you a glass of tea."

"Thank you," she said as I handed it to her and took a seat on the bench next to her.

I could never forget this bench. My mother and I had many important talks here, everything from why the Easter bunny is not real, to sex, to death and dying, just to name a few.

"Why the long face?" I asked with concern.

"One of my patients died today from ovarian cancer. I had been taking care of Mrs. Brooks for six months. Last week, her health was improving. Dr. Nell was even thinking about releasing her to go home to her family. When I arrived at work this morning, the first thing I did was check in on her. I knew by the hazy look in her eyes that something was wrong. I called for Dr. Nell down the hall as Mrs. Brooks begged for me to come back in her room. She squeezed my hand and thanked me for taking care of her. Mrs. Brooks told me I was an angel in the army of the Lord and that she had to go on with him. Almost breathless, she kept repeating it. When she stopped breathing, I administered CPR on her. By the time the doctor and the code blue team came, it was too late. She was gone. I try not to get attached to my patients, but it's hard not to. I take care of people for long periods of time and they become like family to me," she said as her eyes watered.

"Don't cry, Mommy." I wiped her tears away with the napkin. "You know if you cry, I'll end up crying too."

"What do you think my heart is built of? Steel?" She had a smile on her face.

"Yes."

"Why is that?"

"Because you are my mommy," I said, giving her a hug and a kiss.

She held me in her arms. "What am I going to do with you?"

Chapter 27

"Cat got your tongue?" Tory asked.

"I'm fine, just thinking about my drug dose calculations test tomorrow. I need to study a little bit more," I said, sipping on a piña colada.

"Do you need some help?"

Before I could get a word in, he said, "I will help you. Nya, I know what you are going to say—'I do not need any help.' "

"Really, I appreciate it. However, I'm okay," I said, holding up my hands.

"It's all right to ask for help. In college, I took calculus, so I know I can do this. Let your pride go; stop trying to be a superwoman. At times, I know that my queen needs help. I'm your king and hope to be your husband someday. I have to make certain that your needs are met. Don't ever be afraid or hesitate to ask me for help with anything," he said, stroking my hand. "Please, don't make any excuses."

"All right, all right."

Once we arrived at his place, it took Tory no time to solve the calculations. I even gave him a hard one to start off with. After looking over my old quizzes and tests, he knew what my difficulties were.

"You are solving the problem, Nya, but you either word the answer wrong or make careless mistakes. For example, you have a bag of 1000 milliliter of normal saline infused in eight hours. What is the hourly rate?"

"The answer is 125 milliliter per hour."

"I see you did the math correctly on the test you took last week. However, you wrote down 125 ounces per hour. Once you write down your answer, always go back to the question and look at what the instructor is asking for."

"I get so nervous when I'm taking these tests."

"Calm your nerves; you got it." Tory gently patted my back. "Let's practice some more problems. We'll do about forty. Then, I'll see where your confidence level is."

We practiced for two more hours before stopping.

"Would you like some dessert? I have chocolate cake, rum raisin ice cream, and grape popsicles."

"Two scoops of rum raisin ice cream will be pleasing to my taste buds."

"Coming right up," he said, walking into the kitchen.

"I need a mental break," I said, rubbing my temples. "Are you up for a walk?" I looked up as he handed me the cup of ice cream.

"Yeah, let me grab my sneakers."

"This year has certainly flown by. Time sure flies when you are enjoying yourself," I said, kissing him as we strolled along.

"Pretty soon, it will be a solid year for us."

"What do you want to do to celebrate?"

"I have a few ideas running through my head. All you need to do is show up at my house with a smile."

"Do you want your smile with or without clothes?"

"I will take it without clothes."

Being in a playful mood, I challenged him to a race. "Whoever reaches the house last buys lunch on Thursday."

"Babygirl, you've got a deal."

"On your mark, get set, go."

I ran as if my life depended on it. Luckily, I won.

"Don't worry, honey, I'm not going to gloat in your face." I was breathless when I stepped into the house. "I will make reservations at Vivo's."

"You know I let you win, woman."

"Yeah, right."

"Plus, my chest was bothering me. I couldn't get my wind up."

"Stop making excuses. Take it like a man. You lost fair and square."

"Is that right?"

"Yep."

Tory started tickling me and I lost my balance, falling on top of him. Slowly, our tongues started to dance inside each other's mouths.

"I have to let you leave now, because if I don't, I won't let you leave later. Your loving is too good. It makes my toes curl. Down, Oscar, down," he said, talking to his penis. "Sometimes, I think he has a mind of his own."

"Just a few minutes. I won't take long," I said, my temperature rising as well as I pulled down his sweatpants.

"You are absolutely right about that. You come faster than I do. By the time I've put in four strokes, you've already came."

"Don't get mad because I can keep coming and coming and coming," I said, kissing his ear.

"Damn, baby, you know that's my spot."

"You know you cannot resist me," I said, rubbing my pelvis up and down against Oscar.

"Nya, you have a test in the morning. Besides, we ran out of condoms."

"You're right. It's getting late," I said, pulling his sweatpants back up.

"This is harder than you think. I'm going to have to endure painful blue balls for the rest of the night. However, I'll make you a deal. If you make an A or B on the test, I will give you thrusts so good that your vagina will explode and your knees will weaken to the point where you can't even stand up. If you don't rise to the occasion, you will be on probation."

"Fair enough. You're giving me great motivation to go home and practice some more calculations. Goodnight," I said, gently kissing him.

"Bye, baby. Drive carefully."

On Thursday, it was raining hard. I showed up at Tory's office with only a red trench coat, black high heels, a bag full of condoms, and my test paper with a big red 'A' scrawled at the top.

Chapter 28

I was on my way to pick up Yvette from the women's shelter after having come from working out at the gym. I had to go solo on this one. Her car was at the dealership for repairs. Not to mention, she had to work. She really made a difference at the shelter, and the kids absolutely loved her. Yvette's main focus was to get women out of abusive situations and into a stable environment.

Yvette may be little in size, but her voice was definitely heard. Each month, she tried to obtain additional federal and state funding for the living and educational expenses of the families and was now writing a proposal to the Section 8 program for free housing and utilities.

"Hey, Mr. Nickels." His nasty cigar assaulted my nostrils on the way inside the building.

"Hello there, Nya. How are you doing?"

Truthfully, my arms, abs, and legs were saying something else. I was sore beyond belief from my workout. "I'm fine."

"Well, I can see that. If I was thirty years younger and had some hair on my head, I would make you mine, pretty young thing."

"Is that right?" I tried not to crack a smile. I was not actually laughing at him; I just found what he had said to me to be very funny.

"It sure is."

"Isn't it time for you to get off?"

"Yeah, I'm waiting for Harry and Bill to show up. You know on the weekends we have two security guards."

"Well, have a nice evening," I said, waving goodbye.

"You, too, honey."

As I walked past, I could see out of the corner of my eye Mr. Nickels taking a peek at my butt. *Dirty old man,* I thought, shaking my head. *He should be ashamed of himself.*

"Hey," Tara greeted me at the door. She decided to meet up with us at the shelter to join us for lunch since she wanted to drop off some canned goods. "I'm so hungry. Where are we going for lunch?"

"I don't know. What are you in the mood for?" I asked.

"Seafood."

"Where's Yvette?" I inquired.

"She's in her office talking with a new intake. The woman looked pretty shaken up with three shiny bruises on her face. She tried to cover them up with her glasses, but that didn't work. Yvette is trying to make her go to the hospital. The lady told her she couldn't bear to make her kids spend another hour in the emergency room because of her husband beating her. I hate to say this, but at times, I hate to come down here. This is way too emotional for me. The woman had two tearful little girls by her side. My heart couldn't take it if my children saw me getting beat down on a regular basis. It wrecks their mental states," she said with tears in her eyes.

Now, I am next in line to cry. "I hope she places her children in counseling."

"People of color don't go to counseling. What is the point of wasting my money when I can talk to you, Leah, or Yvette for free?"

"Get it right, Tara. *You're* not in favor of counseling, but that doesn't mean the entire black race is not in favor of counseling."

I had to commend Yvette, though. Her heart had to be built of steel in order to handle those domestic situations.

After twenty minutes, Yvette came out with the battered woman. She looked better and even had a smile on her face. This was certainly a place of hope and safety for families. Yvette motioned to let us know that she was coming.

"We'll be in the car," I whispered.

I soon lost my appetite when a man stormed into the building with blood all over his knuckles. He looked as if he had not showered in days, with his scruffy beard. It didn't take a genius to realize he was the husband of the new intake.

"Debbie!" He repeatedly kept shouting out her name in a shrill voice.

Everyone in the building stopped dead in their tracks and turned to look in horror at him.

Where is security when you need them?

Debbie and her girls were nowhere to be found. Yvette had tucked them away in a secure place. Meanwhile a co-worker pushed a red button at her desk to summon for the police. Yvette slowly walked toward the man. "Sir, I'm going to have to ask you kindly to leave."

"I am not going anywhere! I want my kids! I want Debbie! Now! I know that she is here!"

"You are disrupting the daily operations of this building and scaring the children."

"Does it look like I care, lady? So this is the trashy

place my wife was bragging about coming to, just to leave me." He had a devilish smirk on his face. "I found your number on my coffee table that I paid for. My good-for-nothing wife doesn't work. I work hard for my girls and her everyday. I bring home the bacon, and this is the thanks I get," he said, shaking his head.

"Again, sir, she is not here."

The police should be here any minute, I thought. *They need to hurry up.* Tara and I inched our way over to Yvette's side. We had Yvette's back because we didn't know what this lunatic was capable of. And we were not about to take any chances, especially with Yvette's unborn child, Baby Natalie, at risk of being injured.

"You are deliberately trying to keep me away from my family."

Even at ten feet away from him, I could smell the drunken stench on his breath.

"Let me just talk to her, please. Things got out of hand. Tell her that I am sorry, and I will not hit her again if she doesn't provoke me. My dinner was late last night. My food should be ready as soon as I walk into my castle. I don't like to wait." He rubbed his eyes in frustration.

"Sir, we are not going to tell you again to leave."

"Don't tell me what to do—I'm a grown-ass man. If you're going to mess with my family, then I'm going to mess with yours. Say goodbye to that bastard in your stomach, lady!" he yelled, lunging for Yvette.

At that moment, adrenaline shot throughout my body. I felt like an animal that had to protect her family. By this point, Tara and I were only three feet away from him. Amazingly, at the same time, both of us balled up our fists to punch the lights out of him. I punched at his face while Tara swung for his stomach. And I was not finished yet. With all my might, I kicked him in his family jewels. If I had anything to do with it, he wouldn't have any more children in this lifetime to mentally abuse. He fell to his knees in agony. Tara snatched a phone from its cord and started beating the man with it.

By this time, Mr. Nickels ran in with the police. "I was out back taking a smoke break."

Tara didn't stop striking the man until the police had him handcuffed.

"Are you ladies all right?" one policewoman asked.

"I'm fine," I said, taking a deep breath. My hand throbbed as I tried to flex it.

"A paramedic is on the way. They'll take a look at the bruising on you ladies' hands." "What's wrong?" the officer asked Tara, noticing her twisted face.

"Oh, I broke a nail. On top of that, I hope this piece of trash doesn't press charges on us for assault. It can happen, ya' know. I've seen it happen on an episode of *Law & Order.*"

"Ma'am, you do not need to worry about that." The policeman chuckled. "There were too many witnesses here to see what really happened—he threatened the life of your friend and her unborn child."

While we were speaking with the police officers, Yvette was on the phone with Jarvis, who was ready to beat the man down. Tara had to end up getting on the phone just to calm him down while the paramedics made Yvette sit down to assess her pulse, respiration, blood pressure, and monitor the baby's heart rate. She was in a total state of shock.

"Thank you," she said, hugging both of us.

"No one messes with our best friend and little crumbsnatcher," Tara said with tears running down her face.

That was the most I had seen Tara cry in a year.

The paramedics treated our hands with cold ice packs to numb the pain. I still had the energy to knock a few more people out, though.

The director of the shelter, Mr. Hamm, came running in the door. He apologized to Yvette for the whole ordeal and wanted to make sure she and the baby was all right. "From this day forth, there will be two security guards on duty twenty fours a day, every day."

"Who were you talking to?" I asked Tara as she hung up the phone.

"Leah."

Oh Lord, the whole United States will know what happened now. Don't get me wrong. My little sister can keep her share of secrets, but this was a major event to her.

As I predicted, within thirty minutes, Leah, Nelson, Rob, Jarvis, his parents, my parents, Yvette's parents, her little brother, Tara's father, her two brothers, Tory, and the six o'clock news reporters were walking in the door to the shelter.

Mommy hugged everyone in sight, giving Tara, Yvette, and I the tightest hugs. "Now you see why I wake up at the crack of dawn to pray for you all," she commented with tear-filled eyes.

First and foremost, everyone checked on Yvette to make sure she was okay. My girl was fine, but the paramedic called her Ob/Gyn doctor, who decided it was best for her to go to the hospital for monitoring. He didn't want to take any chances with baby Natalie. Her parents, Jarvis, and his parents didn't have any objections. In fact, Yvette's mother wanted her to stay the whole night. As they were all leaving, Jarvis didn't want to let go of Yvette's hand.

* * *

I was extremely exhausted from the day's events. Still, Tara and I provided the three news anchors with a short interview. Afterwards, all three of us went our separate ways with our families and significant others.

John Simmons was charged with disturbing the peace, breaking and entering, attempted murder on an unborn baby, and attempted assault on Yvette. Also Debbie Simmons decided to press charges on her husband for assault and battery.

Good did come out of the situation. After the news stations aired the story, people from all over the country sent donations for the Simmons' family as well as the other families living in the shelter. The police department assigned a permanent patrol for the shelter. And we were even on the second page of the Sunday newspaper:

TWO HEROIC WOMEN SAVE THEIR FRIEND
AND UNBORN BABY FROM HARM'S WAY

Chapter 29

"**H**appy anniversary, baby!" I kissed Tory on his earlobe.

"Girl, you got chills running down my spine."

We were sipping on White Zinfandel. I agreed to have a sip only because it was our one year anniversary. For the rest of the meal, however, I sipped on raspberry ginger ale.

I had put a lot of thought into Tory's gift for the occasion. He loved Stevie Wonder, so I found a boxed collection of his most popular hits. Also, I received a free gift of a DVD full of live performances from the legendary singer and an autographed picture. These items were not cheap coming straight from the manufacturer. Next, I put together a collage of pictures of us. Finally, I bought him an Eternity cologne gift set, another panty dropper on my list.

He gave me a Metro perfume set, pink roses, and a card. That was not all, though. We spent a day shopping at both of the Tyson malls in the D.C. area. I even received a diamond necklace that I had been eyeing for a while. I was eagerly waiting for it to go on sale, but now my wait was finally over since he presented it to me as part of my anniversary gift.

You would think that was enough, right? However, the biggest surprise came when we ended up on the white sand and blue water beaches of Hawaii. I was too excited! Tory said that he kidnapped me as part of his gift for making the dean's list at school.

During the last night of our I-don't-want-to-go-home getaway, we dined at a restaurant called The Volcano. And let me tell you, the restaurant lived up to its name, with all the smothering entrées they had on their menu. Tory decided on the lobster tails, which were huge. *One alone would fill me up.* I chose the grilled flounder and vegetables with a baked potato. For dessert, we had the smothered chocolate sauce brownie with vanilla ice cream and a cherry on top.

"This has been one of the best years of my life."

"I cannot argue with you there, baby," I said, kissing him on his sweet caramel lips.

"You are so sexy with that cocky attitude."

"I wish that we could stay in this paradise forever."

"I was thinking the same thing. Nya, we can make our own paradise." Tory got down on one knee. "Please, make me the happiest man alive. I am the husband you've been dreaming of since you were a little girl. You are the woman that I have always been dreaming of since I was a young man. Will you marry me?" He opened a box which contained a gorgeous two-carat marquise-cut diamond ring.

Butterflies were swarming in my stomach. Tears began flowing down my face. "Yes." I wrapped my arms around him.

"I have one more surprise for you. Since I have been gone so much, it has been difficult on both of us.

However, it has also paid off for the both of us. You are looking at the new vice-president of RADCOM."

"Congratulations! That's wonderful."

"I knew you would be happy."

"I know how hard you've been working."

"Pack your bags. We're going to California."

"We have all ready been here a week, baby. Other people at my job want to take vacation, too; I can't be selfish."

"It's not a vacation, Nya. We will be living there. Next Thursday, I am meeting with a realtor about a house in Beverly Hills. You're going to love it."

"Wait a minute—what about your job in Virginia?" I asked with a puzzled look on my face.

"Two weeks from today is my deadline to move and get the company up and running."

"That's the reason why you have been working there so much." My face turned to a frown.

"Why the long face?"

"I am elated that you received a promotion, but I just cannot pick up and move to California. What about nursing school? What about *my* job?"

"I don't want my wife to be working. I will provide for your every need. Besides, I already looked into three universities that have excellent nursing programs. As intelligent as you are, it will not be a problem for you to jump right in."

"I cannot just 'jump in,' Tory."

He tried to kiss me, but I turned away.

"This is July, which means I am pretty sure the students for fall semester have already been selected. Therefore, I would have to wait till next fall to start their program. The schools are probably very competitive."

"You can take some time off from school. Besides, I want to have kids right away. What happened to Yvette made me realize that life is too short and can be instantly taken away from you."

"I'm *already* in a nursing program. This will be my second year. I'm not about to start over from scratch. Another thing, my credits may not even transfer."

"Well, I did the footwork. I'm pretty sure you will have plenty of time to research the transferring of your credits."

"No, I will not be barefoot and pregnant!" I said, raising my voice.

"What is wrong with you? I thought this is what you wanted."

"Baby, I do want to get married, but I'm not ready to move to California. You already have your degree and I don't. I'm going to get mine, though. We could be engaged until I finish school. Then I will gladly come out to the Hills. I want to have a life with you. But what's the rush?"

Tory sat with a blank expression on his face.

"We are just in our twenties. We've got our whole lives ahead of us. Babies are not in my immediate future right now. I feel that you are being selfish and inconsiderate."

"All right, all right. I understand you want your degree. So how are we going to do this, Nya? I cannot stand being away from you."

"Anything is possible. We can make it work if you are willing. The phone bill will be sky high, though, and we will rack up plenty of frequent flyer miles," I said jokingly, trying to ease the tension in the air.

"When will we see each other?" Tory's tone was more serious than I would have liked.

"Whenever we can . . . holidays, weekends."

"That's not enough for me."

"Tory, you can't have everything your way. I'm not

going to let you take control of my life. Do you know what the word *sacrifice* means?" I yelled.

"Apparently you don't, so look it up in the dictionary. I'm not going to be one of those women who are forty with no degree or job skills wondering what the hell happened, but thinking, 'at least I made my husband happy'. I love the fact that you want to take care of our future children and me," I said, softening my tone. "But I have got to find my way in life, too. Right now, you are doing what you want and loving it at RADCOM. I want the same feeling; I have the same hungry drive for success as you do."

"I know how independent you are, Nya—that's one of the things that attracted me to you."

"I need to earn my own money. I want my own career as well. It's very important to me. This relationship takes two, Tory. Are you willing?"

Tory gently kissed me on my lips. "Mark my words— I may not be your husband today or tomorrow, but we will be married someday."

"I can't be married to someone who does not want to take into consideration my future, feelings, hopes, and dreams." I stared into his eyes.

"I want to spend eternity with you, but I can't handle the long distance."

"We have been dealing with you gone away on business since the beginning of the relationship. It will just be for a little longer."

"I need you by my side every day."

"You don't even see me every day now, Tory."

"Will you at least consider it?" he asked, looking like a puppy dog that had lost its way home.

"There's nothing else to think about. I care about my future and will have input in it. My mind is made up."

"I love you, Nya."

"Hmm, you have a funny way of showing it. You're just going to give up on our relationship. We have something so special, and I love you too. But I can see you're not even trying to budge." I handed him the ring back.

"No, I don't want it; it's for you."

Lord knows I wanted to keep it.

"This ring will only be a painful reminder of what we had."

I asked him, "So we are over . . . just like that?"

"Yes. And please don't even ask me if we can be friends. I don't want to be your damn friend; I want to be your husband. The one who loves you, adores every bit of your body, and consoles you and makes you moan."

"Actions speak louder than words. Thanks a lot!" I screamed, walking away with no idea where I was headed.

"Thanks for what?"

"Thanks for breaking my heart!" I yelled back, trying to hold back the painful tears.

Tory called my name repeatedly, the sound of his voice fading the farther I walked away. I needed to be alone. Since he was not willing to attempt to have a long distance relationship with me, I was through talking. Our relationship was at least worth the try. Sweet nothings in my ear didn't mean a thing. I was not going to try to change Tory's selfish ways, though. Someday, he may change on his own.

Three hours had passed by when I finally realized what time it was. Mentally exhausted, I needed to go to bed. Plus, it was getting dark.

I let the hot water of the shower soothe me. I cried so much that my eyes were red. I managed to pack my clothes and get myself ready to leave the next day before going to bed. It was 1:00 a.m., and Tory still had not returned to the hotel room.

Hours later, the phone rang. It was the front desk

waking me up to catch my flight. I rolled over and found a card and a white rose lying on the bed. Inside the card was a hundred-dollar bill. It read:

I will always love you with all my heart
The money is for food just in case you get hungry while I am gone
I will be back in the morning before we leave to return home

Love, Tory

It was two hours before we were due to leave and his clothes were not packed. I tried to hold the tears back, but I couldn't. I had already used the box of tissue that was in the bathroom. I was glad that I brought my favorite pair of Gucci glasses with me because my eyes were puffy and I didn't want anyone asking me what was wrong.

Tory never showed up, so I left. I had a flight to catch. He was probably hurt just as much as I was. On the flight home, I kept looking down at the ring wondering why this was happening to me. Mommy always told me, "Things happen for a reason."

But I had to question, *What lesson could be learned from a damaged heart?*

Chapter 30

Yvette's baby shower turned out to be a success. Fifty people came to celebrate the coming of Natalie. Yvette couldn't wait to see if this little girl was going to look like her, Jarvis, or a combination of them both. You would think she was having triplets with as many gifts as she received. Yvette had two more weeks before the baby was due, and she had already dilated two centimeters. As a gift, I bought her a car seat and baby bathtub with accessories. I just love it when a baby smells like the fresh clean scent of Johnson and Johnson baby lotion. Tara purchased a stroller, while Leah picked up ten outfits for the summer and the coming fall.

A week later, the girls and I decided to praise the Lord at Second Baptist Church. I put on my finest for the Lord's day. Afterwards, Mommy wanted us to come back to the house for a Sunday feast. It seemed as if every Sabbath day someone was always over to our house for a meal.

Pastor Purns can surely preach and get the congregation up out of their seats and moving up and down the aisles. However, I feel that some people go a little overboard and are only trying to gain attention, such as Ms. Hughs, the woman next to me, who had fallen back almost knocking down her sister and me. Her wig and earrings fell off and three buttons popped off her blouse due to the crash landing on the floor. The ushers rushed in to assist, but she needed more assistance with her loud mouth.

"Jesus! Jesus!" she shouted.

I cringed every time she called His name. Her shrill voice made my ears ache in pain. Tara and Leah could have had more tact if you asked me. I was wrong to think the spirit of the Lord had come upon them as well. Nothing could hold back their tears of laughter.

"Praise ye, saints. Today's word is on blessings," Pastor Purns preached.

"Amen," the congregation hymned.

"What is a blessing? A blessing can be many things. I know one thing—most people want one."

"Thank you, Lord," a woman stood up to say.

"They can come big or small. Today, my main focus of the sermon is financial blessings, saints. I am going to have you talking about me today."

"Come on, preach!" a man rose to speak.

"All my twenty-five years of preaching and teaching the gospel of the word of the Lord, most people want a financial blessing from the Lord. Folks, I am here to tell you that Jesus is not a genie in a bottle. Money does not fall out of the sky. To have blessings in your finances, you have to take control of them. If you spent the rent money and the light money, a financial blessing will not come your way. If those designer clothes and shoes are more important than your tuition money, a financial blessing will not come your way. Let's be honest. We all want to make more money; however, if you are not doing anything to make that happen, it will not come to pass." Pastor Purns stomped his feet.

I had to clap my hands to that one.

"Lots of people do not like their jobs and complain about it. I am here to tell you to do something about it. Find another job, start your own business, or go back to school to make the money that you deserve. Saints, we have to get out of our comfort zone in order to get to where we want to be."

Now I was ready to shout out the name of Jesus. People all over the church were standing and waving their hands.

While I was standing and singing hallelujahs, Yvette pulled my hand. By the look on her face, I knew it was time.

"My water just broke."

Indeed it had, because water was everywhere. Unfortunately, we were jammed in the middle of the sixth row.

"Somebody call an ambulance! Yvette is going into labor!" Leah shouted.

Everyone turned around to see what all the commotion was about.

"Stay calm. I'm right here," I said.

"I am so embarrassed. I just peed in church."

"Don't worry, it was for a good cause. I am sure that God will understand the circumstances."

Within ten minutes, the ambulance arrived. As we were leaving, Pastor Purns prayed for a safe labor and healthy baby as the congregation stretched their hands out to Yvette.

Tara was an emotional wreck.

"The baby is coming," she kept repeating.

I rode in the ambulance with Yvette since I was the sanest person who could go along to keep her calm.

Tara and Leah rode in a car behind us. I instructed them to call Jarvis and the rest of the family.

"How do you feel?" I asked while she was being admitted into the hospital.

"So far so good. The pain is mild."

"Hello, my name is Ms. Reeves, and I will be your nurse for the remainder of the evening."

I helped Yvette out of her clothes and into the hospital gown.

"May I have a cup of water?" Yvette asked.

"No, ma'am. Unfortunately, you cannot have anything to drink until after the baby is born. You can have a few ice chips to suck on, though."

"That's fine. Give me something. My mouth is so dry."

Ms. Reeves and two other nurses moved about to prepare the room for the birth.

"What can I do to help?" I asked.

"You can help me hook up the baby monitor to Yvette," Ms. Reeves answered.

Once hooked up, Natalie's heartbeat came across the sound waves loud and clear. Dr. Monet, Yvette's ob/gyn, came in to check how far she had dilated. Yvette was making good progress, having dilated to five centimeters. She needed to be at ten centimeters before she could start pushing.

"Breathe in and out," I coached.

"Rub my back, please," Her knuckles had turned white from gripping the bed rail.

"Your lower or upper back?"

"Please, my lower back. These labor pains feel like a triple dose of menstrual cramps."

Sweat was pouring down her face, so I pulled her hair back into a ponytail to try to help cool her down.

One hour had passed before Yvette's mother and Jarvis came dashing into the room.

Yvette panted in between her breathing, "Nurse, please give me some drugs."

Jarvis held the digital camera in his hand in close proximity to Yvette.

"Get that thing out of my face! Now!"

When the anesthesiologist came in to administer the epidural, Jarvis almost passed out at the sight of the long narrow needle being inserted into Yvette's back. Within twenty minutes, the pain had ceased, but she could still feel the pressure of the baby making its way down the birth canal. The nurse wanted to wait another hour before checking to see how far along Yvette had dilated. I needed a break, so I went outside to get a Sprite and give the family an update. Tara and Leah were the first ones up in my face when I entered the waiting room.

"How is she doing?" they both asked.

"Last time he checked, the doctor said she had dilated to five centimeters. Five more to go."

Jarvis' parents had cards, flowers, and balloons in their hands, anxiously awaiting the baby's arrival. Everyone seemed to be pacing the floor. One at a time, everyone went in to see her, but Yvette was so out of it.

Two more hours passed before she reached ten centimeters.

"She's ready to push," the nurse said.

Dr. Monet entered after being paged. "Okay, Yvette, it's show time," he said, pulling on his latex gloves.

"Now, when you feel a contraction coming, I want you to push as if you are having a bowel movement," Ms. Reeves said.

"I can't," Yvette said in exhaustion.

"Yes, you can," I demanded.

"Honey, you have to if you want this to be over with and see Natalie," Yvette's mom replied.

"Do it for me," Jarvis pleaded.

"This is how I got into this predicament." Yvette took a swing at the camera. "I told you to get that out of my face! Don't tape me! Tape the baby!"

"She's not out yet."

"Then you'll just have to wait!"

I held one of her legs back and her mother held the other as she prepared to push. Yvette pushed so hard that she almost knocked her mother down.

"Three more pushes," Dr. Monet said.

"One, two, three, four, and five," I declared.

Yvette lay back on the bed to gear up for the last two pushes.

"That's it. One more push," Ms. Reeves said.

From the mirror overhead, I could see the crown of Natalie's head and the beautiful hair that adorned her scalp. The last push did it. She was out and quickly whisked away to be cleaned and assessed. Boy, did she have a set of lungs on her. Natalie's cries were music to everyone's ears. Overcome with joy, Jarvis, Yvette's mother, Yvette and I all started doing our own crying.

Soon, the nurse returned with Natalie, and as Dr. Monet delivered the afterbirth and stitched up her vagina, Yvette counted to make sure Natalie had all ten fingers and toes.

"Is she all here?" Yvette asked.

"Yes, Natalie is beautiful," I said.

Two by two, everyone came in to greet the new member of the family—Natalie Alease Robinson, 6 pounds and 11 ounces.

Chapter 31

A year had passed since Tory and I split. After wallowing in my sorrows for two weeks, but I did pick myself back up. He'd called plenty of times, but I wouldn't return any of his phone calls.

To keep my mind occupied, I poured myself into school and work. I took a summer internship at Creekdale Memorial Hospital and was assigned to the medical/surgical unit. I didn't work for the sake of nothing, though. Those ten weeks of bathing, cleaning up urine and feces, assessing and administering medications earned me eight college credits, putting me on my way to graduating early.

Although Tuesday was the final day of my internship, I paid a visit to say good-bye to a few special people who I had grown attached to. Mommy was right. It was hard not to get close to the patients.

I also got close to several members on the staff as well. The staff gave me a little going-away party to thank me for being an asset to the team. That's what they had written on the inside of the card. I was touched. The most important lesson I'd learned in working on a nursing floor was that teamwork is essential. Overall, my experience at Creekdale was an enjoyable one, and I definitely planned on returning the following summer.

"Honey, give me a call if you need anything. We are all going to miss you. It has been a long time since I have seen a dedicated worker come through those double doors." Ms. Rosen, my mentor, had been more like a second mother to me. She gave me a hug.

"Thank you," I said with tearful eyes. *Oh, how I hate good-byes.*

"Take care."

I had three more weeks before school started back again. And in their opinion, Tara and Leah felt I had to live up those three weeks and party every night. Which is the reason why I was now headed over to the Outback Steakhouse for dinner with the girls.

Yvette was already sipping on a Coke.

"Hey, girl."

I plopped down in the booth. "Hi. Where's my baby?"

"Jarvis' parents have her for the evening. I love Natty, but Mommy needs a break at times."

The waiter approached the table. "Would you like something to drink?"

"Yes, I will have water with lemon and a non-alcoholic peach daiquiri, please."

"Coming right up."

"Have you ordered yet?" I looked around, taking in the my surroundings.

"No, I wanted to wait for the late birds to get here."

Twenty minutes later, Leah and Tara came swarming in.

"Sorry I'm late. Rob was acting cranky. I had to give him a dose of my medicine. I didn't realize it would take an hour and a half. Being sticky and sweaty is not my style, so I had to freshen up with another shower."

"Is he okay now?"

"Yes, I left him in the bed. He's sleeping like a baby."
Yvette looked at Leah. "What's your excuse?"

"I was on the phone trying to talk Toyota out of re-
possessing my new 4runner."

The waiter returned to the table to take Leah and
Tara's order for their drinks and to see if we were ready
to place our meal order.

"Before we get started, I wanted to let you know that
the gentleman at the bar has already paid for your meal,"
the waiter stated.

I looked up to find none other than Darren Edmonds walking out of the door. *The man does not quit.* At
my bank alone—BankFirst was one of his many financial institutions—he held two and a half million dollars
in cold, hard cash.

"You haven't even taken our orders yet," I said.

"I think six hundred dollars will be enough to cover
your meals." The waiter handed me twelve fifty-dollar
bills.

I quickly handed him back one fifty-dollar bill for his
tip, and a huge smile appeared on his face. *Sure, I could
be quite generous with someone else's money.*

"Did he leave a message, or his phone number?"
Tara asked.

"He regrets he had to leave so abruptly. No, Mr.
Edmonds did not leave a contact number."

He probably thought I would tear it up if he had.

"He told me to inform the beautiful Nya Gamden
that he would see her on Tuesday. Mr. Edmonds said
you would know what he means by that. I will get you
ladies another round of drinks, but first, can I take your
order?"

Tara and I both ordered the Drover's Platter; Yvette

wanted grilled chicken, and Leah ordered the porter-house steak.

The waiter gathered up our menus. "The food will take about thirty minutes."

"Damn, he did all that and you're not even dropping the panties yet. Imagine what you would be bringing in if you were," Leah said.

"He at least deserves one date," Tara said.

"I'll think about it."

"Edmonds is really trying to get your attention," Yvette said, slicing the loaf of bread.

"You need to get out more."

"You haven't even been on a date since you came back from Hawaii. All work and no play makes Nya more boring than she already is," Leah chanted.

"Whatever."

"We are all worried about you," Yvette said.

"You haven't been your old self in a long time."

The breakup with Tory did take a toll on me. Maybe it was time for some male companionship in my life.

Tara said, "A lot of men are trying to wine and dine you. I know three in mind who would treat you right, and you know I wouldn't hook you up with any scrubs. Have some fun. Live a little. You deserve it."

"Y'all are right. I sure could go for a vacation as well."

"You took the words right out of my mouth," Leah said. "You know Nelson and I are going to Trinidad to visit his family, and Rob and Tara are coming along."

"It's a 'couple' thing; I do *not* want to be a fifth wheel."

"You won't be. Rob and Nelson will not be with us the entire time. I'm sure they will want to do their guy thing and we'll go do our girl thing. You never know, you might meet a handsome island man who sweeps you off of your seven-and-a-half-sized feet. Besides, there is no need to worry about food or hotel expenses. You know Nelson's parents own a chain of resort hotels." Leah tried hard to persuade me.

It did sound like a good plan, I thought, seeing my aunt, Alberta, worked for US Airways and I could get a plane ticket for a fraction of the cost.

"Honey, please go. Last month Jarvis took me on a vacation to Miami because I was about to have a nervous breakdown. Natty doesn't sleep through the night, and I desperately needed a good night's rest. Look at me now—I feel new and refreshed. A vacation will do you some good."

"All right, all right, I'll go."

Everyone started clapping and cheering as if it was my birthday.

"Ladies, here are your salads. Your food will be out in about ten more minutes."

"Thank you," we said in unison.

"Speaking of men, how are Jarvis, Nelson, and Rob doing?" I asked.

"Jarvis is doing well and working hard at the Ford Plant to provide for Natty and I. Things couldn't be better. Even when I had the baby blues for two months, he was right by my side. He was very supportive and most importantly, didn't pressure me into having sex. Lord knows I didn't feel like being sexual, not even going down on him. The man makes me feel good inside and out; he is my best friend."

"Ahh," I crooned.

Then Leah said,

"I think Nelson may be cheating on me. I don't have any proof, but I keep getting this gut feeling."

"What are you going to do about it?" I asked.

"Nothing for now. I know he loves me, and I am no angel by far—I skip out on him as well. But the man pays all of my bills."

I laughed. "Why do you stay so broke, then?"

"Anyway," Leah said rolling her eyes, "I have the keys to his house, car, and my very own ATM card linked up to his account."

"Jarvis knows better. He does *not* want to feel my wrath. All I have to say are those nine little numbers that give me access to all that is his, and his cutting up ceases."

"I know that's right," Tara said. We were dying of laughter in our seats. I laughed so hard, I almost choked on a piece of lettuce.

"I do see myself with Nelson for a long time. But, right now, I am young and want to just enjoy life."

"Rob's practice is growing, which means his pockets are getting fatter. He is my main squeeze, but I want to fulfill my urges of playing with other men. Like Leah just said, I am young too. He knows how I feel and is cool with it; he just doesn't want me to disrespect him in his face. I can accept that," Tara said. "I don't want to be disrespected either."

To lighten the mood and take my mind off of my thoughts of me not having someone to call my own, I asked, "Is anyone in the mood to go out tonight?"

The vote was unanimous—no. So, instead, we made it a BLOCKBUSTER night.

Chapter 32

Tuesday quickly crept up on me, and I was scheduled to work a full eight hours. I decided to wear a light-green suit with my hair in a bun. I was going for a sexy but professional look. I knew Edmonds was coming for me, and I was ready to have some fun. *What's the worst that could happen? He is handsome; but it's not as if I'm ready to jump his bones or anything.*

Right now, Mr. Tole was in my face begging me to refund him two hundred and forty dollars worth of non-sufficient fund charges. I really wanted to tell him this was not one of those "loans-until-payday" facilities. Besides, even if I did refund the charges, his account would've still been overdrawn for fifteen more days until his social security check came in. There were three customers with similar sob stories waiting to speak to me, and it was already 11:35 a.m. *What is wrong with these people? Is it that difficult to balance an account?* Ms. Stein buzzed me to pick up the phone.

"Yes?"

"Nya, refund Mr. Tole half of the charges. Also, please inform him this will be the last time we can accommodate him."

"Yes, ma'am," I said, agreeing with Ms. Stein, not wanting Mr. Tole to think his behind was on BankFirst's payroll. Then I said to him, "I'll tell you what, Mr. Tole. I can refund you half of the charges this time."

"Please, can't you refund all of them? I am on a fixed income."

Then why are you spending beyond your means? Instead, I said, "I am pushing it with half. This year alone I have refunded you five hundred dollars worth of charges."

"Okay, I don't like it, but I guess I have no choice."

"Thank you, Mr. Tole. Don't worry. Your account will not close." I shook his hand and stood up, giving him the cue that I needed to take the next customer. Otherwise, he would have talked me to death.

After my last customer, Edmonds had not yet arrived and I had the munchies. So, I snuck into the lunchroom, grabbed a bottle of water and crackers, and stared out the window. A candy-apple red Ferrari pulled into the parking lot. Immediately, I thought of Edmonds. He was known for changing his cars like he changed his women, but it wasn't him.

When I returned to my desk, a man dressed in a shirt, tie, and Cache pants was standing around. Since my lunch break was in ten minutes and Ms. Stein, Ms. Pilom, and Rachel, the other financial representative, all had customers with them, I decided to help the gentleman who appeared to look worried. Approaching him, I did not get a good feeling. Sweat was coming down his face profusely.

Maybe it was the hot weather. Maybe I was overreacting.

"Sir, may I help you?"

He looked at me for a minute before speaking. "I would like to open up a new account."

"Okay, step right on over to my desk, and I will be more than happy to assist you."

"All right."

"May I have your name, please?"

"It's John Barker."

"Mr. Barker, what type of account were you looking to open?

"I'm not sure."

"We have a variety to choose from. Do you think you can keep a minimum balance of a thousand dollars in your account?"

"No, I live paycheck to paycheck. I'm lucky if I can keep fifty cents in there. Really, my only purpose for an account is to pay my bills online and make purchases using one of your Visa check cards."

"Now we are getting somewhere. I have an account that meets your financial needs. If you look on this brochure, it describes the convenience of our checking account. Also, here is the schedule of fees. You can make as many withdrawals as you want, whether it is ATM withdrawals, check card purchases, or writing checks. Mr. Barker, I will need at least one hundred dollars and two forms of identification to get the account started. The second ID can be a credit card or anything with your name on it. Also, I will need to do a credit check."

"Let me get the money out of my jacket."

I clicked on the screen to start a new account and set up a customer profile. When I looked back over at Mr. Barker, he had pulled something out of his jacket. I froze in my seat.

"Listen to me carefully," he mumbled. "Can you hear me?"

"Yes."

"Do not scream or I will have your brains splattered on these walls. Don't do anything stupid."

I immediately pressed the robbery button which was located underneath my desk. Luckily, he did not see any of my hand movement.

One of the valuable lessons I'd learned in robbery training was not to try to be a hero. My life, those of my co-workers, and especially the customers' lives were more important than the money. It can be replaced; we cannot. Still, I felt the urge to knock this man's dumb ass out.

Two little children ran over to my desk to get a lollipop. They called me the candy lady and looked forward to seeing me whenever they came to the bank. I acted as normal as possible and handed them each some candy so they could go back to where their mother was.

Barker, if that's even his name, looked so familiar to me. He looked to be around my age. His hands looked as if he never lifted a finger a day in his life. He was the one I saw getting out of the car. Maybe he couldn't afford the insurance premiums on the new sports car his mommy and daddy gave him and had to resort to robbing a bank. *Spoiled rich kids do the strangest things.* By now, my blood pressure was sky high and my hands were trembling.

Barker instructed me to write a note to give to a teller demanding all the money. "None of that funny bait money business."

Line thirty-seven rang on my phone. Little did he know it was security's line.

"Answer it and make it quick. The phone lines are beginning to annoy me."

"Good afternoon, BankFirst. How may I help you?"

"This is security. Are you being robbed?" the woman on the line asked.

I faked the whole conversation, pretending the security department was a customer who wanted to order checks. "Yes, I can definitely get an order for you in forty-eight hours. Thank you and have a nice afternoon." I hung up the phone.

"Good girl. You're getting the hang of things, doing what you're told. Now, get up so I can get my money." He gripped my shoulder.

As I walked over to the teller line, Barker held the gun, which was hidden inside his jacket, pressed against the small of my back.

"Do not—I repeat—do not do anything stupid, or you will make the six o'clock news and tomorrow's newspaper."

I walked over and handed the note to Heather. I was praying she wouldn't freak out and make matters worse. *The police should be here any minute. When Barker runs out with the money, I hope it will be the same time the police, FBI, or any other law enforcement agency pulls up and nabs his ass.* After Heather read the letter, she instantly went into action. While putting the money in cloth bags, she pressed the red button below her station to alert the other tellers that a robbery was in progress.

"Lady, don't be stingy. I know you have some money in your second drawer and coin vault. Give it to me right now."

Come to think of it, his voice sounded quite familiar. Someone who works for a bank would specifically know where excess money is kept.

Everyone stayed calm except Ms. Agnes. She began to scream and beg for Barker not to kill her. Now, I wanted to put a lid on her mouth. Her course of action backfired and agitated him. While holding me tightly close to his side, he pointed the .38 caliber at her.

"Shut your hole, lady, or I will."

Ms. Agnes, the sixty-seven-year-old teller, stood there crying with her hands up. I prayed he wouldn't cause her to have a heart attack. Barker fired two shots in the air to let us know he meant business. He didn't even have to tell the customers or us to get down on the floor because we knew the drill. Tyler, my longtime customer's son, began to cry. His mother tried to console him.

"May I give him a lollipop? This way, he won't be screaming and crying."

"Hurry up." He pointed the gun directly at me. "Walk over to the door with me. And pipe down, old bag. I'm not going to tell you again. Keep it up and I'll be giving away free bullets. Would you like one?"

"No," Ms. Agnes responded with a trembling voice.

After those words, I didn't hear another peep out of her. Barker fired two more shots in the air. The little children started to scream louder. At that moment, Tyler began to choke on the candy I had given him earlier.

Mrs. Roland, his mother, became hysterical. "Please, somebody help my baby!"

Without even thinking, I ran over to Tyler to administer the Heimlich maneuver on him. Within four abdominal thrusts, the grape-smelling candy came up. Expressions of relief came upon everyone's face, even Barker's.

"Thank you," Mrs. Roland said to me, holding Tyler tight. Without hesitation, she assumed the position back on the floor, covering her body over both of her children.

I pleaded, "Will you please let the children go? They're scared out of their minds."

Barker ignored me, concentrating on the sound of the police sirens that were surrounding the building.

"I thought I told you no cops. You must take me for a

joke." He looked at me but pointed his gun at Ms. Agnes. Barker was getting a kick out of the woman being petrified. The smirk on his face was definitely one of undeniable pleasure.

"Everyone, except for the kids and their mothers, get up and walk slowly over to the other side. Form a single line facing me. There are too many people scattered around."

I proceeded to move with the crowd, but Barker stopped me. "You're not going anywhere, pretty thing," he said, rubbing his hand on my butt.

I could see the terror in Ms. Stein's eyes. She didn't want to make matters worse, so she did as she was told.

"Open the front door and let them go. I don't need the extra stress. We will do this nice and slow." He wiped the sweat from his face.

As the door swung open, I could see at least ten police cars in the parking lot.

"I'll pray for you," Mrs. Roland said as she walked out with her son, Tyler, and her daughter closely by her side.

"Lock the door!" Barker yelled.

There was a phone call.

"Hello?" Barker quickly answered. He had the gun pointed in my direction.

"This is the Norfolk Police Department. I am advising you to let those people go and surrender before the situation gets even uglier," the policeman demanded.

"I make the rules. You got it? I want a getaway car in twenty minutes or each and every one of these people is going to have cold blood, starting with the old lady first." Barker didn't give the policeman an opportunity to negotiate before hanging up the phone. He started pacing the floor. None of us moved an inch.

"This is your entire fault. I don't know how, but

you're the culprit responsible for the cops being here. Now you're going to pay."

The next thing I knew I felt a burning, sharp pain in my shoulder and could hear people screaming. From the door that opened to the drive-thru, Darren Edmonds rushed in behind Barker and hit him on the head with his bare hands. Maybe Darren had even been there inside the bank the whole time. I have no idea.

Once Barker fell to the ground, I couldn't resist the urge to kick him in the face. After doing so, it finally hit me that I had been shot. Everything suddenly went black.

Chapter 33

It took me a while, but I found enough strength to open my eyes. I was exhausted and my shoulder was killing me. I looked out of the window to see the sun shining. It was 9:20 a.m. and I was in the hospital. How long had I been here? I had the worst case of "cotton-mouth." I craved for a cup of ice-cold water and a Sprite to quench my thirst.

"Nya," someone called gently.

It was Mommy. Tears began to run down my face. "Mommy," I whispered.

"Don't try to talk, baby. You were shot in the shoulder. You have been in the hospital for four days. Praise the Lord!" she cried with a sigh of relief. "We thought we were going to lose you with all of the blood you lost."

I tried to speak again but could not get any words to come out.

"Don't worry, baby, the best doctors were here to take care of you. Dr. More and Dr. Culchin were able to get the bullet out. Luckily, it didn't hit a nerve or a bone. I've been by your side the whole time. Your father tried to get me to go eat or take a nap, but I could not leave you for a minute." Mommy stroked my hair. "I have been praying for the Lord to heal you."

I could sense other people were in the room, but I didn't have the strength to even lift my head up.

Mommy pushed the button to raise the head of the bed for me.

"Nya, you're awake. Please don't ever scare us like that again." It was Leah. She was sobbing and holding my hand tight. Daddy was holding my other hand. Tara and Yvette were there as well. I was so glad to see all of them.

"Girl, so many people are out in the lobby waiting for you to wake up," Yvette said.

"You almost gave me a heart attack," Tara said. "When I heard you were shot, I drove to the hospital in my pajamas. I knew you were going to pull through. I couldn't imagine losing you. You are my strength to carry on."

"I'm glad to see Sleeping Beauty woke up," Ms. Rosen said as she entered the room.

I started smiling.

"Honey, I love having you around me, but not under these circumstances. Don't worry. I'll have you good as new in a week." She kissed me on the forehead. "Now, may I get you something?"

"Water, please."

"Coming right up. My baby has woken up! Y'all can all come on in here now. Nya is awake," Ms. Rosen announced to the others waiting outside in the hallway.

All of my co-workers, the parents and siblings of Tara and Leah, Natalie, Jarvis, Mrs. Roland, Tory's parents, Mrs. Wellington, and four of my classmates came to hug me and express their wishes for my speedy recovery.

"Tory flew in Saturday but left this morning because he had to return to work. Honestly, Tory took it pretty hard. For the past two days, the boy came to see you at least six times a day. He was so worried about you," Mrs. Sothers explained.

"He left this card for you," Mr. Sothers said.

"Thank you."

"No ifs, ands, or buts—you cannot return to school in three weeks because of doctor's orders. I want you to rest. Please, don't even worry about the clinical time or tests," Mrs. Wellington said. "I'm just so thankful you pulled through."

Ms. Stein said, "I have already talked to your doctors, as well. You can't come back to work for at least eight weeks. I am so happy you made it through. On behalf of BankFirst, Nya, I want to thank you and commend you on your heroism during the robbery. Your calmness kept us sane. I'm so sorry you had to go through such an ordeal."

Flowers, cards, and balloons swarmed my room. I felt so loved.

"Honey, you need to get something to eat and take a shower," Daddy said to Mommy.

"In a few minutes, Willie. I want to make sure my daughter is taken care of."

Just then, Darren Edmonds walked in with flowers and balloons.

"He has come to see you three times everyday," Tara whispered in my ear. It brought a smile to my face. Mommy grabbed the man in an embrace and thanked him for saving my life. Daddy had to darn near pull Mommy off of him to shake his hand to thank him.

"The man saved your life. The least you can do is give the man a date," Leah whispered in my other ear.

"I'm glad to see you are awake." Darren smiled at me and kissed my hand.

"Thank you for saving my life."

"All in a day's work of a gentleman." He placed a card on the table next to my bed. "Read this when you are able to. I'll be in touch."

Right before the robbery, Darren told me he had come in while Barker was at my desk. When he fired the shots, Darren was coming out of the restroom. He hid in the drive-thru until he could make a move to stop Barker. Thank God, his plan worked. Also, Ms. Stein told me Darren performed CPR on me while they waited for the paramedics. He held my hand the whole time and rode in the ambulance with me. Darren didn't leave the hospital until he knew I would be okay, which wasn't until five o'clock Saturday morning.

After talking with my co-workers and Ms. Stein, I found out Barker's real name was John Mithers, the son of one of the most prominent senators in the state of Virginia. The reason he looked so familiar to me was because he worked for the company as an investment banker before he was fired for embezzling over one million dollars worth of clients' money for which he was being prosecuted. He was a gambler and owed past due debts. Mithers was charged with attempted murder and robbery. With the other witnesses' testimonies and mine, Mithers would be locked up for a long time. He was right about one thing, though—I made the six o'clock news and the front cover of the newspaper.

After everyone had left, including Mommy, I decided to read the cards people had sent me. While reading, I heard a knock on the door.

"Are you up for one more visit?" Ms. Rosen asked.

"Yes, ma'am."

Mr. and Mrs. Roland entered. Instantly, I recognized him when he walked in the door. He was a known cardiologist in the area. His hands did wonders when it came to saving people's lives.

"Sorry we are so late," Mrs. Roland said.

"No problem. Thanks again for the flowers."

"It's the least we could do. Earlier, there were so many people in here, we didn't want to impose."

"We wanted to personally thank you for saving our boy," Mr. Roland said.

"No need for any thanks. He was in need and it was instinct to help."

"I know, but I overheard you pleading with Mithers to let the children and me go." Tears streamed down her face. "You put my children's well-being first, and then yourself. I cannot thank you enough. I'm a nurse practitioner and have done CPR and the Heimlich maneuver plenty of times, but I froze when I saw Tyler choking. If you hadn't been there, I don't know what I would've done."

"Honey, don't beat yourself up." Mr. Roland rubbed his wife's shoulders.

"Mrs. Roland, I understand—you are a mother first, then a nurse practitioner. If I were in your shoes, I would have reacted the same way."

"It's so funny," she said with a smile. "Tyler and Sara are telling their little friends the bank lady saved them from the mean man. So how are you doing?"

"I'm feeling much better. I just finished eating chicken noodle soup and sipping on a Sprite."

"Well, we will not hold you. Here's one more thing for you." She handed me an envelope.

I opened it and enclosed was a cashier's check for fifty thousand dollars. My eyes were wide as saucers. "I cannot accept this, Mr. and Mrs. Roland."

"Yes, you can, and you will. It is the least we can do.

Besides, we would rather give it to you than Uncle Sam," Mr. Roland said.

"Don't try to tear it up, either, because if you do, I will have the money wired to your BankFirst account. I know you're going to school for nursing. This money can help out with expenses or whatever else you need. Now, say thank you and give me a hug," she said.

I followed her instructions. "Thank you."

After they left, Ms. Rosen entered. "It's time to take your medicine. This is 800 mg of Motrin. It will relieve the pain and help you sleep tonight."

With a tummy full of food and medicine, I had no choice but to slip into la-la land.

"Now, get some rest," she said and turned off the lights.

Chapter 34

I was up early the next morning. Ms. Rosen came in to change my sheets and help me take a shower. The hot water felt soothing against my skin. Looking at my naked body, I noticed I had lost a few pounds. *Oh well, those little love handles had to go someday.* My shoulder was still sore. She combed my hair and smeared Johnson & Johnson baby lotion all over me. It was a good feeling to be clean and refreshed.

"Now, baby, don't overexert yourself. Lie down and rest. Breakfast will be here soon. How does some bacon and eggs sound?"

"Great!"

Mommy had left a bag for me to put all my cards in. That is also where I put the check. I decided not to tell anyone about the money. For one, I would hear "give me's" and "can I's" from Leah. Secondly, Mommy would have wanted me to donate half to the church. No way! I'm not stingy, and I'm going to give my fair share to the Lord, just not half. Daddy would be the only one cool about it. I decided I would let the money sit in a new money market account until I made a decision of what to do with it. One thing was for sure—most of the funds would be used for a down payment on a house.

I read Tory's card first with the bouquet of white roses on the front.

Dear Nya,

Baby, I love you so much. I could not bear to see you like this. I know you are going to pull through. You are my little trooper. Now I realize you are a precious flower I have lost. Even though we are not together, I will always be there for you if you let me. Whether I am with you or not, I want you to be happy. Mrs. Gamden told me how well you are doing in school. I am so proud of you. Keep up the good work so I can see you walk across the field to get your degree. Call me anytime. You know the number. I have called you several times and you have not returned my calls. I understand you need your space.

Love, Tory

I tried hard not to cry. I missed him so much, especially our late-night pillow talks. Still, I couldn't talk to him. Not yet. My heart was still mending.

Next, I read Darren's card. On the front was a picture of a diamond. It read:

Nya,

You are a beautiful diamond in the ruff. I have admired you from afar and now I am ready to get up close and personal. Get well soon so I can give you a night you will never forget. Don't worry. I will keep my hands to myself. Here's a little something to cheer you up.

Sincerely,
Darren

Attached was a two-thousand-dollar gift card to Nordstrom's. *He had me all figured out.* As I was in the process of dialing Darren's number to express my thanks, there was a knock at the door.

"Come in."

Speak of the devil—I was so glad I had showered, brushed my teeth, and had my hair looking halfway decent.

"Hey."

"Are you up for some company?" Darren asked.

"Yes."

"I brought you a snack."

I opened the bag. "How did you know I love rice pudding?"

"Your mother gave me a history of you from when you were born to the present. She told me it's been your favorite ever since the time you wrote on the living room wall with blue crayon and ate your first vitamin. Mrs. Gamden is some lady."

"I know. That's my mommy."

"Yes indeed. And one who produced a beautiful woman."

"Thank you so much."

"You do not have to keep thanking me."

"No, I need to say this. Thank you from the bottom of my heart for saving my life," I said, tears forming in my eyes.

"Hey now, don't cry because you will get me doing the Niagara Falls up in here, as well. I knew I could beat Mithers down, but my strength was no match for his gun. Out of the peephole of the drive-thru door, I watched as he violated your body and was screaming at you. It took all of me not to keep hitting him over and over again. I wish I could have gotten to you sooner. I know you can hold your own, though. I saw your leg action when you kicked him in the face." He chuckled.

"I was pissed at him for touching my butt and threatening the lives of everyone in the building."

"When do you plan on getting out of here?"

"If all goes well, I'll be released in about a week."

"I would really love to take you out and show you a nice evening."

"Yes, I would like that."

"I'm a patient man. I know you have to get your strength back up. For the next two weeks, I'll be out of town. Will that be enough time for you to get on your feet?"

"Yes. Hopefully, these bandages will be off soon."

"Well, I won't hold you. Here's my phone number in case you need to reach me. Please, don't hesitate to call," he said, gently kissing my hand.

"Thank you for the gift card, Darren."

"You're welcome. I know you will put it to good use." Then he winked and walked out the door.

Chapter 35

The day of my release I was more than ready to go. *Nothing like sleeping in your own bed in your own home.* As Ms. Rosen handed me the discharge papers, I gave her a hug.

"Thanks for everything."

"It was a pleasure having you, baby. Plus, you got some experience with wound care. Remember, do not overdo it and get plenty of rest. Call me if you need anything. I wrote my home number and cell phone number down on the discharge papers."

I wanted to walk, but she wheeled me to Daddy's car. I waved good-bye to Ms. Rosen as Daddy drove away.

"How are you feeling, baby?" Daddy made sure I was secure in the passenger car seat.

"Pretty good. I am hungry for some real food, though. Where are Mommy and Leah?"

"They are at the house cooking up a storm. Leah even gave a hand in the kitchen."

"Well, it's about time."

I was feeling good as new.

* * *

A "welcome home" sign was posted on the door. Mommy invited friends and family over for a Sunday meal to celebrate my homecoming. "Hi, baby," she said as she hugged me. "How are you doing?"

"I'm a little weak. Right now, my shoulder doesn't hurt, though."

"Did you take your medicine?"

"Yes, Mommy."

"Wash your hands. Dinner will be ready in ten minutes."

Practically, my whole family was present. Tara, Leah, Yvette, and Natalie ran up to me. It was good to see my baby. It looked as if she had grown in the past two weeks.

"Hi, Natty." I kissed her on her forehead.

"Hi," she said, giggling bashfully in Yvette's arms.

"You look good," Tara said.

"I sure am glad you're back home because I'm not going to be cooking on a regular basis. It's your job." Leah wiped some flour off her face.

"Ladies, it's time to eat," Mommy announced.

Nelson, Rob, and Jarvis were already sitting at the dinner table with their forks in ready position. They couldn't wait to tear into Mommy's cooking. I said the grace this day, and had a lot to be thankful for—my life was spared and I had family and friends who loved me. It couldn't get any better than this.

"Your mother has been up since six o'clock this morning cooking for you," Daddy said.

I could see why, with all this food on the table. We had fried chicken, fried fish, fried crabs, steamed crabs, crab legs, mashed potatoes, butter beans, peas and carrots, potato salad, tossed salad, string beans, steamed broccoli with cheese, cornbread and homemade rolls.

"What do you want to drink?"

"I want a glass of peach tea, but I will get it," I said, trying to stand.

"No, you will not. Sit down. I'll get it for you. And don't even ask me if I need help in the kitchen. I got it covered. All I want you to do is relax and take it easy."

"Please, come and eat. You have been going non-stop since early this morning, Mommy."

"Don't worry about me. I will fix my plate as soon as I get your tea. Mommy walked into the kitchen.

"How is the heroine feeling today?" Rob asked.

"I'm feeling much better."

"Mrs. Gamden, the food is so delicious," Jarvis hollered in the kitchen after taking a hardy bite out of a chicken leg.

Natty was even gobbling it up.

"Thank you, baby. Y'all eat up. Don't be afraid to get seconds because there is plenty of food."

Aunt Alberta came for dinner, so I knew Mommy and her would be playing cards for hours. Later on, Leah, Tara, Yvette, and I went to Sara's—an upscale soul food restaurant with a bar—for drinks while the guys went to play basketball. I was yearning for the taste of a virgin strawberry daiquiri.

"I saw the Lexus truck in the driveway. When did you get it?" I asked Tara.

"I got it on Friday. Rob gave me half the money and my boss made me an offer I couldn't pass up."

Tara had been saving for months for that car.

"Girl, it has leather interior, a television, and a DVD player in it."

"Don't worry, we took it for a ride," Leah said. "The day you woke up, we went out to celebrate."

"We ended up bumping into the same guys from the Lauryn Hill concert." Then Tara asked, "You know what else happened? Davon's tongue action drove my clit radar wild."

"You two are crazy with the tag team," Yvette said.

"Last night at The System, everyone was coming up to us to extend their wishes for a speedy recovery for you," Tara said.

"We got three times as many free drinks as we normally would." Leah gave Tara a high-five.

"Girl, enough about us. Let's talk about you," Tara said.

"What about me?"

"Two words: Darren Edmonds. When is the big date?" Leah asked.

"I'm not sure; probably two weeks from now. I'm going to give him a call."

"Why so long?"

"He said he would be out of town. I must admit he does have my attention, but I don't like him."

"Yeah, right, I know you are at least attracted to him," Tara commented.

"I am a little bit, but I don't even know him."

"Do you want to get to know him?"

"Yes. Besides, we leave for Trinidad in a week. I cannot wait to have some fun in the sun," I said, trying to change the subject.

"Now you're talking. I want to have sex with Rob on the beach," Tara said. "On a lighter note, Edmonds really likes you."

"I would not say all that. Plus, he has so many women trying to grab on to his balls."

"The key word here is 'try,' " Leah said.

"The man was practically right by your side," Yvette added.

"So was Tory," Tara reminded.

"Every day, Edmonds sent you a bouquet of fresh flowers," Leah said.

"Flowers aren't the only things he gave me."

"What else did he give you?" they said in unison as each of them patiently waited for my response.

I pulled out the Nordstrom's gift card.

"When are we going shopping?" Leah rubbed her hands together greedily.

"Let's go tomorrow. We all have to get our shut-it-down outfits in order for the trip," Yvette suggested.

"It's a good thing I have a day off tomorrow," I said, sighing.

"I propose a toast to the speedy recovery of Nya and hope you get some before the summer is over," Tara said. Then she gulped down her drink of rum and coke in one swallow.

We all raised our glasses and laughed.

After a day filled with shopping, I had about five hundred dollars left that I planned to use for winter clothes and Christmas gifts.

Chapter 36

Now in Trinidad, I gazed out the window at the captivating view of the beach. So far, everything was working out just fine. My room was gorgeous. Aside from the occasional ache and pain, my shoulder was good as new. Luckily, the stitches came out before we left. The weather was at boiling temperatures. However, I knew how to stay cool by swimming in the pool and sipping on peach daiquiris.

"Promise me you will have some fun," I could hear Mommy say when I was leaving.

My bikini matched the color of my drink and attracted a few stares and smiles from guys.

Each time, Leah would say, "Go talk to him."

But my thoughts were with Darren. I was looking forward to our date. I wanted to call him, but I figured he was still away on business.

Tara and Leah wanted to take a bite out of a few men but had to be on their best behavior since they were in the company of their mates.

Tonight, we were going to Nelson's parents' house for dinner.

If it weren't so hot, I would've worn my hair down. Instead, I wore it up in a bun. I had on a white linen suit and crème sandals with matching shell necklace and earrings. Just as I finished dressing, there was a knock at the door.

"Girl, are you ready?" Tara asked. "The guys are waiting for us in the lobby."

I opened the door. "Yeah, let me grab my camera."

"You look cute," Leah said.

"I'm glad to know I moved up from being decent to cute."

Then Leah said, "I am so nervous about meeting Nelson's mother. I've already won his father over."

"Don't be nervous," I said, closing the door behind us; be you."

It took thirty minutes to get to Nelson's parents' three-story house.

"Man, this is a pad you got here," Rob said, taking in the exquisite interior.

"Thank you, thank you."

The butler, who looked old enough to be my grandfather, greeted us at the door.

"Nelson, we have been expecting you and your guests. My name is Zar, and I will be your host for the evening. Let me know if you need anything," he said as we walked inside. "Now, what can I get you to drink?"

"Rum and coke," Nelson said.

"I'll have a watermelon martini," Tara requested.

"Same for me," Leah added.

"Whiskey for me," Rob said.

"I'll have water."

He told me, "I see you are not the drinker out of the bunch. I will be right back with your drinks."

"Don't be a party pooper, Nya; drink something," Leah said.

"Okay, I'll have a ginger ale on the rocks, so it will give the impression that I am drinking something loaded with alcohol. Is that better for you?"

"You don't need to get smart with me."

"At dinner, I will have something." I crossed my fingers. "I promise."

Some of Nelson's childhood friends were there with their dates. The house and island were so beautiful. It made me wonder why Nelson would venture off and leave. Wanting to capture the memories, I took many pictures of my surroundings.

"Ladies and gentlemen, I will escort you to the dining room. Dinner will be served in five minutes," Zar announced.

Dinner turned out to be more of a buffet. We had lots to choose from. I even got my wish of fried plantains.

As Mr. and Mrs. Bole entered the dining room together, Nelson greeted them.

"Mother," Nelson said as he kissed her on the cheek and gave her a hug. Then he shook his father's hand and gave him a hug too.

"This must be the lovely Leah Gamden," she said. "The picture Nelson sent me does not do you justice."

"Thank you, Mrs. Bole. It is an honor to meet you."

"Nelson has told me a lot about you. I regret I missed you the first time you visited. My sister fell ill and I had to go to Tobago to see her."

"It is good seeing you again, Leah," Mr. Bole said.

"This is Leah's sister, Nya, and their friend, Tara," Nelson said.

"Hello, it is a pleasure meeting the both of you," Tara and I said, shaking both of their hands.

"Likewise," Mrs. Bole said.

"Last but not least, this is Rob, my good friend."

"Hello, Mr. and Mrs. Bole. You have such a lovely home," Rob said.

"Thank you," Mrs. Bole said.

Mr. Bole asked, "How was the flight getting over here?"

"Not too long because there were no layovers," Nelson responded.

"Well, I hope you all brought your appetites with you. There's plenty of food to eat," Mrs. Bole said, escorting us to the table.

"Tenille and Cara prepared a fine meal for us," Nelson said as his eyes feasted on all the dishes.

"Hey now, don't you forget about me," Mrs. Bole reminded her son. "I slaved my way through the kitchen too."

"What a pleasant surprise. You have not cooked in a long time, Mother."

"Well, it has been a long time since I have seen my son. This is a special occasion," she said, kissing Nelson on the cheek. "Now, let's eat."

After dinner, Mrs. Bole and us girls decided to take a walk on the beach to work off some of the calories we had consumed. It was so beautiful outside.

I took a big breath of the ocean air. "I don't think I could ever get tired of living here."

Mrs. Bole was a nice woman who was quite down-to-earth. I admired that Mr. Bole and her started a lucrative hotel resort business from scratch. "My family was poor and so was his. I did not want my children to grow up poor."

Even though she was very wealthy, Mrs. Bole stayed

humble. She loved the fact we were all independent women and wished to know a little bit about each of us.

"My son really loves you, Leah. You take good care of him."

"He's my heart," Leah said, pointing at hers.

She truly did love him. At times, I think she felt guilty for stepping out on him. She figured she needed to get the wildness out of her system now before they settled down and get married.

Before we knew it, it was two o'clock in the morning. Time had quickly passed by. I certainly enjoyed myself, and as we were leaving, we thanked Nelson's parents for their hospitality.

"You all are welcome here anytime," Mrs. Bole said.

"Don't worry, gang. We will be back for breakfast," Nelson said as we buckled our seat belts in the car.

When we arrived at the hotel, I called it a night.

"Rise and shine, sleepy head," Leah said.

"Good morning to you. Leah, you must be getting some electrifying sex for you to be up this early and to be so chipper. What is on the agenda for today?"

"We have lots to do. We are going to breakfast. There has been a change of plans. Nelson's parents will be here in twenty minutes."

"Then, it's off to the spa," Tara said.

"Great, I haven't been to the spa in months."

"I know. You've been letting yourself go lately." Leah looked down at me.

"Shut up. No I haven't."

"Your dry cracked hands are the proof."

"Girl, please. I have been at the hospital doing my clinical work. Each time I see a patient, administer medications, or even fluff someone's pillow, I have to wash my hands. I wash them at least thirty times a day at the hospital to prevent the spread of infection. Do you want me to come home and infect Mommy, Daddy, or you with some dreadful disease?"

"No."

"Well, okay then. I need to switch to another lotion, that's all."

"Don't start, you two. Hurry up. I can't wait to get a massage," Tara said.

"The bikini wax is my favorite."

"Make sure you wash your kitty kat," Leah said as I was walking into the bathroom.

"My stuff will never smell like a fish market," I said before closing the door.

Breakfast was scrumptious. I had two heart-shaped banana nut pancakes with a cheese omelet. My shoulder started to ache, but it wasn't anything that a little Motrin couldn't handle. Mrs. Bole joined us for our spa treatment. Our bodies were scrubbed, waxed, and pinched to perfection. When I got my eyebrows arched, I cringed in pain. It hurt so bad my eyes watered.

We each were assigned our own personal masseuse. My masseuse's name was Yuri. His sexy physique matched his name, and he was so gentle with my body.

"You have a nice smile," he said while giving the royal treatment to my hands.

"Thank you."

At first, I was pretty tense. I never had a man massage my body like that before.

"Relax, please; my main job is to make you feel good."

Yuri knew what he was doing. He poured massage oil on my neck and went to work. I almost fell asleep. I didn't want him to stop.

"What happened to your shoulder?"

I told him the story about me being shot, and he expressed pity on my soul.

"It's a shame a stunning woman went through such a terrifying ordeal."

Yuri was extra sensitive on my shoulder. The best part of the massage was when he concentrated on my back and my feet. For two whole hours, Yuri's hands danced with my skin.

"I hope to see you again."

"Oh, don't worry. You will." *I wish I could have a session with him every day.*

"On a more personal note, may I take you to dinner?"

"No, thank you, but I appreciate the offer, though."

"Here is my number in case you change your mind," he said grinning.

Not wanting to appear rude, I put the number in my Bebe bag, but did not dare tell the girls about this one because I didn't want to hear their mouths.

After lunch, we went snorkeling. It was so much fun. I made the guide stay right with me in case a shark or some kind of creature with teeth tried to have me for dinner. I figured it would eat him before me, and give me time to get away.

By the time we finished, I was in need of a nap. Tara, Rob, Leah, and Nelson, on the other hand, were all feeling frisky. I didn't want to admit it, but I was in need of some sexual healing too. We all decided to go back to our rooms for the rest of the afternoon to rest up before dinner. Tonight, we were going to Rasta's, a popular nightclub.

When I got back to the room, I decided to call Mommy.

"Hello?"

"Hey, Mommy! What are you doing?"

"Hi, baby. I just got in from work. Are you having a good time?"

"Yeah. Today, we went snorkeling and to a spa."

"That's good to hear."

"What's going on at home?"

"Nothing much. I'm about to fix a couple of tuna sandwiches. I don't really feel like cooking tonight. Your father went to the doctor today. He has hypertension. His doctor put him on Prinivil. Also, he has to cut back on fats and start exercising."

"Well, I guess I'm going to have to become the 'nag patrol' about exercise, taking his medication on time, and eating healthier, just like I did when I forced him to stop smoking."

"Your father begged me not to tell you because he knew he had it coming." Mommy laughed.

"I'm concerned about Daddy. I want both of you to live long, healthy lives. Besides, I don't think I could take it if something ever happened to either one of you. I would probably end up in Tidewater Psychiatric Institute."

"Your father knows you mean well."

"Well, Mommy, I'm going to lie down for a little while. I love you, and tell Daddy I love him too."

"Okay, baby. We love you too."

When I woke up and looked at the clock, it was 7:00 p.m. I had an hour to get ready. While I was dressing, I listened to Beenie Man and Sean Paul, practicing my wind and getting pumped up for the club. For dinner, we decided to eat at the hotel and order lobster. *What the hell, it was free.*

"Have one drink tonight," Leah pushed.

"Here we go again."

"Please," she begged.

"I'll think about it". I turned my attention to Tara. "Your hair looks good."

"Thanks. Tonight, it's going to be cool, so I figured I would try my luck and wear it out."

I knew my curls wouldn't hold up, so I wore my hair in a bun. It was too hot for me.

While the guys were talking about a soccer game, Tara, Leah, and I started reminiscing about our childhood. We couldn't stop laughing about the time Leah got a crayon stuck up her nose, how Yvette accidentally super glued her hand to the door, and how in the tenth grade, I got a paper airplane stuck in my hair. Let's say, at the time, I did not find it funny, and the culprit paid dearly for it.

At 10:30 p.m., we headed to the club. It was packed. I even saw celebrities such as Halle Berry, Denzel Washington, and Meryl Streep. I knew they were on vacation. Still, I had to capture a Kodak moment to add to my collection.

After all the excitement, the bar was the next stop.

"What are you drinking?" Nelson asked me.

"It better not be ginger ale."

"Why are you riding me?" I cut my eyes at Leah. "Okay, I will have an amaretto sour."

"That's more like it."

"Don't hate because I am not an alcoholic like you."

"Whatever," she said, laughing.

The drink had me feeling nice off the buzz. The DJ was playing all of our songs. *Murder She Wrote* came on and we reported to the dance floor. It felt good to let loose and kick back. I was putting it down. The DJ continued to play songs by Sean Paul, Bob Marley, Sizzla, Capelton, and Elephant Man. I took a break, but got right back up when he played "Liar's Deed," my favorite reggae song. As I was grooving to the tunes, someone came up from behind. He was rocking with me to the beat of the song. It was none other than Darren Edmonds.

"You can wind almost like a true Trini gal," he said.

After the song, I was ready to talk. "What are you doing here?" I asked with a smile.

"This is a vacation for me. I am here to visit my family. You are looking at a fourth generation Trini man. Believe it or not, my great ma-ma is alive and well and lives here. She is my heart, so I come to check up on her at least twice a year."

"Well, I am here on vacation as well."

"I can see that." He paused for a moment. "Hmm, you take my breath away," he said, gazing into my eyes.

I was trying not to get lost in his. The eyes always did something to me.

"Since we both are here for a little while, I would love to take you out."

"Okay."

"How does tomorrow night sound?"

"Great."

"Is eight o'clock all right with you?"

"It's fine. I must say, though, you are a very persistent man."

For the past two years, Darren had been sending flowers and cards to my job every fifteenth of the month, religiously. I knew it was him, but I decided to play the naive role.

"You can't blame a man for trying."

"Well, I figured I should give you a chance since it is a new century."

After we engaged in some small talk and laughter, I gave him my number and hotel information. As he embraced me in a hug, my nose soaked up the distinct aroma of his Versace cologne. I didn't want to let him go, but I had to play it cool.

He held me back away from him. "You look stunning tonight."

"Thank you."

"All I ask is for you to bring your beautiful smile with you tomorrow. Bye, now," he said, waving to Tara, Leah, and I.

"When are you two going out?" Leah asked as I sat back down at our table.

"Tomorrow night."

"That's what I'm talking about!" Tara gave Leah a high-five.

"Girl, we have to get you ready for tomorrow," Leah said. "And don't even try to get out of it."

Chapter 37

Slowly but surely, eight o'clock steadily crept up on me. Tara did my hair in beautiful curls coming down my back. I stayed under her portable hair dryer for three hours. Damn near killed me. However, I took a stand when they wanted to put makeup on me. "I don't need any makeup except for my lip gloss."

Leah begged, but I declined. I pulled out a shut-it-down outfit for the night. It was a strapless baby blue Versace dress. I had a silver purse and sandals to go with the dress.

Tara looked through my bag and hers for accessories. "What jewelry are you going to wear?"

"My diamond earrings, pendant, and bracelet, of course."

"You look gorgeous," Leah said, like a proud mother whose daughter was getting ready to go to the prom.

"Thanks. You don't think it is too much, do you?"

Leah shook her head. "No way."

"Girl, please tell Nya to enjoy herself and have some fun," Yvette told Leah from the other end of the phone. Leah had to call her and tell her the news, even if it was an international call.

Leah laughed. "Now here is Yvette in another country telling you to have a good time."

"You know the drill—call me on the cell phone to make sure I am safe."

"What time do you want us to call?" Leah asked.

"Around 10:30."

I was so nervous, and for what? Leah and Tara were hyping things up bigger than what they really were.

"What are you two and the guys doing tonight?"

"We are going to sail around the island in the yacht. If you are here in the morning, be ready to spend tomorrow in Tobago. It is more exquisite there than Trinidad," Leah said.

"The guys are waiting for us in the lobby," Leah announced after answering the hotel room phone.

We all exchanged hugs.

"Have a good time!" I shouted after them.

"Please do the same," Leah said as she and Tara got on the elevator.

There was a knock on the door. I looked through the peephole. Darren was right on time. As I opened the door, his eyes got real wide and I could tell he was trying to keep his composure.

"You look amazing." He hugged me and stepped inside. Then he handed me a bouquet of white roses and a reggae CD.

I was grateful because I didn't already have this one in my collection. "Thank you."

I could see he went all out in his casual Armani suit. When we arrived downstairs, a stretched Excursion limousine was waiting for us.

"Would you like a glass of champagne?"

"No, thank you. I don't drink."

"Fair enough. I also have ginger ale in the refrigerator. Would you prefer a glass of that instead?"

"Yes."

"I know you are wondering what I have in store for you tonight."

"It did cross my mind."

"We are going to a restaurant called Libby's. It's along the shore. I'm sure you will love it."

"Good evening, Mr. Edmonds," the host said.

"Hello, Jahad."

Jahad was an older man who appeared to be in his sixties. He looked as if he still didn't miss a beat.

"This is Nya."

"It is a pleasure meeting such a pretty lady," he said and kissed my hand.

"Thank you very much."

"You look so familiar."

"I do?"

"Yes, you favor—"

Darren cut him off. "We will be seated now."

"Okay, very well, then," Jahad said, nodding his head.

"Do you mind sitting outside and enjoying the ocean view?"

"No, not at all. Mr. Jahad is a very nice man," I commented after we were seated.

"Yes, he has been a long-time friend of my family. I have known him since I was a little tot. So have you been enjoying the island?"

"Yes, very much so. We went snorkeling and swimming the other day. I plan to go jet skiing, as well.

"How is your shoulder doing?"

"It's coming along well. The wound has healed with minimal scarring."

"Hello. My name is Sophie, and I will be your waitress. It is nice to see you again, Mr. Edmonds."

"Thank you."

"Our specials this evening are lobster in a wine sauce and grilled swordfish. Now, what can I get you to drink, madam?"

"I will have a ginger ale."

"And you can bring me a bottle of red wine."

"Very well."

"Now, I'm not trying to get you drunk, but would you like to try a glass of red wine? If you don't like the first sip, put it to the side."

"Well, I'll give it a try."

I figured what could one glass of wine hurt? The man was trying to show me new things and I liked that.

"I know you are young. But how young? Come on, let me see some identification, please." He laughed.

I already knew he was thirty because I had pulled up his bank profile plenty of times on my computer. I alone had opened three accounts and a hundred-thousand-dollar equity line for him.

"I'm twenty-one."

"I'm not trying to go to jail or have a hit out on me from your father."

I began to laugh.

"How did you celebrate the big 2-1?"

"My friends took me out for a nice dinner and I received some wonderful gifts. To be honest, I thought I would feel more grownup and mature, but, actually, I feel the same."

"The only time you will feel grownup is when you have a child to be responsible for."

"Are you speaking from experience?"

"Not my own, but from someone else's. After my

brother Simore had my nephew, he became more responsible and mature." He paused. "You know when I first met you, I noticed you were very mature for your age."

"Thank you. I have no time in my daily planner for nonsense." We both chuckled.

"How is school coming along?"

"Very well. I go back in three weeks. First, I have to be released by my doctor."

"I have seen you work your magic at the hospital."

"When did you witness that?"

"I have a vending machine contract with most of the hospitals in the area. I saw you walking a patient down the hall one day."

"Don't you have workers to load the drinks and snacks into the machines?"

"Yes, but that day my manpower was down. Plus, it keeps me humble, so I don't get a big head. I'm willing to do what it takes to have a successful business and a satisfied clientele, just like you are willing to go the extra mile for your patients. In fact, you go above and beyond. I know the director of Creekdale Memorial and he raved to me about how Ms. Rosen and you saved the life of a burn victim by administering CPR when the electricity had failed." Without warning, he caressed my face. His hands felt soft against my skin. "You have the face of an angel, Nya."

I felt a little uncomfortable with him touching my face. It was a bit too soon. And I guess he could sense my discomfort because he quickly pulled back.

"How does the wine taste?"

"It tastes as if grapes are rolling around on my tongue."

"I'm glad you like it. I would like to propose a toast

to a beautiful relationship, professionally and personally."

We touched glasses.

Nice touch, I thought. *But you don't have me hooked yet.*

I ordered the seafood linguini, and Darren ordered the lobster in wine sauce. Everything was so tasty and well prepared. I only had one glass of wine. I sipped on water for the rest of the dinner. For dessert, I had fresh strawberries glazed with a light cream sauce. When it got close to 10:30 p.m., I excused myself to the restroom to await the call from the girls.

"Hey," I answered.

"How are things going?" Tara eagerly asked.

"Good. We just finished eating, and I think there is more in store for the night."

"Call us if you need to."

"Thanks. I will. Bye."

Apparently, Darren had the same idea the gang had. We took a little cruise around the island in his yacht. It was him, the driver, and me, of course. Darren was quite romantic. "May I have this dance?"

I reached out for his hand.

While we slowly danced under the stars, the music system on the deck played a variety of jazz, Luther Vandross, Anita Baker, Babyface, Otis Redding, and reggae love classics. I felt at ease in his arms. I could have stayed out there all night.

Darren reached down and gently kissed me on the lips.

I pulled back with a look of astonishment.

"Nya, I apologize. I didn't mean to make you feel uncomfortable."

I looked into his eyes and paused. Then, I kissed him back. *Certainly, kisses do not hurt.*

Chapter 38

The next day, I played it simple with my clothes. I wore a fitted white T-shirt that crossed in the front with Cache pants and my beige sandals. The gold hoops made me look sexy with my bun. Yeah, it was going to be another scorcher outside and I wanted to make sure I would be as cool and comfortable as possible. My overnight bag was packed. Unable to decide on which bathing suit I wanted to wear, I packed both, figuring the gang and I would go swimming in Tobago, where, I'd been told, the ocean water was crystal blue.

I stared over at the colorful bouquet of exotic flowers delivered that morning while I was having breakfast with Leah and Tara, who, by the way, bombarded me with never-ending questions on how my date had gone with Darren.

Punctual as always, Darren was at my hotel room door. "Are you ready?" he asked.

"Yes."

"Did you bring a helmet?"

"No. Will I need one? We don't have to go if my life will be at risk," I said with a touch of fear in my voice.

"Just teasing."

I let out a sigh of relief.

"Relax, you are in good hands."

The parachute ride was exhilarating.

Afterwards, he invited me over to his place for lunch.

"I could not wait to see you again. Right after you left, I wanted today to come as quickly as possible."

"I have a few questions."

"Shoot."

"What do you want from me?"

It could not be sex. You could get it anytime from anyone, I'm sure.

He held my hand. "I want a healthy relationship. I enjoy spending time with you."

"I enjoy you as well. Next question—are you involved with anyone else?"

"No."

"Do you have any children?"

"None." There was a moment of silence. "Nya, do you have any more questions?"

"No," I answered, satisfied with his responses.

"Well, if there is anything you need to know, please do not hesitate to ask me."

"Well, there is something I need."

"What's that?"

"For you to always tell me the truth."

"You got a deal," he said, shaking my hand.

I just hope he lives up to it.

"I need something from you, as well, Nya."

"I'm listening."

"Don't believe those rumors you heard about me."

"Have no worries, because I am one to form my own opinions."

"What is it thus far?"

I smiled. "The verdict is not in yet."

Darren definitely had exquisite taste. His entire home was decorated in Italian style furniture. While he was in the other room talking on his cell phone, I cleaned up the kitchen and washed the dishes.

The cook had prepared grilled swordfish and grilled vegetables with rice. I was definitely getting in my protein intake.

"You don't have to do that," he said, re-entering the room. "The cook will be back soon."

"No, it's all right; besides, I'm almost done."

"Would you like dessert?"

"No, I am too full from lunch. Maybe later."

Darren came up behind me and started slowly rubbing my neck. I think it was becoming one of my spots. It felt so good, especially since my other ones had not been touched in ages. I stopped drying dishes and bask in the pleasure.

He whispered into my ear. "I know what you need. Let me give it to you. I have dreamed of having you in my arms many nights."

I pulled him close to my lips. His cologne made my vagina wet. Darren carried me all the way up to his bedroom.

"I want to take my time with you. Relax," he said, his tongue sliding down my neck.

All of a sudden, a bolt of pain shot through my shoulder. "Ouch," I cried out.

"What's wrong? Did I hurt you?"

"No, it's my shoulder. Please, I need my medicine. It's in my bag downstairs," I said with tears in my eyes and still trying to be brave.

"I'll go get it for you."

Darren quickly returned with the bottle of Motrin in one hand and a glass of water in the other.

"Thank you so much."

"Don't cry. I'm here for you. Let me help ease your pain." He ran to the bathroom. He came back with a hot cloth and put it on my shoulder. I hesitated at first. After the heat penetrated my aching shoulder, it started to loosen up. With a bottle of lotion in hand, he said, "Let me rub your shoulder. It will make you feel better. I certainly cannot have a woman in my company shedding tears of agony."

"Please, be gentle."

"Shhh . . . lie down; I want you to get some rest for tonight's festivities. I don't want to go anywhere if you are not feeling better." He rubbed my hair.

As the medicine kicked in and his rubdown relaxed me, I soon fell asleep.

Several hours later, I woke up. With Darren nowhere to be found, I decided to take a shower. My shoulder was feeling much better. The intense pain came from me forgetting to take my prescribed medication. I told myself I would not make that mistake again.

What am I going to wear tonight? I thought, looking through my bag. *Yes, this looks hot.* I held the orange linen set up against my body. I knew my midnight blue bra and thong set would make Darren's eyeballs pop out, forcing him to take a second, third, and fourth look at me. I decided to wear my hair down. My feet needed a rest, so I slid them into a pair of brown, low-heeled sandals.

I turned around and found him standing right in front of me.

"What?"

"You look gorgeous tonight. The orange color brings out your radiant skin tone. Not to mention, that outfit is showing all of your curves. I'm trying hard to resist my everlasting impulse to lie you down on the bed and make sweet passionate love to you."

"Good answer."

"Is your shoulder feeling better?"

"Yes."

"I don't want you to do too much."

"Are you ready?"

"Yes, the jet is waiting."

My phone rang.

"Good evening, Leah."

"Wow, each day we have been on the island, your attitude becomes more and more laid back. You finally understand the concept of having a good time, huh? Anyway, I wanted to let you know we are on our way now."

"Okay, I will see you then."

The restaurant, Island Treasure, had a live band. Rob, Tara, Leah, Nelson, Darren and I danced the night away. We stopped for a moment to eat their hardy feast of seafood. I even surprised myself by having another glass of wine.

After two-and-half hours on the dance floor, the gang and I were tired, except for Leah, of course. Nelson and Darren began telling stories about the island and how both of their families started their businesses from the ground up.

Darren and I decided to go back to Trinidad while the others stayed in Tobago. After reaching our destination, we took an hour walk on the beach. What a day!

"I had a great time."

Darren smiled back at me and took my hand. "May we sit please?"

"Yes," I said as he spread a blanket down so we wouldn't get sand in our clothes.

I was gazing at the moon in the sky. At that very moment, I was so happy. I didn't want the feeling to ever go away.

"Now, *I* have some questions for *you*." He rubbed my thigh.

"I'm listening."

"Why didn't you give me a chance two years ago?"

"You came across too arrogant for me. Now that I think about it, maybe I should have taken your arrogance as a higher level of confidence. Also, I wanted to keep it at a professional level."

"Are you still with Tory?"

"No, we parted ways about a year ago. He received a huge job promotion which made him migrate to California."

"I would see you two out together all the time."

"Did it bother you?"

"Yes, I wanted you to be mine—then and now. Do you still love him?"

Darren's words were giving me goose bumps.

"He will always have a place in my heart."

"Are you two going to get back together?"

"No," I said sternly. *Enough with the twenty-one questions about Tory.* I wanted to forget about him. My heart still hurt whenever I thought of him.

"I see it's still a touchy subject. It's in the past, though, Nya. You are my lovely jewel to hold now. Matter of fact, that is going to be my nickname for you—Jewel." He gently caressed my arm. "I knew over time I could win you over."

"I admire that about you."

"You're looking at a man who goes after what he wants."

"I love your ambition and persistence. You are one of the most known entrepreneurs in the United States. You're a positive force in the black community. Let the truth be told—you have inspired me to reach for the stars and make my dreams become reality." I smiled.

"Thank you. Let me tell you something. There are two kinds of people on this globe—the have and have-nots. I am not cut out to be without success, luxuries, and living comfortably. I have worked long and hard hours to get to where I am today and continue to do so. I had to climb up the success ladder my own way and on my own terms." He paused and then said, "I can see you're getting cold. Let's go inside the house," covering me with the blanket.

My body yearned for him to warm me up even more. Once inside the house, I took off my clothes piece by piece and led him into the bedroom. It worked. Darren's eyes were glued to my lingerie set. He gently squeezed my butt. I began to unbutton his shirt and take off his pants as he caressed my hair.

"I cannot tell you enough," he said, running his fingers up my legs, "how exquisite you are inside and out."

Darren slowly removed my thong and bra and caressed my breast as we kissed. I caressed his cobra and sucked on his fingers. My vagina was throbbing and dripping of wetness. He teased each one of my breasts with his tongue. A chill traveled the length of my spine.

Gently, he laid me on the bed. "Let me taste you." His hands drifted down to my clit.

"Yes," I moaned.

Darren gave me a sample of sexual healing. Now, I was ready for more. His condom-wrapped cobra slid right into me. He wasted no time in giving me those deep, long strokes. As I came, I called out his name over and over again. Then, he picked me up.

"Where are we going?"

"Heaven," he proclaimed, kissing me.

I wrapped my legs tight around his back as he rode me up against the wall to ecstasy.

Chapter 39

Shortly after our return to the States, I got back into the groove of things with school. It was hard at first after being spoiled by lavish gifts of designer clothes, money, and attention from Darren. He had even given me a cashier's check in the amount of ten thousand dollars to help with my expenses of school and for the wages I had lost not being able to work because of my injury from the robbery.

I thought about what a great time I had with him. He had brought sunshine into my life. I was a little disappointed that he would not be returning home with me due to the fact he had bought some property in Long Island and had to close the deal by the next day. But I completely understood.

After sitting out one more week—doctor's orders—my days returned to normal and consisted of clinical rounds, medication worksheets, care plans, and written tests. Much to my delight I would be working under Ms. Rosen again. I knew she was going to give me an 'A'.

The same day I returned to school was also my first day back to work. Darren and I agreed we would keep our relationship strictly professional at the bank. When

I arrived at work, the security guard greeted me at the door. I could tell Mr. Wood was waiting for me. I was surprised. The only time I see the man is if he is sending an employee to the unemployment line.

"Nya."

"Hi, Mr. Wood."

"I wanted to personally welcome you back to work." Mr. Wood shook my hand. "How is your shoulder doing?"

"It's good as new."

I was overjoyed to see my desk not stacked with papers a mile high.

"Welcome back, baby. I'm so glad you came back," Ms. Pilom said, hugging me.

Yeah, so glad I came back so you wouldn't have to do your job anymore. I know the deal.

"You are a hot commodity right now. Ms. Stein wants to see you in her office."

"Thanks."

"Hi, Ms. Stein," I said after knocking and entering.

"Nya, it is so good to see you." Ms. Stein hugged me. "Did you bring the doctor's note stating you can come back to work?"

"Yes, here it is."

"How is your shoulder feeling?"

"Fine. I finished physical therapy last week."

A gentleman with a badge in his hand and a woman dressed in the sharpest navy-blue suit were also sitting in her office.

"Nya, this is Gary Tiller, the detective working on the robbery case."

He shook my hand. "Hi, it is nice meeting you."

"Mr. Tiller is here to take a statement from you and prepare you for the trial."

"I gave a statement at the hospital."

"The trial is in thirty days. I want to ask you a few

more questions. The police department wants to do everything by the book with this case so Mithers can be locked up for a long time for what he put you and everyone else through."

"Okay, I am more than willing to help."

"This is Karen Sworn, the bank's psychiatrist," Ms. Stein said.

"Hello, Nya."

"Hi."

"She is here to meet your counseling needs," Ms. Stein explained.

"Have you been having trouble sleeping, having nightmares, or waking up in cold sweats?"

"Yes, I keep having recurring dreams of Mithers shooting me," I said with my arms crossed.

"This is what I am here to help you with."

"To be honest, I just want my life back to normal. Do I have to go down to the police station and answer your questions?"

"Well, I wanted you to, but we could do it right here if it makes you feel more comfortable."

"Thank you. I would like that."

"I came to introduce myself and wanted to set up a convenient time for us to meet," Ms. Sworn said.

"I don't know with work and school."

"You can go during work hours," Ms. Stein offered.

"How does tomorrow morning around nine o'clock sound to you? You can come to my office," she said.

"Sounds good to me."

"Here is my business card. Call me if you have trouble finding my office."

"Thank you. I will," I said as she was walking out.

"I will only take up an hour of your time," Mr. Tiller said.

"Would you like for Mr. Wood or me to sit in?" Ms. Stein asked me.

"Yes," I answered, thinking I needed all the moral support I could get.

Mr. Wood brought lunch for the whole branch. I ordered my favorite, coquitos. All day long, customers were coming up to me to see how I was doing. I have to admit, I missed them and my co-workers.

"Nya, there's a call for you on line twenty-eight," Heather said.

"Thank you. This is Nya, how may I help you?"

"Hey, baby. How is your first day back going?"

"Pretty good. I will fill you in with the details when I get home. What's for dinner?"

"Lasagna with tossed salad."

"Ooh, I cannot wait to sit at the table tonight. I love you. I will talk to you later, Mommy."

"Okay, have a good afternoon."

"I will."

I looked out of the window to see leaves falling from the trees.

Hmm, fall is coming. Just like in life, another season is ending and another is ready to begin.

Chapter 40

"Hello?"

"Hi, Nya, this is Mr. Coles. How are you doing?"

I could tell something was wrong by the sound of his voice. "Is everything okay, Mr. Coles?"

"Tara and I are at Newhaven Memorial Grounds. We went to put fresh roses on her mother's grave because today is Mary's birthday. Nya, I have been out here since eight o'clock this morning, and it is now one o'clock and she still will not leave. At first, I thought she was talking to Mary. You know, telling her all the latest events. Then, she went into some kind of trance. For at least two hours, she repeatedly kept saying, 'Momma, talk to me, please.' I have tried to get her in the car. The only three words she keeps saying to me are 'in a minute.' A minute has turned into five hours. My baby misses her mother so much. I don't know what to do. I was hoping you could talk some sense into her. I would call Rob, but I don't have his phone number."

"Don't worry, Mr. Coles, we're on our way."

I called Rob and he agreed to meet us there. Usually, a week or two before Tara's mother's birthday, she would not be her normal self. Even though Mrs. Coles

died five years ago, Tara acts as if she only lost her yesterday. It is very difficult to get her to talk about her
feelings towards her mother, but I was going to at least
try to reach out to her today.

"Thanks for coming."

Rob, Yvette, Leah, and I all walked over to the grave-
site and sat next to Tara. She kept rocking herself back
and forth with tears falling from her eyes.

"Hey."

"Hi. Doesn't my momma's tombstone look beautiful? I wiped the old flowers, leaves, and dust off of it.
There's nothing too good for my momma. So what are
y'all doing here?"

"Well, your father called me because he is very worried about you." I handed her a Kleenex.

"There's nothing wrong with me. Really, I'm fine."

"Baby, come on. Get up. You hungry? We can pick up
your favorite at Bangkok Garden," Rob offered.

"I'm not hungry. I want to stay right here with my
mother; she needs me."

"What's wrong?" I asked.

"Nothing," she said, tears rolling down her eyes.

I handed her another tissue.

"I don't need another tissue. I want to be alone with
my mother. When I am ready to come home, I will call
my father to come get me."

"We are not leaving you out here like this," I said.

"It's freezing out here," Leah added.

"So what? I will be okay."

I pleaded with her. "Please, Tara, let us help you.
What's been bothering you?"

"I am so angry and I have been angry for so long."

"What are you angry about?"

"My mother is dead and she is never ever coming

back. I miss her so much. Each of you has a mother. I want mine too. Mommy, why did you have to leave me?" she screamed at the headstone. "Why? Why?"

She continued, "For the past week, I have been having these dreams where I see my mother in my bedroom, the kitchen, the bathroom. She comes up to me and hugs me tight. Mommy starts talking, but I can't hear her. The last two dreams I could read her lips. She is trying to tell me she loves me. Then, she goes back into the light. I always wake up when I am trying to follow her into the light. Talk to me, Mommy. Please, I'm listening. Right now, I feel like I don't want to go on," Tara said, shaking her head.

"Your mother would not want you to stop living your life," I said.

"Well, I didn't want her to die, and she did and left me. I am so angry!" Tara screamed at the top of her lungs.

She kicked and screamed for the next two hours as we all took turns rubbing her back.

"Tara, get it out. It's all right to cry," I told her. "We all know how much your mother meant to you."

Finally, Tara's lungs gave out and we knew she was exhausted. That's when we all headed to her father's house and her doctor came over to examine her. He doesn't usually make house calls, but he was more than willing under the circumstances. Aside from the minor bruises as a result of her pounding her fists on the ground, she was fine. The doctor gave her a sedative to help her sleep better, and she slept like a baby. Rob spent the night at her house, not letting go of her hand the entire time unless it was to go to the bathroom. At that moment, I realized how much he truly loved her.

When Mrs. Coles died, Tara never grieved. She didn't

cry once, not even at the funeral. For too long, those feelings had been bottled up inside of her and needed to come out. Her doctor recommended she attend counseling sessions. This time, I hoped Tara would not object to the doctor's vital prescription.

Chapter 41

"Right there. Oh," I moaned. "Yes, oh," I said breathlessly as I shivered in pure pleasure.

"Jewels," his pet name for me, "you give me a workout every time," Darren said, smacking my butt as I got up to tinkle.

I laughed. "I see you like to break a sweat."

After work, I had gone over to Darren's house feeling a little frisky. Last month, to my surprise, he gave me a key to his house. He had just gotten back from Baltimore. My honey was trying to expand his real estate business statewide. I gave him another five years to be worldwide.

"I'm going to get a bottle of water. Would you like anything while I'm down there?"

"Yes, fix me a chicken sandwich, please."

"Do you want it with or without mayonnaise?"

"I want a dab of mayonnaise."

"Okay."

"Jewels."

"Yes?"

"Can you bring me a glass of water with that?"

I had worked up an appetite myself, so a chicken

sandwich didn't sound bad to me at all. As I was preparing the food, one of his cell phones started to vibrate. (The man had three cell phones—don't ask me why.) I looked at the name on the display, not being nosy, just curious. One missed call from Gabby. *Hmm, I wonder who she is. Maybe, she is a family member.* I didn't have any proof of him cheating, so I wasn't going to sweat it. Besides, she might be a business partner. Business equals profit; profit equals money.

"Thanks," he said as I handed him the food tray. "How was your day?"

"Chaotic, but nothing I couldn't handle. I was down three tellers today. One was in a car accident, the other in training classes, and the third teller was out sick with strep throat. So I had to get on the teller line. With today being the third of the month, I was busy with military personnel, public school employees, Norfolk City employees, welfare, social security, and public assistance recipients all coming in to cash their checks. The line was a mile long the whole day. And as if my day wasn't bad enough, Ms. Agnes, bless her heart, doesn't know when she breaks wind. I don't know whose stench is worse, hers or Mr. Palox, my clinical patient."

Darren burst into laughter.

"What?"

"You are so funny."

"It's the truth. Thank God I am off tomorrow. I need a mental break day from school and work."

"Hang in there. The semester is almost over."

"I cannot wait," I said, kissing him on the lips.

"What are your plans for the weekend?"

"The girls and I are going to New York to shop. Also, a new boutique called Rubie's has opened up on 100th Street in Manhattan. My sources tell me this store has the latest in winter and spring fashions."

Darren began choking on his sandwich.

"Drink this water."

He continued to cough.

"One more sip. Are you all right?" I rubbed his back.

"Yes, I'm fine. A piece of chicken went down the wrong pipe. So you said you were going to Rubie's?"

"Yeah. Have you heard about it?"

"Yes, my sister told me their clothes were fair, but nothing spectacular."

"That surprises me. They received great reviews in all of the fashion magazines. But I don't know now. The girls and I may end up taking it off our list of places to shop."

"What are your grades looking like?" he asked with a smirk on his face.

"I am bringing home all A's and a B. The B is in geriatric nursing. Let's just say that treating an older individual who is impacted is not my calling."

"You know I take your word for it." Darren handed me an envelope.

"What is this?" I asked with a large grin on my face.

"Keep up the good work, Nurse Jewel."

I opened it. Inside there was a cashier's check for six thousand dollars and four one-hundred-dollar bills. "The check is for the clothes you are about to buy."

"The check is more than enough to cover my expenses."

"My jewel has to eat too."

I crawled over to him on the bed and placed a soft kiss on his full lips. "Thank you."

"You're welcome."

"What do you want to do tonight?"

"Hold that thought," he said as his cell phone rang.

"I'm going to go take a shower."

He nodded in agreement.

I was not in the mood to dress up. An orange turtleneck with Baby Phat jeans and my brown cashmere coat would keep me warm in the chilly air.

"How does a movie sound?" I asked as Darren entered the bathroom.

He didn't answer, so I turned around. His facial expression looked as if he had lost a puppy.

"What's the matter?"

"I haven't heard from one of my men who delivers and restocks my vending machines. He is nowhere to be found. It has been three weeks now. No one has heard from him."

"Have you called a family member?"

"Yes. I called his wife and she hasn't heard from him either. He had a nasty habit of drinking, and sometimes he would even drink on the job. I got Baker help, and he was regularly attending the AA meetings."

"If you need to cancel with me tonight, that's fine. I understand."

"No, his wife has already filed a police report; there is nothing much else I can do."

"Have you hired someone else to cover his routes?"

"No, not yet. I figured he would turn up like he always did. Will you do me a favor?"

"What's that, honey?"

"Will you cover his routes for me until I find a replacement? Think of this as a business wager. I will compensate you for your time. I know working part-time at the bank is not putting enough money in your pockets."

"I know, but I make do with what I have."

"I am willing to pay you $600.00 a week for your trouble."

"I will only have time to make the deliveries first thing in the mornings."

"It will not be a problem. I will let my clients know the delivery time has changed."

"And I will not have time to unload and restock the machines."

"Not to worry, the security department of each corporation or business does that for me. All your pretty self will have to do is deliver the boxes to their rightful owner."

"I want to help you in any way I can. I guess you've got yourself a deal," I said, shaking his hand.

"Now, what movie are we seeing tonight?" He grabbed the soap and my ass at the same time.

Chapter 42

What a day! For the past three days, we shopped until we dropped, catching a lot of sales in the process. I brought with me an empty suitcase to pack all of my new clothes in.

"Would you like something to drink?" the flight attendant asked.

"Yes, I will have a ginger ale, please. But can you please add a little bit of orange juice in it?"

"Sure, not a problem."

For some reason, I was not feeling so good. A sudden rush of nausea had come over me. Luckily, I had a pack of crackers in my purse.

"Would anyone else like something to drink?"

"A rum and coke for me," Tara ordered.

"Water," Yvette requested.

"An apple martini for me," Leah said.

I called home to make sure Mommy was still picking us up. "Hi."

"Well, hello to you."

"Hi, Mom," Leah, Tara, and Yvette all screamed into the phone and into my ear.

"What did you girls do?"

"You mean, what didn't we do? We got a little taste of luxury staying at the Waldorf in Manhattan. Yvette's uncle is one of the customer service managers there."

I shared my shopping experience with Mommy of how the girls and I tackled down every department store, clothing store, and boutique. On Saturday, we went to Brooklyn for cheesecake at Junior's and shopped at the Fulton Mall. The best part of the day was Fulton Street and the Village. I can always find trendy clothes for cheap prices. I didn't go too overboard. But I did pay six hundred dollars for a pair of D&G boots and four hundred dollars for a Fendi purse to add to my collection. Later that night after shopping, we went to Club Hypnotic.

After finishing my call with Mommy, I felt the urge to go to the restroom. As I got up, I almost fell down.

Thankfully, the flight attendant caught me. "Are you all right?"

"Yes, thank you so much. I lost my balance."

When I returned from the restroom, Tara said, "We need to have a group talk."

I lightly shook Leah to wake her up. The girl can fall asleep anywhere.

"I want to thank you guys for being there for me. I feel as though a weight has been lifted off my shoulders from all of the anger. Counseling is going really well. The therapist, Mrs. Wittle, who Mrs. Gamden recommended, is the best. She is helping me work through my anger. Daddy, Rob, and my brothers have come and sat in on several of my sessions. I have to admit, I do love Rob with all my heart. He has been there for me through thick and thin."

Yvette handed Tara a tissue to wipe the tears.

"Thank you. Girl, these are tears of joy. I can finally move on with my life now."

"We will always be here for you." Leah held Tara's hands.

"I know. I love y'all too. Come on, everyone, group hug."

Chapter 43

I reported to Darren's warehouse bright and early. I didn't have to be at work or school until 9:00 a.m. each morning, so my side job worked out perfectly. I had to get up an hour earlier to prepare for the day. It was well worth it for the money I was getting, though. I was going to do it for free, but my honey insisted I be compensated. He did more than enough for me already.

Darren introduced me to Raymond Gilles, his business partner and right-hand man.

"It is nice to meet you," I said, shaking his hand. Then I asked, "Do I have something on my face?"

"No, it's just so hard not to stare at such beauty."

"Thank you."

"Darren, you definitely know how to pick them. You remind me of—"

"Are the boxes ready?" Darren asked. "Remember, Nya, each client has to sign on the bottom line. Their signature guarantees they received the boxes."

"Okay."

"You have six runs to make and they are all in the

same area. Call me if you have any problems." Then he kissed me.

"Have a good day! By the way, here is your week's pay plus a two-hundred-dollar bonus for the hell of it."

"Thank you."

I finished the run in forty-five minutes with no problems then dialed Darren's number. "Hey, honey, everything went well."

"Did anyone give you any problems?"

"Not at all."

"Great. Listen, Jewels, I am on the phone with my broker, trying not to lose all my money in the stock market. Call me tonight."

"Hugs and kisses all over."

"Bye."

Raymond made the deposits for Darren so he could pick up the signed paper on his way out of BankFirst. After several months, my relationship still remained on the down low with my co-workers. Ever since returning home from Trinidad, I was getting white roses twice a month.

"These came for you," Ms. Pilom announced. She placed a vase filled with a dozen of chocolate red roses on my desk. "You must have some man's head spinning." She laughed.

I opened the card to read it.

She leaned over my desk. "What does the card say?"

"None of your business."

"Well, excuse me. I have to get my work done anyway. I'll see you in the meeting, girl," she said and walked to her desk.

"Hmm."

The card read: *Always Thinking of You.* I didn't have the slightest clue who sent them to me, and I didn't have time to sit around guessing. I had a meeting to attend.

Mr. Wood had called a meeting for suggestions on ways to boost our sales goal. I didn't know how Ms. Stein did it. She was responsible for a million-dollar sales goal of new money to walk in the door each month. To my surprise, she never stressed like the other branch managers. She always told me, "God will provide a way." That was a testimony in my eyes.

Chapter 44

"Ms. Gamden, Dr. Hicks will see you now. Hi, how are you doing, today?" the nurse asked.

"Well, I don't feel like getting a pap smear this afternoon," I said as I followed her.

She giggled. "Who does?"

"I have been putting it off for too long."

"Let me get you to take off your shoes so I can weigh you, please."

"Okay."

"Right now, you weigh one hundred and thirty-four pounds," she said after fiddling with the slider on the scale.

"I have put on a few pounds." I pat my stomach.

"I need you to go into the bathroom and urinate in this cup. After you finish, please go to room three and take off everything except your bra. The doctor will be in shortly."

"Thank you."

It seemed like an eternity waiting for the doctor. I hated waiting in the examination room because it was always so cold in there. Goosebumps covered my body. The thin paper-cloth dress didn't keep me warm at all.

To pass the time, I picked up a copy of the *Ladies Home Journal.*

After about fifteen minutes, there was a knock at the door.

"Hello, Dr. Hicks, long time no see."

"Hello to you," she said. She strolled over to wash her hands in the sink.

"How did my test results come out?"

"Well, your blood levels are normal. You don't have a yeast infection, bladder infection, or bacterial infection, but you are pregnant."

My mouth dropped to the floor. "What?" I gasped. "How could this be? I got my period last month. Are you sure?"

"I'm positive. I had the nurse test your urine twice to be certain. As far as your period goes, you can still menstruate while your body is transitioning from normal to a gestational period. Did you have any breast tenderness or nausea?"

"Now that you mention it, I have been a little queasy lately. My breasts are sore, but I just thought it was PMS. They are always sore the whole time I am menstruating."

"I'm going to give you a sonogram and check your cervix to see how far along you are. Please lie back and relax your muscles; I know this is uncomfortable for you."

I took a deep breath.

"From the look of things, you appear to be about six weeks pregnant. Your lab work has already been shipped out to be tested for STDs and cervical cancer. I will notify you by mail of the results. If there are any problems, I will call you. Everything looks great, though."

I wanted to cry, but the tears would not come. This was not the best time to be having a baby. In three weeks, my last semester of school would be starting. Darren would never agree to me having an abortion. He didn't believe in it. One night, he told me his last love had a botched abortion and could never conceive children again. She left him because she couldn't bear the fact she could not give him children. I didn't want to keep this from him. He had a right to know because it was his baby, too.

"I know how overwhelming this is for you. Here are some brochures about pregnancy and adoption, with phone numbers you can call for support. Also, here are two phone numbers for local abortion clinics. In the state of Virginia, you have up to thirteen weeks to have an abortion."

"Thank you for your help," I said, getting dressed.

"Go home, weigh your options, and really think about what you want to do. Call me if you need me. On your way out, the nurse is going to give you some prenatal vitamins."

When I got into my car, the tears began. I could not understand when I conceived. I was careful to take my pill every morning. In addition, we used condoms. I dialed Darren's number.

"Hey, Jewels, how was your day?"

"Okay." I took a deep breath. "I have to tell you—"

"Hold that thought," he said, cutting me off. "On second thought, let me call you back."

"This is important, Darren—"

Apparently, he forgot to press the end call button on his phone. I heard another phone ringing in the background, and Darren answered.

"Gabby, how is my gorgeous wife doing? Of course, I miss you, Bambi. I've told you time and time again I am taking care of business in Virginia. It's a gold mine for real estate down here. I know you're frustrated because you haven't seen me in two months, but hold on a little longer and I'm going to build you the house you have always dreamed of in New York. I have got to make the money first. Of course, I am going to come to Rubie's for the fashion show. I wouldn't miss it for the world. I know all the celebrities will be there. Of course, I love you. We have been together for ten years, and I'm not going anywhere. How could you question my love for you? Yes, we can spend some time together in Virginia. When I first bought you here, you said you didn't like it. Listen, Gabby, I would love to sit and chat, but I have another call coming in. I'll call you later."

I heard the door shut.

"Hey," a voice said. I could tell it was Raymond.

"Hello, my friend."

"Why the long face?"

"Gabby is upset because we haven't spent much time together. She's always on my case about something. I give the woman any and everything her heart desires. This is the second home I am building for her. And what thanks do I get? Grief! Not to mention, Tracy didn't even get to Tory's dick. She almost seduced him, but he stopped her because he is in love with Nya. Now, I have minimal dirt on this guy. I was so happy to learn he moved all the way across the country. Besides, he and Nya already broke up. Now, if I were to tell her anything, I think it would still bother her to know Tory had his hands on another woman while they were together. To top it off, he fired Tracy. I refused to pay her for an incomplete job. The girl had the audacity to tell me to pay her five thousand dollars plus an extra five hundred for her troubles. She was lucky to get a thank you. I refused to give her the extra money, and she threatened to tell Nya everything. She made me so angry I hit her with the first thing in sight, a frying pan. The boys had to come wrap her up and throw her body in the James Lake."

"I can't believe you killed her. That's exactly what you get for thinking with your dick. I know you were fucking Tracy too—don't lie."

"It was just two times. I was drunk and horny. Believe me, I truly regret it. She kept throwing herself at me. We did it a couple of times, and she thought she could be my woman. I don't think so. She was strictly a STD, something to do."

"I don't know how you can sleep at night. As far as Gabrielle, it's been a while since you've spent some quality time with her. You need to go see her."

"It's not easy handling two women."

"Two very sensuous beautiful women at that."

"Gabby is and will always be the love of my life, but I think I'm starting to fall in love with Nya."

"It doesn't help any that she looks just like Gabrielle."

"She favors her."

"Favor her, my ass. Pretty women are at your disposal anytime you want, yet, you don't want them; you want Nya."

"That's beside the point. We need to keep our eyes on the prize. Nya is moving as many shipments as four of my men put together. No one will ever question her; she looks too innocent."

"What if she gets into trouble?"

"I have the best lawyers money can buy in Virginia. In less than a month, we'll have reached our financial goal. I can't have my bride-to-be doing my dirty work."

"You already have one wife."

"In the country of Trinidad, you can have as many wives as you want. I'm ready to have children. A son would be the ultimate gift from Nya. Gabby is unable to have children, so I have to settle for the next best thing."

"How do you know Nya wants to get married to you or have your children?"

"The marriage idea will take a while. However the part about the kids, I've already got that worked out. I've been poking tiny holes in my condoms for the past two months. Nya should be pregnant soon."

"Man, you are just as scandalous as a woman."

Darren laughed. "I have to work hard to get what I want."

"Well, I'm going to Jillian's and have a couple of beers. In the meantime, I will work on finding a replacement for your bride-to-be."

"Mrs. Nya Edmonds—doesn't it have a ring to it?"

"Yeah, whatever you say." Then I heard the door close.

I immediately hung up the phone. I burst into tears and beat on my steering wheel. *How could he do this to me? Why did he lie to me? Why didn't he tell me he was married? Why would he put me at risk for danger? Most importantly, what was so special about those packages?* So many more questions were running through my mind when my phone rang. It was Darren. I pulled myself together to camouflage my emotions.

"Hey."

"I apologize for cutting you off. Now, what does my princess have to tell me?"

"I scored an A on my pharmacology test."

"Congratulations!"

"Thank you, baby."

"How's your day going?"

"Grueling."

"Well, I will come by later to tuck you in."

"That's music to my ears."

* * *

I knew just the person I needed to see. I stormed into Safar's office.

"Can I help you?" the receptionist asked.

"Please, I need to see Safar."

"I do apologize, but Safar is not taking any more appointments for the rest of the day. I can schedule you an appointment with her later in the week."

"No, I need to see her now please."

"Ma'am, I have a two o'clock opening on Wednesday or an eight-thirty on Friday."

By then, I had walked into her chambers.

"Ma'am, come back here. You cannot go back there without authorization."

I didn't care what the lady said. My life was on the line. I was going to fight until the end to hold on to it.

"I have been expecting you, Nya."

The receptionist finally caught up with me. "Safar, she just waltzed back here."

"Clara, it's all right. Please, shut the door as you leave."

The receptionist nodded and walked out.

I burst into tears, my head buried in Safar's lap. "What am I going to do?" I asked her over and over again.

She handed me a tissue. "Nya, look at me. I have told you before you are a warrior and a true fighter. Darren is an evil man and will stop at nothing to get what he wants. You got tangled up in his lies and deception. As far as the child you are carrying, you are the only one who can make the final decision. The answers lie within your heart. Someone is going to pay you a visit. Pay very close attention to what he tells you. He will be the one who helps you take Darren down. Do not tell anyone about those packages. You don't want to get anyone else involved. You are going to live a long life filled with joy and happiness. This situation is going to make you stronger. Dry your tears." She rubbed my face. "Go home and get some rest; you will need it."

"Thank you," I said hugging her. I reached into my purse and pulled out two hundred dollars to show my gratitude for the priceless wisdom she had given me.

"No, my child, this one is on me." Safar held up her hand.

"Thanks again," I said and walked out.

On the way home, I decided to stop at Chili's to pick up dinner. I called Darren to let him know I couldn't make it tonight because I had to study for my tests. Mommy and Daddy had Bible study, so I was pretty sure she wasn't going to cook tonight. And I was not in the mood for leftovers. I hadn't eaten a decent meal all day and I could feel the nausea creeping up. I ordered my favorite, Monterey Chicken, to go. I asked the bartender, "May I have a glass of cold water, please?" and waited for my order to be prepared.

"Coming right up, miss."

"Thank you."

As I was waiting, a man approached me.

"Nya Gamden?"

"Yes?"

"My name is Brennon Gilles. May I have a few moments of your time, please?"

My guard was up, thinking he might be one of Darren's henchmen. I didn't want to be caught up in any mayhem. "May I ask who you are?"

"I am the chief detective in the country of Trinidad." He showed me his passport, Trinidad identification, and his police badge. I could tell the badge was the real thing because Nelson's uncle had one like it. I decided to take a seat.

"What do you want with me?"

He had an envelope in his hand. He laid the items out on the table. There before me were at least a dozen pictures of me delivering packages. "Is this you?"

"Yes."

"I am working with the DEA on an investigation regarding Mr. Darren Edmonds."

"What does it have to do with me?"

"A lot. Inside each and every one of these packages is at least ten kilos of cocaine. Each one has the currency value of forty thousand dollars. For several months, five days a week, you have been delivering these packages. Darren is the wholesaler. The clients break the cocaine down and do whatever they want to it. Some have others sell it in the streets, while others snort it or smoke it up themselves with friends and family. Each week, you are making Darren at least a quarter of a million dollars."

"Sir—"

"Call me Brennon."

"Well, Brennon, I swear to you on my mother's grave I did not know. He has a lucrative vending machine business. I thought I was delivering drinks and snacks to the clients."

"You are. But underneath the last layer of the box is another layer containing the drugs. Don't worry. We have no intention of indicting you or charging you with conspiracy. Still, we need your help. I'm going to give it to you raw. Some cops stop at nothing to get to the man they want, even if it means damaging the lives of innocent people. Don't beat yourself up over this . . . because you didn't know."

"Here I was thinking I was helping my man out and all along he was using me."

"In all reality, you could be charged with conspiracy,

intent to distribute a narcotic, and distribution of a narcotic. If convicted, most likely you would receive up to twenty per charge. Plus, the amount of cocaine transported into your possession is a vital factor in determining how many years you would get. Right now, you have worked yourself up to two life sentences with no chance of parole."

I burst into tears. "Sir, I don't want to go to prison."

"This is my investigation, so what I say goes. I am fully aware you come from a good home and are going to school for a nursing career. You have your whole life ahead of you, and I am going to make sure Darren doesn't take that away from you."

"Darren says he has other men making deliveries?"

"He does, but they deliver marijuana and ecstasy. You, on the other hand, deliver the one that makes the most profit. For many years, the Trinidad government and the DEA have been watching his every move. Believe me, we want to get him, but the evidence must stick in order for him to get some hard time. Darren has no idea we are on the prowl for him. I have dedicated my life to bringing him down. I have a personal and a professional vendetta against him. Ten years ago, I was the happiest man alive. Ever since the age of seven, I have been in love with Gabrielle Yuston. Now, her last name is Edmonds.

"Everyone called her Gabby as a nickname." He pulled out a picture from his wallet. "She is the most beautiful woman I ever laid my eyes on."

I have seen this woman before, I thought. Instantly, everything started to click. *She's the woman who called Darren's phone that night.* Also, even though he suggested I not make a pit stop in Rubie's, the girls and I went anyway. Her portrait was hanging in the front of the shop. I alone spent at least six hundred dollars in her boutique. Each one of us bought something. The saleswoman was so helpful and informed us Gabrielle oversees each item that is for purchase in her store. As we were leaving, I distinctly remember she was coming in. The woman had style. To my relief, I never mentioned to Darren I had gone into the shop and I never wore any of the dresses I bought in his presence.

"Darren and I were the best of friends. He knew the eternal love I had for this woman. Finally, my senior year of high school, I got up the nerve to ask her on a date. Eventually, we fell madly in love. Within a year, I asked for her hand in marriage, and she gladly accepted. Little did anyone know Gabrielle was seven weeks pregnant with our child. Like any man, I was hoping for a son.

"The night before the wedding, my best friend Darren gave me a bachelor party. We had strippers and all the alcohol on the island, it seemed. The strippers did a couple of routines and left with some of our mutual friends. After the party was over and all the guys left, Darren wanted us to share in a private toast. 'To my best friend Brennon and his beautiful bride, Gabrielle, may you two have a happy and fulfilling life,' he toasted.

"I drank the champagne and gave him a handshake. I was so honored for him to toast to my happiness. Within a few minutes, I started to get dizzy and the room began to swirl. Then everything went black. To this day, I still don't know what drug he snuck in my drink to put me in such a state of incoherence. All I can remember is waking up with two women I had never seen before in my life all over me. One was kissing me while the other gave me head. I was too weak to move. I asked them who they were, but they wouldn't answer me.

"Then I heard a voice scream out my name as the sound of glass breaking on the floor echoed in my ears. It was my beautiful Gabrielle. She screamed at me over and over again, asking me how I could do such a thing. I couldn't seem to get any words to come out of my mouth. She said Darren had told her I was sick, and so she was bringing me over some chicken noodle soup to make me feel better. She had tears in her eyes as the bowl fell to the floor.

"Same time, the police rushed in, saying they received an anonymous tip I had a controlled substance in my room. Half of pound of cocaine was found in between the mattress.

"Before storming out, Gabrielle spit the words 'I hate you' in my face. A week later, Darren came to visit me in jail, and I asked him why he had done that to me. I thought we were friends; I grew up with him. That is when he informed me he secretly loved Gabrielle too. He told me he thought it was the only way he could make Gabrielle stop loving me.

"To make a long story short, I was sentenced to five years in a maximum pit hole. I served three because of good behavior. Six months after my sentence hearing, I received a letter from Gabrielle telling me she had an abortion and was marrying Darren." Brennon spoke these words with tears in his eyes. "She felt he was a better man for her and wanted nothing else to do with me.

"Eventually, I cleared my name and became a police officer. For the past six years, I have been watching Darren's every move, waiting for him to slip up. And finally, he has. My law enforcement agency in Trinidad, as well as the DEA, believes he is supplying the entire states of Virginia, Maryland, North Carolina, Georgia, and Florida with cocaine and is behind a lot of unsolved murders in the area. The head of John Baker, one of his deliverymen, was found in the Elizabeth River. From the results of the investigation, it is assumed he was digging into Darren's stash.

"Now, I am here to avenge the death of my unborn child and the love that Gabrielle once had for me. Please, I need your help to bring Darren Edmonds down."

"What can I do to help you?" I was still overwhelmed from all that I had just digested from Brennon's story.

"All I want is your job. You said you told Darren you would do the deliveries for a little while—so step aside; one of my men will do it."

"His right-hand man, Raymond, hangs out at Jillian's most of the time. Him and Darren are the ones, who give me the packages," I told him. "Maybe if you get in good with him, eventually, you could get in good with Darren."

"Now, slowly but surely, you have to wean yourself from the job. Act as normal as possible because you don't want him to think anything is wrong." Brennon gave me a strange look.

"What are you looking at?"

"I'm sorry, but I can see why Darren fell for you. You are very beautiful in your way. You resemble Gabrielle very much too."

"I don't understand if Darren has a legit and lucrative business, why does he deal cocaine?"

"He does so for power. What do men with power want more of?"

"More power." I realized I had been played for a fool.

Brennon and I exchanged phone numbers.

"Call me anytime. I know this is a lot to take in, but I am going to be here for you. No more lives will be destroyed because of Darren."

"Thank you. I appreciate your sincerity."

Just then, the bartender walked over with my take-out order.

"Sit down. Please eat. You look a little pale."

"No, I need to get home to study for my test and sort this whole thing out in my mind. I feel like such a fool." I made a feeble attempt to stand, but fell right back down in my seat.

"Are you sick?"

I shook my head.

"Bartender, can you bring a glass of ginger ale for the young lady?"

The bartender nodded.

"On second thought, maybe I do need to eat. All I had to eat today was a bowl of oatmeal and chicken salad." I began to cry again. *Is this what an emotional breakdown is? If so, I am very close to having one. Or a nervous breakdown.*

"Nya, I apologize for upsetting you. It was never my intention."

"It's not you. I am pregnant with Darren's child. I overheard in a conversation him saying he purposely got me pregnant because Gabrielle is unable to have children."

"What are you going to do?"

"I can't have this baby. By no means am I ready to be a mother. This baby was conceived out of a tangled web of deceit. I am so angry right now I want to beat the crap out of Darren!" I barked, balling my hands up to form tight fists.

"Look, whatever you want to do, I support you one hundred percent."

"I know three things for sure: One—I am not going to jail; two—I am not going to jail; and three—I am not going to jail. I have worked too hard to get to where I am today. I have five months before I graduate and nothing is going to stop me. He could have caused me to lose my license. You can't be a nurse with a felony charge."

"I thought you would see things my way."

"How did you make it through prison knowing you were an innocent man?"

"Faith. I knew one day justice would be served. It was not easy, and there were plenty of times I wanted to break down, but I stayed strong—just like you have to do now."

After I finished my meal, he offered to walk me to my car.

When we reached my car, he said, "I will be in touch. Remember, keep things as normal as possible, and I mean *everything*. Don't worry. I will never come to the bank, your school, or your house. I will always let you know when and where I want to meet. Darren cannot know I am here."

"My lips are sealed. Have a good night."

"One more thing."

"Yes."

"This dilemma will be over before your graduation. Consider it an early present."

I spoke no words in response. The large smile on my face said it all.

Chapter 45

For the weeks that followed, my bogus relationship couldn't have been better. I was playing my role to the tee and continued to do the drops for Darren. He was even happier with our sex life. I rode him with such force he could barely hold on. I did so not to reach ecstasy, but to release my hatred toward him.

Deep down, I was in fear of my life. I didn't know what Darren was capable of—a lot of money was at stake. Darren was even giving me an extra five hundred dollars a week for my services. At first, I refused, but he insisted that the money was for a good cause since I was trying to do something with my life, and he wanted to be the one to help me accomplish my goals. Actually, I believe he was giving me the money out of guilt. A mere eleven hundred dollars was pennies compared to the hundred of thousands of dollars I was knocking him off with a week.

One evening, Darren and I were eating dinner at Tokyo's, a Japanese restaurant.

"Jewels, your butt is getting bigger. I can tell it's because of those back shots 'Big Daddy' has been giving you." He laughed.

"You are so silly."

"Did you get your period?"

"Yes, last week my monthly visitor came."

Darren picked up his chopsticks. "You didn't mention it to me."

"I hardly spoke to you at all last week because you were in New York on business." *Whew!* I was so thankful he bought my lie. "How is business going?"

"I am almost ready to break ground on the Long Island project. These will be top-of-the-line luxury homes."

"Let me see. Do you have a blueprint?"

"No, Jewels. When everything is done, then you can feast your eyes upon them." He reached over and kissed me.

I pecked with him a little bit to make him squeal and to keep everything normal as Brennon instructed.

"I have a little something for you."

From out of his briefcase he pulled a ring box.

I stared at it in astonishment, hoping he was not trying to propose to me.

"Go on. Open it."

My hands trembled. "Okay." I was still reluctant to open the box. "The ring is beautiful. Thank you so much." He put it on my finger. "Thank you for being so understanding when I am away on business. You know I hate being away from you. This is a little token of my gratitude for you putting up with me."

Thank goodness . . . it's not an engagement ring, after all.

"I'm going to have to go away for a little while longer, Jewels. Here is your salary for five weeks." He handed me an envelope. "After today, though, I won't need you to do the runs for me anymore. Raymond found another guy to do it. Besides, my queen should not be working in the first place. Plus, I know the hospital needs you more than I do. It was nice doing business with you." Darren laughed.

"The pleasure was all mine," I said, batting my eyes. "And I understand about you having to go out of town. Honey, I know you are making money and expanding your real estate business. Pretty soon, you will be international. Take all the time you need; I will be right here for you."

"Jewels, you make me feel so good."

This three-carat princess-cut ring is making me feel even better.

Later on that night when I got home, I couldn't wait to call Brennon.

"Did our friend tell you the good news?"

"Yes."

"Keep it up and this will be over sooner than you think. My man is the best of the crop in law enforcement. He definitely knows how to play the role. Get some sleep. I can hear you yawning on the phone. I will see you in the morning, Nya."

"Goodnight."

Chapter 46

"Ms. Gamden, these papers are legal documents stating you want to have an abortion. Please sign at the bottom," the nurse said.

"Yes, ma'am."

"With that all taken care of, how will you be paying today?"

"Cash."

"Your total is three hundred and fifty dollars."

I handed her the money.

"Do you have someone who will be driving you home?"

I looked at Brennon. "Yes."

"Your blood and urine tests are normal. It's a good thing we fit you in today. In two more days, you would have been too far along to have an abortion in the state of Virginia."

"I was still deciding whether or not to keep my baby, but I'm ready to get this thing over with."

"Well then, come with me, please."

"Nya, it's time to get up. Here is a prescription for Tetracycline. This drug will prevent infection. Since you are Rh negative, I gave you a RhoGAM shot. No intercourse, douching, or baths for two weeks. How do you feel?" the nurse asked.

"I have cramps," I said slowly.

"Take this ibuprofen; it will relieve the pain. Let me take you back to the lobby."

Brennon held my hand as we walked out the door. "Are you all right?"

"I will be later. I need to lie down."

I had purposely arranged the appointment for that week because Leah went to Atlantic City with Nelson, Mommy and Daddy went on a cruise, and Darren was in New York. I didn't want anyone to suspect anything was going on with me.

"Do you want something to eat?"

"I could go for some Chick-fil-A, the kid's meal, please, because I can never finish their larger-size meals."

During the ride, the anesthesia, which was still in my system, caused me to fall asleep. When I finally awoke, I was at the Marriott in Hampton. Brennon was sitting in the chair.

"What time is it?" I asked.

"Six o'clock."

"Why did you let me sleep for so long?"

"As long as you were breathing, I didn't want to bother you. I figured sleep was the best thing in your condition. How do you feel?"

"One quarter of a million bucks."

"Your food is on the table. Don't worry, it's hot and fresh. I only returned with it a little while ago."

"Thank you."

"Are you ready to go?"

"Yeah, I have to use the bathroom first though."

We decided it would be best if I rode a cab home in case Darren had someone spying on me.

"Thank you so much for being there for me."

"No problem. You know I am here to help in any way I can. Are you straight? Do you need anything?" He pulled out a wad of cash.

"No, thank you."

"At least let me pay the cab fare."

"Well, okay."

"I will be in touch," he said, and the cab pulled slowly away from the curb.

Chapter 47

Each day it got harder for me to look at Darren's face. School was my outlet to this madness. I was getting antsy with anticipation. In three more weeks, I would be a part of the graduating class of 2005 and would be taking my boards in July. Ms. Rosen had already offered me a job at Creekdale Memorial Hospital making sixty thousand dollars a year to start. *Cha-Ching!*

I had taken my last final, and the students and I were huddled in Room 343 to see what our scores were. Finally, Mrs. Wellington came in to post the grades on the blackboard. I was so nervous I completely forgot what number I was assigned. *What is my number?* Then a light in my head went off. I remembered it was five. I began to sweat as I ran my finger down the sheet to find my number. I received a 94 on my written exam and a 99 in clinical. I screamed so loud I know the whole building heard me. I had stuck it out another semester to earn credits towards a master's degree, and I still graduated on time. Maria and I hugged each other.

"Congratulations!"

"Congratulations to you too!"

I headed straight to Mrs. Wellington's office and knocked on the door.

"Come in. Oh, hello, Nya."

"I wanted to personally thank you for everything," I said with tears in my eyes.

"Don't thank me; you did all the work. And there is a 'no crying rule' in my office." She giggled. "I am so proud of you, Nya."

"Thank you."

"Now, hold your head high and remember everything I taught you." She gave me a hug. "I will see you at graduation."

I am going to party tonight. I raced home, praying I would not get a ticket, and barged in the front door. "I made it!" I screamed at the top of my lungs.

"I knew you would," Mommy said.

Daddy smiled. "Congratulations, pudding, I am so proud of you. Now that you are going to be a big-time nurse, I know you will take good care of your mother and me during our golden years."

"Girl, come over here and give your mother a hug. My baby's graduating."

"Darren dropped off something for you; it's on your bed—can you buy me a new car now?"

"No, Leah."

"I'm just playing. Congratulations. I love you," she said, giving me a hug.

"On a more serious note," Daddy said, "we need to talk to you."

"About?"

"Well, the sheriff's office came by the house today to drop off your court summons for the Mithers' trial. You ready to testify?"

"Yes, I will be able to handle it. The psychiatrist has helped me get through my nightmares."

"The Mithers' family is ready to settle on the civil suit," Mommy said. "Mr. Holmes wants to see you next week to discuss the details."

I sorted through my mail. "How many pennies are they trying to dish out?"

"Eight hundred thousand dollars plus the cost of medical and counseling expenses."

"What do you think?"

"Well, it's more than you were hoping for," Mommy answered.

"Tell Mr. Holmes I said yes. Mommy, please schedule an appointment right away so I can sign the papers."

"Will you buy me a car *now*?" Leah was more serious this time.

"No. But I will tell you what I *am* going to do. I'm going to send Mommy and Daddy on a second honeymoon. You two have always wanted to go to Las Vegas again—well, here's your chance."

"Thank you, baby."

Daddy hugged Mommy. "Sin City, here we come."

Then I turned to Leah. "On second thought, I may help you out with half for a car. I don't want to talk about the case anymore though; we will deal with that later. Promise me you all will be at the trial right by my side."

"You know we will," Leah reassured me.

I immediately called Darren to thank him for the gift he had personally delivered to my home. He was ecstatic about my grades and the graduation.

"Jewels, put on your best smile—I am giving you a party; you deserve it. I want to see you in a dress too." He had bought one of my favorite designers, a soft pink Chanel dress with the back out. He knew how I like my dresses styled. "A limousine will pick the girls and you up at eight o'clock."

Since this was a special occasion, I decided I would wear my hair down.

"Uh-oh, somebody has combed their hair tonight," Leah said while we cruised in the limousine, which was equipped with a TV, DVD, a mini bar, and a little refrigerator.

"Where are we going?" Yvette asked.

"I don't know; Darren is surprising us."

"You mean *you*," Leah said.

The car stopped at Federico's, a very expensive Italian restaurant. Darren was anxiously awaiting our arrival. He looked debonair in his white suit. My closest friends and family all were there to celebrate my graduation.

Once Darren got the bill, I started to feel kinda bad for him. Shit, Leah and Tara chug-a-lugged on a bottle of champagne that cost five hundred dollars. Ooh, it must have slipped my mind. *Money wasn't a thing to him.*

Raymond handed me an envelope. "Congratulations."

"Thank you."

"How did the food taste?" Darren asked.

Instead of my usual, I had ordered grilled chicken with linguini in wine sauce. "Tasty."

"Jewels, I am so proud of you. In the short time we have known each other, you have blossomed into a gorgeous woman with a heart of gold." Darren lit his Cuban cigar.

"Thanks, baby."

"Come on over with me to the bar; we need to talk."

"All right. But can you wait until I finish my strawberry cheesecake?"

"No."

"What's the rush? We have all night."

"Come on over, sweet thing, and bring your dessert with you."

"This is what couldn't wait—your graduation present." Darren handed me a card. Enclosed was a cashier's check for fifty thousand dollars.

"I know the girls and you want to go on a trip and live it up. This will cover your expenses."

"You are too much. This dinner party was enough," I said, kissing his cheek.

"Nothing is too good for my Jewels."

Darren nodded to Raymond, who exited the restaurant and quickly returned with a bag with Tiffany's written all over it. Raymond handed the bag to me and walked back to the table.

"This one comes from the heart."

The first box was a diamond charm bracelet. The second box was a necklace made of diamonds with a charm that read JEWELS. It was beautiful. I guess he did really love me in his own sick and twisted way.

"Thank you so much."

"Now, I've got to run," he said. "There is a very big business deal going down tonight. Please don't be upset. I was hoping the goodies from Tiffany's would make up for me having to leave."

"Will I see you later on tonight?"

"No. I have to head straight to New York to finish the Long Island project. Right now, I don't know when I will be back."

I tried my best to look disappointed. "I understand."

"Go have some fun tonight. I know The System is going to be packed. You and your crew are already on the VIP list. Fix your face; let me see a smile."

I showed my pearly whites. He kissed me and gave me a hug. In my heart, I knew it would be the last time I would see him alive.

Chapter 48

The line at The System was two blocks long. The bouncer immediately let us in with no problems; we even had our own VIP reserved table.

"Damn, I'm glad we're here, so I can work off all the food I ate," Tara said, rubbing her stomach.

She and Leah were drunk as two skunks.

"Don't hurt yourself or nobody else on the dance floor." I waved my bracelet and pulled at my new necklace and charm, showing them off.

Leah brought my arm closer to her eyes. "It's gorgeous."

"Darren must really love your butt to go all out like this," Tara said. "Is he coming out tonight?"

"No, I don't think so, but with him you never know. Keep your eyes wide open to see if he makes an entrance into the building though."

It was reggae night, and they also announced a special guest would be in the house tonight.

Three hours, later, Yvette and I gave up our dancing shoes. I never wind so much in my life, but sometimes you got to let loose and get high off of life.

"What are you ladies drinking?" the bartender asked.

"I want a Coke," Yvette said.

"I'll have a strawberry daiquiri." I dug in my purse for money. "How much?"

"The drinks are compliments of Mr. Edmonds. He called early this afternoon and said he was picking up the tab for you and your guests. By the way, congratulations on your graduation."

"Thank you."

I began to wonder who the special guest was. Usually, one would hear screams and hollers when somebody important walked up in the club. As the bartender got our drinks ready, the special guest stopped at the bar.

"So, what will our special guest be having this evening?" The bartender winked at him.

"You know, my usual," he answered.

As I turned to fulfill my curiosity as to who the special guest was, I found myself staring right in the face of Jay-Z, my favorite rap artist, standing only three feet away. He looked over at us. "How are you ladies doing tonight?" "We are enjoying ourselves," I said, trying to keep my cool. "How about you?"

"I'm having a good time."

"I just want to congratulate you on all of your success and let you know I love your music. I admire you for making something out of nothing; it is a rare commodity."

"Thank you very much for your support. The new ladies, Rocawear summer collection will be in stores soon."

"You have a nice night," I said as Yvette and I walked back to the table with our drinks in hand. My heart was racing a mile a minute.

Leah and Tara were still shaking it on the dance

floor, so Yvette and I decided we would wait to tell them
who we saw when they sobered up.

Another hour had passed. It was getting late and I
was tired.

"Hey, Yvette, why don't you stay the night? This way,
we can have breakfast in the morning. I've been so pre-
occupied with school I need to catch up with my girls."

"Okay, I just have to call Jarvis and let him know the
deal."

Tara and Leah came back stumbling to the table drunk
out of their minds. I helped walk Tara to the door while
Yvette helped Leah. As we were leaving, I felt someone
caress my hair softly. I turned around and no one I
knew was in sight. Only one person touched my hair in
such a way—Tory.

Chapter 49

Darren and Raymond were dead. It was in all of the papers. Their bodies were shipped to Trinidad to be laid to rest. The article was very vague and said both died a sudden death. Darren's survivors were Gabrielle, his wife, and an eight-year-old daughter from Trinidad, who currently lived in New York with her mother.

I didn't want Darren to die, but Brennon felt it was the only way to get his vengeance. *When you get back at someone who didn't have the slightest clue of what was going to happen, it is the sweetest revenge.*

The memorial was three days ago. I played my role. The girls gave me their condolences. Everyone was shocked to learn that Darren was married. Tara gave me the same "all-men-are-dogs" speech, which I took in stride.

Two weeks had passed before I heard anything from Brennon. He told me to meet him at the Rivermont Hotel in Room 301. When I arrived, he greeted me with a hug. "How are you?"

"Feeling much better. I graduate on Saturday."

"Congratulations, I knew you could do it."

"What happened?" I asked, dying to know.

"My man Lufus got in good with them and started selling kilos of cocaine in New York. Lufus gave Darren an offer he couldn't refuse."

"How much?"

"Forty thousand for each kilo," he said. "There has been a drought up north. It's a means of supply meets demand. The deal was set, and everything went according to plan. Honestly, for years, I have had dreams of putting one bullet in his forehead, but I thought a life sentence in prison would be far worse. I came up behind Darren to enjoy the pleasure of personally arresting him. That's when he saw me out the corner of his eye, turned around, and shot at me. Twenty shots from twenty different DEA agents landed in Darren. His last words were that it was the only way and that he never meant to hurt me. Unfortunately, Raymond got caught up in the crossfire, trying to desperately protect his friend.

"But that's not all. I saw her. After ten long, grueling years, I saw Gabrielle. I explained everything to her. She heard me out from start to finish. She felt remorseful about the abortion. For so long, she had lived a lie. Thankfully, Darren didn't leave her high and dry. She gets all of his property and money, and business is booming at her boutique. She always had an eye for fashion. We are working on a friendship."

"That's wonderful. I'm so happy for you."

"Well, I'm not going to hold you up. Besides, I have to tie up some loose ends with the local DEA department. Let me walk you out to your car."

"Thank you."

"For what?"

"For setting me free from evil and keeping your word."

"You are a gorgeous woman; any man would be lucky to have you."

"Are you saying that because I favor Gabrielle?"

"No, I am saying it because of who you are." He handed me a bag.

"What's this?"

"Take it. It was going to get burned anyway. I trust you will use it wisely." He had a smirk on his face.

Enclosed were twelve ten thousand straps of hundred-dollar bills.

"You keep it," I said, outstretching the bag toward him.

"No, I have plenty. My family owns all the alcohol stores in Trinidad. Believe me, we are okay. Take care of yourself, Nya. I'll be in touch."

"Bye."

Right away, I went and donated twenty thousand dollars to the Battered Women's Shelter. I sent it unanimously. The rest of the money I placed in a safety deposit box at my bank until I decided what to do with it.

Chapter 50

"We will now call the Health Sciences," the dean said. "Christine Eden." There was an eruption of clapping. "Nya Gamden."

I walked across the stage like I was floating on air. My friends and family not only clapped, they yelled and screamed at the top of their lungs. I think we were the loudest family. Leah even had a bullhorn to enhance her voice. *She is so crazy.* I repeatedly kept hearing shouts of "That's my baby," compliments of Mommy.

I had reserved a table for twenty at the Fisherman's Wharf for after the ceremony. I didn't want Mommy to do all that cooking. On Sunday, she would be preparing me a feast anyway.

I settled my civil case with the Mithers' family to the tune of eight hundred thousand dollars. Since they were a high-profile family, they wanted this swept under the rug as soon as possible.

I decided to take my boards a week early because I was eager to start working at the hospital with those tiny babies. Obstetrics was where my heart was. When taking the test, I was so nervous I was shaking. I still managed to pull myself together and ended up scoring a 90.

Having worked at the hospital for three weeks, I had just gotten off from a twelve-hour shift and had enjoyed every minute of it. *Nursing is so rewarding.* On my way home, I decided to stop off at Wal-Mart for a few items. I grabbed a shopping cart. People were everywhere. I knew it was going to take me forever to get through the checkout line. *Let me think, what do I need? Rum raisin ice cream, juice, oatmeal, and Vitamin E.* I picked up the rest of my items and headed toward the juice aisle. As I turned the corner, someone who was not paying attention slammed into my cart. "Hey." It was Tory.

"Hi."

"Are you here visiting?" I asked.

"No, I moved back here about two months ago. I loved California, but the holder of my heart is here. Once I got the company up and running, my old boss moved to California, leaving no one here. So, it worked out perfectly. I would've come back anyway—I hope you like the roses I sent you."

"Thank you," I said, trying hard not to smile.

"Once again, I apologize for slamming into your cart."

"I thought you learned your lesson the first time."

We both busted out laughing.

"I didn't contact you when I first got back in town because I figured you didn't want to deal with me. After all of this time apart, I came to realize I was selfish for trying to plan your life and asking you to give everything up for me. If I could have one wish, it would be for you to be my wife. If you give me another chance, I promise, you will not be sorry. I am more than willing to start from the beginning and work my way back into your heart. Anything is better than not having you in my life, Nya. I love you so much."

"I love you, too," I said, hugging him. It felt like home to be back in his arms again in the juice aisle.

EPILOGUE

For about two weeks, Tory and I tried the "friend" thing. The sexual tension built up so much he could not wait to get his hands on me. Believe me, the feeling was mutual. Even though I tried to fight it, I never stopped loving him.

Tory is now the president of RADCOM. He proposed to me for the second time and I gladly accepted, receiving a sparkling new four-carat diamond ring and a gorgeous house with all the trimmings along the Chesapeake Bay.

As for me, I have had the honor of bringing sixty-two newborns in this world thus far. I plan to work for another year and then return to Old Dominion University for my master's.

John Mithers was convicted of all charges and sentenced to life without parole.

As a gift, I paid off my parents' mortgage and helped Leah buy a brand new Montero Sport with the money I received.

Each week, the girls and I get together to catch up.

The following year, Yvette graduated from Old Dominion University with a psychology degree. She is now the director of the Women and Children's Battered Home Shelter. Also, she wants to open a pregnancy center for teens. It was much to her surprise someone sent a generous donation unanimously. Jarvis and she married on July 11, 2005, and are expecting their second child, Michael, this winter.

Leah and Nelson are still going strong. He opened another Caribbean restaurant in the Tidewater area. Business couldn't be better. Leah oversees both of the restaurants. She is trying to get rid of the fifteen pounds she gained from eating stewed chicken daily. Since they love to travel, both have gone on countless trips together all over the globe. Neither of them is ready to get married yet. She still tries to put a hole in the dance floor whenever reggae music is played and is set to graduate this fall.

Tara and Rob are engaged. Finally, she gave up her cheating ways for a good man. Rob bought her a brand-new, green C-class Mercedes Benz. However, she still kept her Lexus truck. She graduates from Old Dominion University this upcoming spring. Counseling has turned her life around, enabling her to look at things in a more positive light. Once a month, Rob goes to the sessions with her.

Brennon and Gabrielle have started a relationship. Since she is unable to have children, they are looking to adopt in the near future. She still has her boutique shop in Manhattan, and he works as a detective for the New York Police Department. He calls me from time to time. Finally, he gets to live his life the way it should have been.

And to all, a happy end.